ABSOLUTELY NOW!

Best wishes

Lynne Franks

ABSOLUTELY NOW!

A Futurist's Journey to Her Inner Truth

LYNNE FRANKS

Century · London

This edition published by Century Books Limited 1997

1 3 5 7 9 10 8 6 4 2

Century
Random House UK Ltd
20 Vauxhall Bridge Road, London SW1V 2SA

Arrow Books Limited
Random House UK Ltd
20 Vauxhall Bridge Road, London, SW1V 2SA

Random House Australia (Pty) Limited
20 Alfred Street, Milsons Point, Sydney,
New South Wales 2061, Australia

Random House New Zealand Limited
18 Poland Road, Glenfield
Auckland 10, New Zealand

Random House South Africa (Pty) Limited
Endulini, 5a Jubilee Road, Parktown 2193, South Africa

Random House UK Limited Reg. No. 954009

A CIP catalogue record for this book is available from the British Library

Papers used by Random House UK Ltd are natural, recyclable products made from
wood grown in sustainable forests. The manufacturing processes conform to
the environmental regulations of the country of origin.

ISBN 0 7126 7835 2

Typeset by SX Composing DTP, Rayleigh, Essex
Printed and bound in the United Kingdom by
Mackays of Chatham Plc, Chatham, Kent

Contents

Acknowledgements

Thanks and love to all the wonderful teachers and friends I have met during my journey including Denise Linn, Gabrielle Roth, Sister Maureen and the Brahma Kamaris, Paul Howie, Frances Graves, Hazel Henderson and Brian Bacon. Thanks also to Gail Rebuck and all the team at Random House for their constant support and encouragement; Marina Cantacuzino for her unstinting good humour and hard work and Valerie Wade for suggesting the title as we ran to catch a plane.

Finally my beloved family. My mother Angela, my father Leslie, my son Joshua, my daughter Jessica and my partner Tom Blakeslee. I love you all very much.

Introduction

In June 1992 I let go of everything I always thought had mattered – material wealth, successful career, a high profile, a long-term marriage and my religious practice. It was like jumping out of an aeroplane and not knowing if the parachute would open, yet realising that if I stayed on board the aeroplane would burst into flames. I knew that without making this major shift I would destroy myself on both a physical and a spiritual level. I wanted to find out how to live my life in a balanced and connected way, from a point of love instead of fear.

I realised I'd spent my working life constantly sacrificing happiness in the present for some far-off goals in the future. It was time to find my truth and learn to live it.

I'd started what was to become the UK's highest-profile PR agency when I was just twenty-one years old and for more than twenty years I'd been living a rollercoaster life of launches, hype and hysteria so cleverly parodied by Jennifer Saunders in *Absolutely Fabulous*. I'd represented my clients' views and beliefs as my own, run a manically busy company of fifty energetic young people and managed to raise two children in my spare moments. After losing two close friends, also PRs, from cancer, I knew it was a matter of life and death for me to get out before I burnt out on some kind of PR funeral pyre.

As I embarked on an intense and often dramatic spiritual journey, I discovered techniques and philosophies based on ancient and modern wisdom that showed new ways for people to communicate with each other, new ways for business to interact with community, and a responsibility for mankind to honour and respect all living things especially the planet on which we live – Mother Earth.

My global journey took me to the UN women's conference in Beijing; a holy mountaintop in India where I discovered the power of Shakti – the divine woman; the empowering Celtic sites of Ireland, Scotland and Wales; the redwoods of California where I danced to African drums; and to Midwest America and a Native American Vision Quest and sweat lodge.

My journey took a new turn as I formed friendships with ethical business chiefs, Anita and Gordon Roddick of The Body Shop and Ben Cohen of Ben & Jerry's ice-cream; met visionary statesman Vaclav Havel at a business conference in Prague alongside David MacTaggart, founder of Greenpeace; and spent time with spiritual leaders including Ram Dass, Mother Meera, His Holiness the Dalai Lama and Dadi Janki of the Brahma Kumaris World Spiritual University.

This is the story of my journey and the answers I found along the way.

The *Ab Fab* Years

'I'm working on a comedy series about a fashion PR who is a Buddhist with two teenage children, but she has nothing to do with you' – was how comedian Jennifer Saunders broke the news to me about *Absolutely Fabulous* when I bumped into her at a film launch.

'But everyone will think it's me. After all, the press knew I was your PR and it certainly sounds like me,' I said after a few seconds of stunned silence.

Jennifer was defiant. 'I'm perfectly capable of coming up with an original idea of my own,' she said sharply.

A year later, at the very time I was reassessing my life, *Absolutely Fabulous* came on air and I realised that the consumer-led world of hype that Jennifer had so cleverly parodied was indeed a true and accurate reflection of my own frenetic lifestyle.

By now I had seriously started to question the value of my success and wealth and what it meant to be acclaimed as the PR guru of the 1980s. I was starting to feel a personal need for a far deeper understanding of myself and the world I inhabited. For me *Absolutely Fabulous* was a rite of passage, marking the end of an era and satirising a way of life which I now saw as empty and unsustainable.

Ever since being a teenager I'd been in a hurry to get on with my life. I couldn't wait to leave school at sixteen and go to work but my mother insisted I do a secretarial course first. She sent me to the best secretarial college around, where I met other north London Jewish princesses all equally interested in boys, dancing and clothes. I spent my time clubbing, spotting the newest fashion looks and dancing every week on TV's first youth music programme *Ready Steady Go*. My big claim to fame was my *Ready Steady Go* dancer's membership card which carried my photograph together with the rules – no spitting, chewing gum or wearing jeans.

I was always obsessed with street styles and trends and from the ages of fifteen to eighteen went from being a 'rocker' wearing tight jeans, ponytail, high heels and hanging around funfairs with boys in leather bike jackets, to being a north London mod. Blue patent lavatory-pan-heeled shoes with straps around the ankles, tightly pleated long granny dresses from British Home Stores and a full-length navy leather coat from C&A were amongst my most treasured possessions. I wore them with pride when my friend Hilary and I ventured down for the 'mod and rocker' clashes on Brighton beach or to London West End clubs.

I loved dancing all night to soul and R&B music – and still do. At my fortieth birthday party held at a huge specially decorated film studio during the height of the *Ab Fab* years, 500 of us ate designer cous-cous from Kensington Place, the newest, trendiest restaurant in town, and danced all night to James Brown. 'Do you think we'll be dancing to the same music when we're in our eighties?' one of my friends asked me. 'I will, for sure,' I told him. James Brown himself must have been well over pension age when I saw him perform a two-hour live show in Mallorca in '96 and he was still strutting his stuff to Sex Machine. I intend to do the same.

In my first job at a solicitor's, in between typing out revealing details from people's divorce statements, I would go shopping in Oxford Street trying on and buying the latest white cut-out Courrèges-style boots and striped jersey minidresses. On weekends as a special treat I'd

2

queue at the newly opened Biba shop where I bought my first 'designer' outfit – long lilac jacket, flared trouser suit with a lilac and white gingham shirt and long collar. I also shopped at the trendy new shops in Fulham and Chelsea owned by other designers who later became friends and clients – Ossie Clark, Alice Pollock and Zandra Rhodes.

I was a typical London sixties mod with a Vidal Sassoon symmetrical hairdo, dressed in a Biba dress and matching scarf, with false eyelashes on top and bottom, loads of make-up and panstick on the lips. I looked like a Jewish Twiggy. Life was about boys, clubs, music and fashion.

Gaining more confidence as the months went by, I left the safe confines of the solicitor's office and got a job temping for a glossy advertising agency. There were certainly lots of fashionable-looking people working here: I was in my element – and when I spotted the cute guys working in the art department I decided to stay a while. I got transferred to the PR department without even understanding what PR was and soon after got involved promoting products like Cadbury's Drinking Chocolate to the press and public.

My first solo event was to take a coachload of pop stars drinking hot chocolate along to Hampstead Garden Suburb to sing carols for the Christmas edition of a teenage pop magazine. As this was a predominantly Jewish community, the people looked very confused when they opened their front door and saw Unit Four Plus Two singing 'Away in a Manger' – particularly as it was still only October. We had to shoot then because of the magazine's long lead time.

I stayed at the PR company for a year or so but eventually plucked up the courage to telephone the prestigious *Petticoat* magazine, the first teenage girls' weekly. I was interviewed by their glamorous and rather intimidating beauty editor, Eve Pollard, who was looking for a secretary. Eve, later to become one of Fleet Street's first woman newspaper editors, took me on and very soon was encouraging me to start writing little pieces of my own, as well as helping her out on photo shoots, like one showing readers how to paint hippie flowers all over their body.

3

Soon I was promoted to writing a regular page about what was happening in 'swinging' London. I worked alongside the awesome Janet Street-Porter who had just left architectural college and was a seriously trendy person. Tall and toothy, she was the most confident person I'd ever met in my life. She knew everyone, had been everywhere and seen everything. Dressed in the shortest, most stylish clothes around, she was extremely kind yet scared the living daylights out of me. Like many of the other pioneering young women journalists in the offices of *Petticoat* and its sister monthly magazine *Honey*, she became a high-flyer in the media and TV world. Looking back I see the offices as a training course for ambitious young media women.

My days were spent at previews, launches and promotions and what little time was left over I'd spend with my boyfriend, the manager of a fashionable menswear shop in Carnaby Street. It was as if I'd died and gone to heaven. We spent every evening in the most happening sixties clubs in London, usually the Speakeasy or the Bag O'Nails in the West End where I had press golden memberships. It was an incredible time: we'd catch all the big names jamming together. Many times I saw Jimi Hendrix either collapsing from drugs or jamming with Eric Clapton or members of the Yardbirds and the Animals. The Beatles were often there too but they'd sit quietly in a corner; they were still shy boys from Liverpool.

Trouble was, I spent so much time going to these trendy clubs that I didn't have enough energy to do my work and I'd arrive in the office exhausted every morning. One day the editor, Audrey Slaughter, called me in and told me that she thought my personality was better suited to PR than journalism. In hindsight it was good advice but at the time I wasn't keen on the idea – I didn't want to become a pushy PR person like the ones who used to ring me up all the time.

By mutual consent we decided I should get more experience in journalism elsewhere and I went to Freeman's mail-order company to work on their in-house publications. I was no longer in the glamorous world of King's Road fashion but a big corporate institution in south London. From meeting pop stars I was interviewing warehouse men about their fifty years of service. Instead of going to the latest fashion show I was travelling to Scotland to interview a Freeman's agent who'd just bought her first trouser-suit and whose husband was painting the Forth bridge. In her small terraced cottage by the bridge she pointed out how once he'd finished he had to start all over again going the other way. 'A job for life,' she said proudly.

I worked at Freeman's for about two years and it was here that I learnt to write and edit, managed to give up smoking because of their stringent no smoking policy, went out with most of the good-looking men who worked there and discovered how to sneak in the back way when I was late for work after all-night raves. Eventually my eccentric hours got too much for my boss and she persuaded me it was time to move back to the world of mainstream magazine journalism.

One day, while going for an interview, I bumped into PR man Ben Coster. He offered me a job as a temporary assistant. Out of desperation I went to work with him for a week and stayed about six months. I found out that I quite liked PR, especially if it was about fashion, and it helped that I was working with some of the same girls I'd met during my stint on *Petticoat*.

It was now the early seventies and Ben Coster was doing PR for an embryonic London Fashion Week. One day as I helped on the press desk at the designers' show I was approached by an exotic creature dressed in a brown Lurex siren suit, matching turban and high heels.

'Yahh, hi, my name's Katharine, are there any important journalists here?' she asked in her plummy, Cheltenham Ladies College accent.

I was fascinated. I'd certainly never met anybody who looked and spoke quite like her before. 'Yes, *Vogue* and *Harpers & Queen*,' I told her. I guided the journalists over to the beautiful embroidered suede and leather outfits designed by Katharine and her partner.

They made an extraordinary pair – Katharine with her tailored, sophisticated jacket and trousers draped perfectly on her six-foot rangy body and tiny, feminine Ann Buck with her scalloped shell-pink waistcoats and tiered skirts adorned with pastel ribbons and bows. I rapidly became friends with both of them. The beautiful tall one I soon discovered was designer Katharine Hamnett and she and Ann were soon to become my first clients in my own PR agency. Katharine with her incredible energy and enthusiasm suggested that I should start my own PR business, and their company Tuttabankem would pay me £20 a week.

By this time I was living with my boyfriend Paul Howie, an Australian, whom I'd met at Freeman's when he was working there as a buyer. We'd first become friends through work, particularly after Paul started giving me samples of suede miniskirts and crêpe hot-pants. I knew he was quite a flirt at work and was happy for our relationship to stay platonic.

On our first date, several months after he left Freeman's, he took me to the ballet. I thought it was such a sophisticated thing to do, especially as he was dressed so coolly in his flared cotton loons and open-toe sandals. We started to spend more and more time together until finally we ended up in bed and I moved into his trendy west London flat the next day. Paul was a weekend hippie with his long hair, moustache and tie-dyed T-shirts which he exchanged for a three-piece suit and floral shirt and tie on workdays.

I'd always gone for different types of boyfriends, usually as unconventional as possible. I specialised in French DJs from the West End clubs, foreign students or non-Jewish north London mods. I was strictly against going out with Jewish men, and it seemed mutual. All the ones I knew seemed to want beautiful manicured princesses hot for a husband, but I'd always wanted a career and was much too inde-pendent to follow my Jewish girlfriends into early engagement. I was too competitive for most Jewish men – they wanted to get engaged to their mother, not their father.

Even Paul had seemed somewhat too normal for me, although I soon discovered he was as much of a rebel as I was. We were madly in love and even though I knew he'd been quite a ladies' man through-out an earlier marriage, naively I thought it would be different for us.

'Why don't you work from home here in the flat?' he generously offered when I told him that Katharine had suggested I start my own business. Despite my nervousness I decided to go for it. I could always find another job it if didn't work out and he was prepared to pay all the rent.

Katharine Hamnett was also in the early days of her business and rarely managed to pay my £20 a week fee on time. Luckily I soon picked up some other clients and my workload began to grow. I had an old car which I paid for by having a Saturday morning secretarial job. I would put the press samples in the back and drive around to the magazines showing them to fashion journalists. I worked from our battered kitchen table with a notepad and an answerphone.

My second client was an avant-garde boutique called Brave New World based in Notting Hill Gate near where we lived. I'd noticed it opening and one day, sounding far more confident than I felt, I went in. 'I love your clothes,' I said to the nonchalant crowd of fashionable young things lying around the shop. 'I have a PR agency and it would be great to represent you.'

One of the young middle-class boys who owned the shop said they'd give me a try. They must have been about as naive as I was. Before long I became friendly with their peroxide blond designer, Brent Sherwood, who was convinced he was the reincarnation of Marilyn Monroe. His own clothing, as well as his designs, was mostly leopardskin, gold lamé and Marabou feathers, which went brilliantly with the fun designs of Mr Freedom that Tommy Roberts had just opened down the road.

My first visit to the Paris ready-to-wear collections was with Brent and we were so broke we went on the train and ferry. The French customs officers stopped us when we arrived. 'Open your case,' they ordered my androgynous companion, obviously disturbed by his fully made-up face first thing in the morning. They got more than they bargained for as stiletto heels, women's underwear, and an assortment of different coloured slimming pills spilled out of his bag.

As soon as I made some money I moved to a cheap one-room

office in Covent Garden, then still a fruit and vegetable market. I took on staff and gained more space. It seemed to be a very rapid expansion: I'd started to build up a momentum in the business and nothing was going to stop me.

After a year or so, in 1976, Paul decided he would like to start his own business too. I helped finance him and he found a shop next to Chelsea football ground at the less fashionable end of Fulham Road. It became the first avant-garde menswear shop in London. All of our fashion designer friends, including Katharine Hamnett and Wendy Dagworthy, designed their first menswear for the Howie shop. Paul designed his own range of colourful hand–knitwear and in just a short space of time it became the hang-out for many of England's top pop stars and men about town.

I'll never forget the first editorial we got in the *Sunday Times*. We stayed up until two in the morning to get the paper as soon as it came on the stands. Brilliant fashion editor, Michael Roberts, who had written the piece, photographed the outfits looking like tramps' clothes. What could have appeared dowdy looked extraordinary. A beautiful tweed overcoat had been tied up with a piece of string in the middle – but somehow it worked. That, and a subsequent editorial in the *Evening Standard*, launched the Howie business.

We sold jewellery for men, got knitwear designer Betty Barnden to make sweaters featuring people's faces taken from photographs – very popular with pop stars – and wild designer Fred Spurr, one of the Royal College of Art's most talented students, designed black plastic PVC jumpsuits covered in battery-operated light bulbs. We were the talk of the town. Paul would stand in the shop six days a week explaining the clothes to his stylish customers while I got as many magazines and newspapers as possible to write about them.

The PR company meanwhile was still growing in leaps and bounds, moving every few months to larger and larger offices in Covent Garden after the fruit and vegetable market had moved out. My biggest chance for expansion came when I was approached by Murjani, the American company that produced Gloria Vanderbilt jeans. It was the first time a celebrity had endorsed a pair of jeans and it was a huge success in the States. Finally I was given a proper budget and was reluctantly persuaded by the men from the Murjani marketing company to use that year's Miss World contestants as models for a fashion show. I had to pick my own winners, get them out of their old-fashioned stilettos, put their collars down and modernise them.

The jeans had to appeal to the most avant-garde fashion editors as well as to the more conventional Debenham's store buyers who had an exclusivity on the range. As always, what the press wanted and what the buyers wanted was miles apart. The press's priority was glamorous stylised photographs; the buyers, understandably enough, wanted clothes they could sell. I worked on this show with the top stylist, Caroline Baker, who had the knack of turning the ordinary into the extraordinary. It was an interesting exercise and culminated in a party at the House of Lords with Gloria Vanderbilt, the 'poor little rich girl' who was herself part of American social history.

Soon after that I got a chance to break out from just promoting frocks through fashion editor Kathryn Samuel. On her recommendation I was approached to do the PR for some friendly guys who were opening a bike shop in Covent Garden. They in turn introduced me to Raleigh, who took the agency on to make cycling fashionable for young women. We had bicycles in nearly every fashion show and fashion shoot in town. Our brief expanded to include bicycles as a way of life for everyone and included launching BMXs to children. The ingeniously offbeat Vicky Pepys – part of the Lynne Franks PR team for many years – arranged for bicycles to be present in the most unlikely situations. Showing the newest collections of Raleigh bikes every year alongside designer fashion collections gave the staff in our busy offices little room for manoeuvre.

I was now in my late twenties and I decided it was the right time to have children. It was my Jewish mother instinct. I'd always loved babies and somehow ignored the fact that my work schedule would hardly allow me time to be an attentive mother. I knew somehow that I'd have a boy and a girl, that their names would be Joshua and Jessica and that they would be beautiful. Joshua was born in 1976 and Jessica in 1978. Both times I rushed back to work straight away and employed an endless stream of nannies. It was a crazy time. I'd be working hard all day and then up all night with the kids. I was travelling constantly – Milan, Paris and New York at all the designer collections – throwing parties, organising my staff, arranging fashion shows and launches, writing press releases and working out endless budgets.

Now I regret that I didn't spend more time with my children when they were young. But work was such an all-consuming passion that it took priority above all else. I didn't even consider it could be any other way. And it wasn't that I was ambitious to be rich or famous or have power or money: I was just completely obsessed with what I was doing. To this day, I really don't know why. It was about being the best PR in London. Somehow I trapped myself in this role. I knew my business was a success and I just couldn't stop working.

Perhaps I got it from my parents, who worked extremely hard and always made sure I worked for my allowance money. Even when I was very young I was only given it if I'd done all the chores expected of me, like making my own bed or clearing away the dishes. It certainly instilled the work ethic in me. By the time I was twelve I'd graduated to working in my dad's butcher shop. Every Saturday and often after work I'd weigh up the meats, cut up the mince, wrap up the barbecue chicken and take the money in an atmosphere rank with the smell of dried blood on sawdust and hanging carcasses at the back of the shop. My father supplied saltbeef to all the 'nosh bars' in London so there were always huge barrels of brine with sides of beef that needed constantly turning.

My parents worked so hard that we never took holidays together. Instead my sister and I were sent off to holiday camps, which we hated. My best memories of early childhood are of going with our grandmother on holiday to Brighton where my younger sister Sue and I entertained the old Jewish ladies on the Hove seafront by singing 'Que serà serà' and 'Sisters'. Dad would come on Sundays to take a walk along the Brighton seafront. It was here that the north London Jewish crowd gathered at weekends to talk about old times and show off their children. They had last met in the 1930s having a wild time dancing to big bands at Jewish weddings until the war split them up. By the time the 1950s came along they were married with small children and had started up their own businesses.

My father knew everyone and everyone knew him. He was a lively, large, good-looking man who loved telling jokes and entertaining his friends. At the time I was embarrassed – now I appreciate what fun he was.

But he started getting what were then called nervous breakdowns, subsequently diagnosed as manic depression, from the time I was four years old. I got used to him being regularly hospitalised and receiving electric shock treatment. He was at his worst about the time of my O levels so I'd help my mother after school instead of studying for my exams.

My mother was small and rather fragile looking but as I watched her moving these huge carcasses and sides of beef around with seeming ease, I was in awe of her strength. She is a highly intelligent woman who as a schoolgirl before the war had been determined to be a journalist. It was understood that somehow I would try to take over where fate and circumstance had forced her to leave off. I was never interested in following an academic path. I spent more time organising school dances in aid of Oxfam. Meeting old schoolfriends years later I was told that I had always been the one to tell them what the latest music was, or the latest fashions. I suppose it was inevitable that I ended up trend forecasting and event organising as part of my PR career.

In 1978 Paul and I opened Mrs Howie, the first fashion shop in the Covent Garden area. We found a large old banana warehouse and asked architect Ben Kelly to design it. It had a rubber floor, sail-cloth on the walls and clothes rails made out of warehouse clamps. With its post-industrial tones of blue and grey it was way ahead of its time and soon it was featured in all the magazines as London's first high-tech shop and the centre of the London fashion scene.

I bought interesting and often unsellable fashion from art students as well as from young designers in Paris, London and Milan. I bought for the shop the way I do for myself – irresponsibly and indiscriminately – and then got as much publicity for the clothes as possible. Sometimes they sold brilliantly – like the hundreds of pairs of land army breeches that we bought from army surplus stores. But often they didn't. Again our clientele consisted of pop stars, and we'd always try and be super-cool as David Bowie or Bob Geldof with a very young Paula Yates wandered in. Paul designed regularly now and we sold his men's and women's collection through the shops as well as to other top retailers. The American stores in particular loved what they called his *Annie Hall* men's look for women, and his hand-knits.

We had designer studios downstairs, a menswear department, Walker's shoes and the Lynne Franks PR offices at the back. Japanese tourists and TV crews arrived daily and our genial giant shop manager Charles in his oversized dungarees charmed them all.

Many wonderful characters worked for us when they were just out of school before moving on to major international careers. John Galliano was our Saturday boy while still a student at St Martin's College of Art; leading international photographer Mario Testino sold our shoes; and Daniella Milton, who now works with Anjelica Huston in Hollywood, was our office junior.

Covent Garden became the creative centre of London, its old market buildings the ideal spaces for fashion photographers, designers and graphic artists, as well as for dance studios. Other fashion shops started springing up all around us and soon we were hanging out with many other highly energetic ambitious young people.

We became famous for our parties, which I would give at the drop of a hat. 'OK, time for some fun,' I'd say, giving my driver, Dave, wads of cash to buy themed flowers, drinks and food. I'd list the names of my favourite journalists, designers and pop stars to my enthusiastic staff, who'd immediately start ringing round. Clearing away our press samples to the downstairs back room, we would get in the best DJ and sound system in town and danced till we dropped. Once when we decided to have a red and green theme for our Christmas party an over-enthusiastic fashion student continually poured lethal red and green cocktails into everyone's glasses. Friends complained of green pee and multicoloured puke for days.

Most nights turned into some event or other after we closed the door of the Covent Garden shop. Although I'd always banned cigarettes, I was relaxed about joints and our staff and friends would often sit around till late at night drinking bottles of wine and getting stoned while we regaled each other with tales of the hysterical things that had happened that day.

We also spent time hanging around the Zanzibar, a private members' club and forerunner to Groucho's, where we'd meet up with our Covent Garden friends. It seemed great fun at the time but there was a price to pay. The nights when I sat around the office were nights I didn't go home to my children and Paul started to neglect his business. I started getting worried as his lunch hours turned into all-day and night binges where the novelty of getting out of it with his pals and the attractive Zanzibar waitresses was more appealing than running a fashion company.

'Don't go out for lunch,' I'd beg him as I juggled telephones, staff and often the children. 'I won't be long,' he'd assure me as he made his escape, often with binoculars over his shoulders, on his way to his other great love – a day at the races.

Meanwhile, the PR company was getting busier and busier. I was working for many of Europe's most innovative fashion designers. The eccentric Vivienne Westwood became a client in the days of punk fashion which she helped create with her erstwhile partner and former Sex Pistols manager, Malcolm McLaren. She lived near me in south London and would often cycle round to see me on her home-made bike late at night to chat in her flat Lancashire vowels about the responsibility of motherhood and running a business as we played with my small baby daughter.

Katharine Hamnett remained a client and was by now becoming a major international star. I started working with Body Map, a company run by talented design duo Stevie Stewart and David Holah, who hung out with the most interesting young artists in town like dancer Michael Clarke, filmmaker John Maybury and singer Boy George. They were all slightly younger than me and had emerged out of the London art college and squat scene. It was the early 1980s and London fashion and music was about to undergo a huge revival. Lady Di was our fashion ambassador and the international fashion set considered London once again to be the mecca of street style it had been in the sixties.

I'd always considered fashion shows quite boring and made a point of trying to put as much entertainment value into the presentations as possible. The Howie catwalk shows were put on in an east London pub using local kids as models, in St Paul's churchyard in Covent Garden and at gay discos. We used models on roller skates to show Paul's designs of Superman and American football style giant knitwear, an example of which is now in the V&A. The press loved our brightly coloured Howie Diffusion striped T-shirt dresses, which were copied all over the world. Our shows were a great success but the follow-up business details were never given enough attention. We grew too fast too soon, with Paul more interested in having a good time than organising clothing production.

The Body Map team got their friends to help with their shows and they were the height of eighties camp. They would regularly use the 'trannie' look with David and his friends dressed in high heels and wigs. Stevie's mother and other beautiful women in their forties would model alongside David's five-year-old niece, with Boy George and his cohorts parading down the catwalk or sitting in the front row of the audience in their latest outfits.

It was the time when Leigh Bowery, Trojan and other club personalities were crossing the cultural boundaries of fashion and art. I went with them to hit New York by storm in the mid-1980s. We stayed at Morgans, then New York's newest and most stylish hotel just opened by Studio 54's Steve Rubell and Ian Schrager, went to all the happening night spots in town and together with nightclub queen

Suzanne Bartch promoted high-profile fashion extravaganzas. London had come to New York. Sadly, so many of the characters of that time didn't make it – drugs, crazy nights and AIDS claimed many victims.

Eventually Paul's neglect of the Howie business took its toll and much to my horror it went into high-profile bankruptcy. I'd always imagined that the fashion manufacturing business would make a lot more money than PR but that was not to be. The PR agency took over the lease of the Long Acre premises; it was now of a size that needed all the former shop space for offices and press showrooms. We were working in many areas of consumer products and retail and I seemed to spend most of my time running from one client meeting to another. I had a big car with a telephone and eventually my own driver, and would work from the back of the car as I spun around London making calls and doing paperwork. Paul had started freelance designing and was travelling around the world finding new production sources. We had no time for ourselves, and very little for each other.

The success of the PR company was due largely to the unique creative energy that emerged from the team. Hundreds of bright young women and a few men moved in and out of our doors as part of what I would call the Lynne Franks Training College for PR, but a nucleus of ex-fashion-students, journalists and retailers, including Christine Bryan, Heather Lambert, Debra Bourne, Sarah Beerbohm, Vicky Pepys and Australians Ann-Marie Fitzgerald and Harriet Ayre-Smith, worked with me for a number of years in building up the agency. We were plugged into youth culture and knew what was happening in the street. When we crossed over into the mainstream I still had the ability to know what people wanted before it happened.

In the early 1980s several of Britain's top designers complained to me that there was nowhere central and prestigious to hold their catwalk shows. I suggested we should put up a giant tent like the one in Paris and went all over London looking for the right site.

Initially the tent was at the Commonwealth Institute in Kensington High Street until the lawn began to sink and we moved to the Duke of York's Territorial Army headquarters in King's Road. That was really the start of London Fashion Week. I convinced Mohan Murjani, my client from Gloria Vanderbilt days, that it was important for his international prestige to sponsor the events, and the Murjani Tent was born. I also got other clients like the British Fashion Council, Swatch and Harrods to sponsor the tents – a 'win-win' situation for all. The tents were the highlight of British fashion for years until industry politics meant that they had to move to the less glamorous environment of Olympia and the designers gradually left to show in Paris or Milan instead. Now that the focus is back on London, the tents are in the elegant grounds of the Natural History Museum.

I took London Fashion Week very seriously. After all, I was the one who had to make sure that self-important fashion editors sat in their allocated A-row seats while lesser publications were allowed the rows behind. The irony was that you often had the worst view in the front row because that was where the numerous photographers would be positioned. I was also the one who had to make the photographers crouch down as low as possible and turn pushy Italian buyers protesting 'No English' out of the press seats. We had to create excitement and hype, making sure that there were no empty seats while throwing out all the fashion victim gatecrashers. *What a nightmare!*

I took to changing my own outfits so that I would be dressed appropriately for the different designers – sometimes three times a day. I felt this was only polite, although unknown to me it caused great mirth amongst the press. I made sure I gave my favourite designers flowers at the end of the show, often with tears in my eyes. I knew the sweat and toil as well as the tremendous financial sacrifices that had gone on to make these catwalk shows a reality. These would perpetuate the designers' high profile so that they could sell more frocks, get their pictures in the paper and try and make enough money to pay for the next season's show.

Celebrity clients are an important part of this game: the number of famous faces in the front row of a show add to the designer's international kudos. Although often the most creative and best trained, the British designers were always under-capitalised and lacked the professional management and licences of their European counterparts. They went in and out of business, lurching from one drama to another, and I cared passionately throughout it all.

I worked with many of the major international designer names over the years including Donna Karan, Romeo Gigli, Jean Paul Gaultier, Edina Ronay, John Galliano, Jasper Conran, Calvin Klein and Ghost. Creative, stimulating individuals, most of them could laugh at themselves and at the insane system we were part of. Beautiful clothes and sensual fabrics are enjoyable to wear as well as to design. It is the machinery around them that feeds ego and illusion, and creates insecurities.

The stress of running the business, keeping a home and family going and watching Paul lose his sense of direction was unbearable. As a result I started unwinding with cocaine in the evenings. We'd visit friends and in between lines of coke would spend most of the night rolling joints, drinking wine and talking fifteen to the dozen with none of us listening to each other. It was the frenzied 1980s and I was spinning round in circles poisoning my body and soul with negative drugs and negative people. I was hyper all the time and although able to do my job well was putting excessive stress on my personal life and well-being. I lost all sense of reality, spinning faster and faster on a mad merry-go-round of adrenalin.

It came to a head for me when a crowd of us went away to the country for the weekend to celebrate a friend's fortieth birthday. He took so much cocaine that night that he had what appeared to be a heart attack the next morning. Although he recovered I decided that enough was enough. I was in my early thirties and wanted to live a long, healthy life. It was time to clean up my act.

A few years earlier I'd met a woman who was to become one of my closest friends and mentors. Alan Flusser, a leading American menswear designer, and his sweet wife Marylise had become friends of ours through the Howie shop. We knew that they had been practising a form of Japanese Buddhism for some years and believed it had kept

17

them sane in the madness of the fashion industry. They had often told me about their friend, fashion stylist and PR Kezia Keeble, who was another Buddhist. Alan said she reminded him a lot of me.

I was in New York and seven months pregnant with Jessica when I first met Kezia. The Americans good-naturedly thought of me as a British punk with my pink and orange hair, big leather jacket, Brook's Brothers' man's shirt and tie, an expandable pleated skirt, socks and Walker's shoes.

Paul and I got on immediately with Kezia and her younger husband, also called Paul. We'd go to Studio 54 together and hang out at their office-cum-apartment eating healthy food. Kezia was a tall, statuesque woman usually seen at fashion shows wearing a large checked blanket coat and with her baby daughter, Cayli, strapped to her back. Paul Cavaco, a stylishly dressed young American of Spanish Cuban descent, was half her size and when I met them again at the Paris collections the family was turning heads among the fashion glitterati.

While on holiday with them at their home in the Hamptons, I noticed that Kezia would disappear for hours on end. When I asked her where she had been she explained that she was chanting Nam-myoho-renge-kyo to stop a plummeting rogue satellite falling on to a populated area of the world.

She explained that by chanting Nam-myoho-renge-kyo you could alter situations and change your karma – in other words change old patterns and bad habits that had accumulated over many lifetimes. She then showed me a scroll called a Gohonzon. It was enshrined in a Japanese-style altar and had on it a mixture of Chinese and Sanskrit characters. She explained these were symbolic of the different states of being and came from the lotus sutra, one of the teachings of Shakamuni, the original Buddha. Nam-myoho-renge-kyo, the teaching of a thirteenth-century Japanese Buddhist priest called Nichiren Daishonin, was written down the centre and she told me the scroll was an object of worship that reflected our highest intention like a mirror.

'By chanting to it every day,' she told me, 'you can fuse your entity with the mystic law of the universe and manifest your potential. Nam-myoho-renge-kyo means "I devote myself to the mystic law of cause and effect through sound and vibration."' I wasn't quite sure what she meant and didn't yet feel ready to follow her path, but I kept an open mind as I'd seen what a powerful effect it had on her and Paul and on Alan and Marylise. Since I'd stopped practising Judaism as a teenager I'd never been interested in following any religion but now, seeing how much benefit my friends seemed to be gaining, I wondered whether this might give me the inner peace I was looking for. Juggling a highly pressurised job, a young family and a busy social life was starting to take its toll.

Several years later I felt ready to explore the idea of chanting. My stressful life together with my decision to keep away from a cocaine lifestyle made me ready to look for an alternative path. I started chanting with another Buddhist, designer Jeff Banks, while on holiday and he taught me how to recite the morning and evening prayers and liturgy. I learnt to repeat part of the lotus sutra with Japanese phonetic pronunciation taken from Chinese writing of the original Sanskrit five times every morning and three times every evening. After I came back to London Jeff introduced me to his ex-wife, pop singer Sandie Shaw. She too was a Buddhist and she took me to meetings at other Buddhist friends' homes where I practised the rituals and studied the philosophy and history behind them. I felt better than I had for years and after about three months of commitment I was given my own Gohonzon to chant to.

For the first time I started understanding the eternity of life through reincarnation. I had always had a great fear of death, but now I understood the Buddhist realisation of the impermanence of life but the continuation of soul. I began to believe in a divine energy, a cosmic force to which we are all individually connected. I learnt about the logic of karma – that we experience the effects of our own causes – and how to take individual responsibility for changing the pattern of my life.

Every morning and night I sat in front of my black Japanese lacquer altar and chanted. In the mornings I would go to my Gohonzon with a shopping list of problems I needed solving, usually about work, and would end up, 'Oh, by the way, we must save the world too.' I attended meetings and would hear the other Buddhists pour open their hearts and tell of all their problems. They made me feel very lucky. I would even say I had no problems: that I was happily married with two wonderful children and a successful business. I was in denial.

These Buddhists came from many backgrounds. They were mostly aged between thirty and forty, and of mixed nationalities, race and cultures. There were teachers, dancers, social workers, house-wives, postmen and plumbers. The media cottoned on to this re-emerging interest in Eastern philosophy and religion and focused on a number of high-profile practitioners, including myself, Boy George, Tina Turner and Sandie Shaw. *The Face* magazine wrote of Designer Buddhists chanting for a new Porsche, and the rest of the media followed suit. I am sure that my constant encouraging of most of the British fashion industry to follow my example and chant for happiness added to the hysteria.

In the mid-eighties the Nichiren Shoshu Buddhist organisation that I belonged to put on an exhibition for peace called Choose Life. I took Katharine Hamnett along and she was inspired to design what she called her 'Choose Life' big slogan T-shirts. Giant-size, bright-coloured T-shirts in cotton and silk appeared everywhere, sporting slogans like SAVE THE WHALE, HEROIN FREE ZONE and the famous 58% WANT PERSHINGS OUT. She wore one under her jacket at a London Fashion Week reception at 10 Downing Street and exposed it as soon as she was standing next to Mrs Thatcher. Cameras flashed and the picture went out all over the world. Not quite what Mrs Thatcher had in mind when she agreed to host the party.

About this time Katharine and I went to offer support to the women protesters camping outside the American nuclear weapons base at Greenham Common. She took along piles of US GO HOME T-shirts which her Knightsbridge boutiques, not wanting to offend their American customers, had refused to sell. We gave them away to the women, who were delighted to wear them.

I asked some of them why there were no men there. They explained that there had been at the beginning but the men always got involved in some form of confrontation with the police so they'd been asked to leave. In the media, the Greenham women came across as mad, angry men-haters but the reality was that many were quietly spoken teachers, housewives, nurses and mothers who cared about the future of the planet. The women of Greenham and the Katharine Hamnett T-shirt series which I promoted were, I believe, major forces in the start of a consciousness shift which had repercussions throughout the world.

I'm certain that Live Aid in July 1985 was the result of Katharine's Hamnett's T-shirts followed by celebrity endorsements of good causes. Soon after Live Aid, I worked with Bob Geldof, Harvey Goldsmith, Jasper Conran, his assistant Christina Vierra and Kevin and Sue Godley to create Fashion Aid at the Albert Hall. It was the first time that we'd got major international designers to come over or send their top models with their newest collections for a joint show in England. The Duchess of Kent was there and all the designers did special T-shirts. Kevin Godley made a film which went out all over the world and we created the most extraordinary fashion show. In the Katharine Hamnett scene, introduced by Annie Lennox, all her friends including me wore yellow and red slogan T-shirts and danced on the stage together with African drummers, Hindu dancers, flags, poles and a Mrs Thatcher lookalike with handbag and pearls. It was a great experience.

Another celebrity cause I worked on was with Sting and his wife Trudi Styler's Foundation for the Amazon Rain Forests. Trudi even managed to persuade notorious rivals Gianni Versace and Giorgio Armani to participate jointly in a fashion show in London. I helped with the press and became a trustee of the Foundation, continuing to work with her on various other projects. A cause becomes much more sexy if there is celebrity involvement!

Celebrity endorsement started attracting sponsors, becoming part of a new area of cause-related marketing. One of the first high-profile events along these lines was Reebok's sponsorship of the Amnesty International Human Rights world tour in the autumn of 1988 which starred Sting, Bruce Springsteen and Peter Gabriel. Lynne Franks PR was the press agency for the musicians as they travelled across continents raising awareness of the Amnesty message. Reebok, of course, were delighted with the association with both the rock stars and the cause.

We were involved in creating publicity for many important social messages or charities. We launched Green Consumer Week in the mid-1980s, when the British consumers were first made aware of the power of their purchase. We worked on a number of AIDS aware-ness campaigns as well as with Comic Relief, Greenpeace, Oxfam and other charity fund-raising activities. We kept our fees down or did away with them altogether and I felt that in some small way we were doing more than just increasing our own or our client's bottom line.

By the mid-1980s Paul and I decided that he should come into the PR business and help me run it. It seemed as if the shock of his own business collapsing had made him straighten up his act. His logical brain and good management skills were just what the PR agency needed. He took over the administration, finance and personnel and finally we were able to use our mutual skills in a working partnership that was enjoyable and beneficial. The company became a major force in the marketing services world with large offices in Marble Arch and more than fifty staff.

Paul had a master plan to build up Lynne Franks PR so that we could sell it to a larger agency. He explained that the only way we'd make capital would be to take advantage of the eighties madness when service businesses would buy smaller ones for vast amounts of money and let the principals retire after a suitable time lag. I was reluctant at first because I was so locked into being a workaholic that I couldn't see any other way of living. But finally Paul convinced me and deals started coming our way. He'd also decided to become a Buddhist to help save our marriage and consequently our relationship became far closer.

We moved to west London and were able to spend more time at home with our children. We held Buddhist meetings regularly at our house and seemed to have survived the worst of the 1980s. We talked a lot about business, the children and our Buddhist activities – but avoided talking about our relationship.

At about this time we were contacted by the advertising agency for Brylcreem. They had a bright young female creative team who realised that Brylcreem had the potential to become very fashionable and needed a dynamic PR campaign to run alongside their trendy ads. Beechams, the traditional pharmaceutical company who owned the brand, were cautiously enthusiastic.

I developed the 'Brylcreem Boy' campaign as a kind of male beauty contest with street-cred, advertising it through shopping centres and at Boots stores. We held regional heats at the 'in' clubs in town. We were not only looking for the cutest boys around – with great hair, of course – but also for boys with personality, brains and ambition. We code named it 'Bril' and there was certainly no shortage of boys wanting to enter. The competition continued successfully for several years, building momentum and gaining widespread TV and media coverage. It was interesting to see similar boys' beauty shows on the new girlie shows on British TV in the mid-1990s. I'm not sure now of the political correctness of male or female beauty contests but then they were just a lot of fun.

We launched Swatch watches in the UK and made sure that all the pop stars and presenters on MTV wore them. On one occasion I turned the Piazza at Covent Garden into a huge outdoor Swatch graffiti art gallery for thousands.

Then there was the challenge of Harvey Nichols. In the early eighties the Knightsbridge department store had had quite a staid image. Together with their brilliant in-house team, led by their marketing director Mary Portas, we completely changed that image in the media. It became the place where every fashion victim in town had to shop – to the point where it was even lampooned as Edina's favourite store in *Ab Fab*.

The eighties went through a phase when the media turned retailing tycoons into stars and then knocked them down again. I worked for the best of them. Ralph Halpern of the Burton Group, George Davies of Next and Gerald Ratner of Ratner's jewellery stores were all my clients and friends at different times. These men were exciting to work with and we got high on the mutual energy exchanged. I think it was a lesson for them, and me, that a high profile for a businessman is not always a good thing.

One day Gerald Ratner called me into his Mayfair office. Peering at me over the top of his tennis-court-size desk he told me he'd been asked to do a major speech for the Institute of Directors. Gerald was a very funny man and he told me his joke about Ratner's jewellery costing the same as a Marks and Spencer's prawn sandwich but not lasting as long. I told him I thought it was a bad idea and his speech should be about caring for his customers and staff. He looked at me as if I was mad and I feared the worst. Sure enough, he made his joke and it totally misfired. It was repeated for days by the British press and brought the king of the cheap jewellery trade tumbling from his throne.

Ralph Halpern never really got rid of his 'five times a night' superstud press image, although in many ways it didn't do him much harm either. He too was a highly creative and dynamic character with an entrepreneurial spirit that would freeze his minions into fear. I found his need for armed bodyguards particularly amusing: I wasn't quite sure who he thought was out to assassinate him.

George Davies was by far the shrewdest when it came to charming the press. His problem was that he didn't manage to charm his directors in quite the same way and was ultimately ousted in a boardroom coup. We worked closely together for a number of years and I found his good taste, quick mind and creativity a joy. We launched Next Directory as the first mail-order catalogue for the middle classes. Beautifully designed by Tim Lamb, the catalogues were a work of art and cost a fortune. It was George's promise of a 24-hour telephone delivery service that really caused a revolution in the mail-order business. Under the eye of his then wife Liz Davies the clothes were well designed and good quality, the promise of delivery more or less achieved and the publicity enormous. For the first time in my career I arranged an embargo date on a story. George and I had reasoned that, apart from the considerable impact, it made much more sense for the public to be able to get the goods when the stories were published. The fashion press had a bad habit of showing clothes much earlier than they were available in the stores, just to be first with the story.

The press were appalled but kept to the embargo, with the notable exception of Liz Smith, then fashion editor of *The Times*, and Next took the unheard-of step of issuing an injunction to stop *The Times* publishing. In one weekend in the spring of 1988 all over the country newspapers, magazines and television stations were talking about the Next mail-order phenomenon.

In 1991 Lynne Franks PR moved to even larger offices in west London's Harrow Road. Originally an old car spray warehouse, the building was converted by designer Ben Kelly. We were the first offices in the media world in London to have a no-smoking ban; it was even publicised in *Time Out*. We had comfy sofas, flowers, a sound system and MTV in reception. When we first moved to Harrow Road I felt a strange energy from the police station next door so I got a little Burmese lady called Mrs Wong to come in and feng shui the building.

Feng shui is the Taoist art and science of living in harmony with the environment which for centuries the Chinese people have used to design cities, build homes and bury their dead. It's like psychic interior design. Mrs Wong got me to hang paintings of flowers, change the position of mirrors and put up wind chimes outside the main doors. Adding these touches I felt changed the energy of the building. The Chinese believe that the way the furniture is placed, the way the doors open and the way mirrors and pictures are hung can bring health and good fortune to the family or business. Their business community frequently consults feng shui masters when choosing offices or moving to new premises as it is thought to determine the prosperity of the business.

Although my home life seemed more settled, I was still very busy with clients and wasn't spending nearly enough quality time looking after myself. I would rush for a massage, or acupuncture, or to some other kind of therapy without having time to enjoy the benefits. I would jump into my car to rush to a session, arrive late feeling neurotic, get patched up just enough to keep me going for the next twenty-four hours, and rush back late to my next meeting. I wasn't eating the right food, was always in a hurry and often did my Buddhist chanting on the run or in the office. I wasn't the only one who seemed to be living my life in this mad way. I would observe other women friends and colleagues rushing to the gym or for a massage in a panic. Why were we all living like this? I wondered. Often I didn't even have time to relieve my bladder as I rushed from meeting to phone call to therapist to meeting. If only I'd kept some of that time just for personal space, even a couple of minutes between meetings, I later reasoned, I could have saved myself a fortune in the latest anti-stress cure.

Around this time I got a late-night phone call from my friend Kezia Keeble in New York. She was very sick with cancer. Down the line came a frail voice with an urgent message: 'The world is in chaos,' she said, 'and I'm not going to be here to help stop it self-destruct. You have to do something about it.' It was an awesome appeal, and one that terrified me. I had an image in my mind of Kezia handing me a pennant dedicated to love, peace and hope and I took her words to heart. Perhaps the time had come to start directing my skills towards creating a better world rather than the promotion of a new frock.

Surrounded by telephones, diaries, people and possessions, Kezia was similar to me in her need to plan and control every aspect of her life. But when she was faced with something she couldn't control – the cancer ravaging her body – she finally realised the truth. That's when I finally became aware of what Buddhism could have shown me if I'd had the time to listen. It was from her pain, awakening and personal growth that I understood that only by changing the pace of my life and letting go would I find happiness. The ultimate gift she gave me was the beginning of an understanding of the eternity of life and death. It made me begin to feel responsible about what I was going to do with my life. At last I saw that there was a lot more to living than work and that I should take time for myself and the people I loved.

We decided to sell the business and, although there was an extended arrangement whereby I could stay on as long as I wanted, I started longing for my freedom. Who was Lynne Franks and who was Lynne Franks PR? I was experiencing an identity crisis as well as bereavement from my creation – the business.

After several months of negotiation Paul brilliantly concluded an advantageous deal with the corporate PR group, Broadstreet, who bought us before getting in trouble for overspending and being taken over in turn by French advertising agency BDDP. Paul was happy but I grieved and went to bed with sedatives. Three days later, realising this wasn't my way, I dragged myself up and got some acupuncture. It gave me the energy I needed and I was able to pull myself back together. I was determined to take this chance to lead a different kind of life. I'd existed on my adrenalin for so many years that I'd forgotten what it was like to slow down.

For the first time we had money – even after we'd paid all our tax. We bought our dream home in Maida Vale and spent a fortune decorating it. It was as if we were children being given unlimited access to a toy shop. We just spent and spent. We needed staff to keep this large house and our lifestyle going so we employed a chauffeur, a cook, a gardener and a housekeeper. I no longer went shopping for food myself, and if we had a dinner party I'd hire extra people to come in and do the cooking for me. Often we entertained key players from the worlds of politics and business, together with well-known show-business personalities, but always we kept it informal and often ended up dancing around the dining table. We travelled first class, stayed in the top hotels and ate in the most expensive restaurants.

The only thing that kept me grounded was my Buddhist activities. Paul and I held discussion meetings together, went on study courses and participated in local community events. The children also got involved when our organisation put on an ambitious modern production of *Alice in Wonderland* based on Buddhist principles, at Hammersmith Odeon. Less elaborate but more intense was a production of *Aladdin* which Paul wrote and we both appeared in with our local Buddhist group. Several hundred people, including many of my fashion friends, saw me appear as the Empress of Maida Vale – 'very big in government circles' – and watched as the scenery collapsed, we forgot our lines, the sound system blew and the costumes fell apart. I got very strung out, wanting everything to be perfect as usual, until I saw what a wonderful afternoon everyone was having.

We'd always wanted a second home in the sun and at last we had enough money to buy one. It was when I was staying with some friends in Mallorca and visiting Katharine Hamnett that I drove through the beautiful village of Deia and realised I'd come home. I asked Katharine to help me find a house there as soon as possible.

Meanwhile I was still working in the agency with an agreement to stay a further two years and still living the same crazy life. My back finally gave out under the tension and I couldn't stand without a stick.

One day I was lying in bed unable to move when I picked up the *Evening Standard* and read an article about a woman called Denise Linn, a Native American shaman who was visiting England and doing a workshop on spiritual healing over the coming weekend. I believe you get the right signs when you need them and now something resonated inside me. I was supposed to be going on a Buddhist course that weekend but at the last minute it had been cancelled. With the children and Paul away and with my first free weekend for many years I quickly booked in.

*

I was starting to realise that business success, money and possessions did not necessarily make me happy. The inevitable accompanying stress, lack of quality time with my family and friends, and always living in the future created an emptiness and lack of centre that was destroying me.

2

Letting Go

For the first time in my life I was completely alone. I was on the top of a mountain outside Seattle with only a bottle of water, a sleeping bag and a drum. Elsewhere on the mountaintop were my two young teenage children and husband as well as other members of the Vision Quest workshop. Apart from a brief night-time visit from my daughter I didn't see another soul for twenty-four hours.

During the day I watched the eagles circle below me. Then I took my clothes off. I sensed the primeval blood of my female ancestors, the blood of women of all time, running through my veins. As night came I made a circle with my urine to keep out the wild animals, put my sleeping bag in the middle and wasn't scared of the spooks that I'd always imagined in the dark.

Ever since my childhood I'd been scared of being on my own. I'd shared a bedroom with my sister, moved in with Paul when I was twenty-one and always been surrounded by colleagues, friends or children. In that twenty-four hours I realised that my fear of being alone was really a fear of facing my own mortality. There was nothing to be scared of apart from my own fears. In fact I relished being on my own. I didn't want the silence to end.

At dawn the next day I started making my way back to the meeting point. Twenty of us appeared, coming from all directions. None of us had watches or compasses but we all sensed where to go and how to get there. All of us in one way or another were deeply changed. I reunited with my husband, my children and other friends and we performed a ritual to signify the end of the Vision Quest.

Some months earlier I'd gone to a workshop by healer and teacher, Denise Linn, looking for some way of learning to heal my stress-induced painful back.

I'd hobbled on a stick into the Kensington hotel where the workshop on spiritual healing was being held, feeling nervous and self-conscious. I had never gone to any kind of New Age event and didn't expect to know anyone there. Despite always sounding so confident I had an underlying shyness which surfaced in unfamiliar surroundings and with new people. I looked at the other eighty participants, mostly women, wishing the floor would swallow me up. They seemed normal enough, so instead of walking straight back out of the door I gingerly sat on one of the chairs.

Immediately a friendly dark-haired woman about my age turned my way. 'Aren't you Lynne Franks?' she said. I panicked. I'd been spotted. She introduced herself as the beauty editor of a national newspaper and took me to meet her friend, who was also a well-known beauty and health journalist. They were friendly and relaxed and told me that they had attended shaman and healers' training courses before. They explained that many journalists covering their areas came to this type of event as part of their research in alternative healing and found them very useful. These two women were part of my own media world; I started to feel at ease.

We were taken into a large adjoining room, where I first spotted Denise Linn. She was a beautiful woman in her early forties with the dark hair and aquiline features of her race. 'We are going to learn the power of Native American healing,' she explained, 'by visualising the four elements and the four directions in a meditation as well as various other healing techniques.'

As the weekend progressed Denise took us through various processes where by using music and her own voice she put us into deep relaxation through a gentle form of hypnotic suggestion, in order to get in touch with our inner selves. We were able to explore our animal totem and other archetypal imagery from our unconscious, and working with drums, ritual, Native American songs and dancing opened ourselves up to joyful transformation.

In a state of deep relaxation I was told to summon up an image of the animal or bird I most identified with. I saw a red fox, which Denise explained was wary and protective of its cubs. I'm not sure, looking back, if I really let go enough to bring up a true symbol from my unconscious or was influenced by a photograph I'd seen but I do believe it can be a useful exercise and it is taken very seriously by Native Americans and other indigenous people as a way of connecting with nature and the spirit world.

By the Sunday evening, far from feeling in pain, I was spinning around dancing to Indian drums in the hotel gardens. I felt so good I wanted more, so I introduced myself to Denise at the end of the workshop. At once we seemed to connect and later I found out that we share the same birthday. She told me about the residential retreats she did out in the wilds near her north-west American home and I determined to take my family to one. So here I was, several months later, learning how to make my own drum and build a sweat lodge.

A sweat lodge is a traditional Native American structure where rituals and prayer sessions take place. Shaped like an igloo, it's made from bent branches, traditionally covered over with buffalo skins for insulation, although these days plastic sheeting or blankets are often used. Large rocks are heated outside on fires and then brought inside to create an intense sauna-type heat.

Originally many Native American tribes would take peyote, the small buttons from the desert cactus, or other forms of hallucinogenic ritual herbs. Shamans saw visions in the swirling steam and received messages from their gods and ancestors. Our sweat lodge ritual, however, was far simpler and without hallucinogenics. Calling in the four elements of earth, fire, water and air, we sang traditional chants and prayed to the gods to rid us of our daily fears and negative patterns. We followed Denise's refrain: 'As we sit in the still darkness, this is the time to cleanse and heal all negativity. It is time to transform hate into love, resentment into forgiveness and shame into understanding.' I felt the words reverberate in the deepest part of my being.

In the event, having been most concerned for my children, I was the one to end up with problems. I started to hyperventilate, but, never one to give in easily, insisted on sticking it out until the end of the first session, at which point I rushed outside and plunged into an ice-cold stream. At that moment I felt very disconnected with my body and began to breathe rapidly. I later learnt that in rebirthing rapid shallow breathing and intense heat are used to let go of old birth traumas and open up to new energies. The strange feeling seemed to last for hours but I'm sure it was no more than a few minutes. My children held me until I became grounded. Then I went back into the sweat lodge for the next session, this time making sure I sat next to the door.

During the rest of our week I continued to face fears through various trials of endurance, including river rafting and jumping from high cliffs into small pools of water. We were taught how to heal each other through simple exercises and group energy, and used vision circles to help us see our future. For this we divided into small groups. One person would lie down in the centre while those on the outside projected into the future predicting where they saw that person's life in five years' time. When it came to my turn an Australian woman claiming psychic powers put her hands on my stomach.

'Never mind five years, my dear,' she said. 'If you don't change your life drastically in the next two years you're going to get very sick indeed.' I took her advice seriously, knowing that changing my lifestyle was now a matter of life or death.

I'd been planning a slow move from the fast lane for a while but time was running out. My body was often in pain, particularly my stomach, throat and back where I seemed to hold my stress. I ate the wrong foods, took very little exercise and spent most of my time in a state of anxiety. Another warning to me was the serious illnesses and subsequent deaths of my two best friends in PR, Kezia Keeble in New York and Jean Bennet in London. Both women, only a little older than me, had children the same age as mine and had been my friends for many years. Like me they were passionate about their work and lived under enormous pressure.

I was planning to stop working at Lynne Franks PR after my two-year contract was up. The Vision Quest made me determined to get out even sooner. Since my week in the wilds of Washington State I also realised I needed to get out of London and spend more time on my own in nature. Although Paul and I seemed to be getting on very well in the States, regaining some of our old intimacy, we reverted to our bad old patterns when we got back to London. We stopped communicating, as my crazy schedule took over again and he spent hedonistic evenings with his friends. I'd lost track of who I really was. I wasn't sure if I liked the person I'd become. Even I was confused about how much of the Edina character in *Absolutely Fabulous* was really me.

But now I knew I was creating whatever was happening to me, and that any changes had to come from within. The fact that my life had become just one big rush was nobody's fault but my own. Life seemed full of confrontations and tension. Sitting in heavy traffic and running late from one meeting to another was making me ill. Trying to control my life and everyone around me was obviously not the answer. And I'd seen what it had done to Kezia and Jean.

In theory I had everything I thought I wanted – a large house, a big car, a successful business and a wonderful family – but inside I felt I had nothing. Although my marriage seemed on the surface to have improved, it was a plaster on a very deep wound. Too many years of unhappiness had been pushed under the carpet and both of us fought shy of confrontation in our newly formed friendship. My inner landscape was barren.

In my work I was perpetuating a system I no longer believed in and had lost my true connection with self. I'd forgotten what it was like to be a human *being* because I was too busy being a human *doing*. How could I possibly get excited about the latest frock length any more? I felt I was drowning in an ocean of illusory glamour instead of diving into the ocean of knowledge. Buddhism had taught me that each individual can create one small ripple in the ocean and affect the whole planet for good or bad. I wanted to learn how to create that ripple and dedicate myself to communication based on love, not hype.

Newspapers, magazines, movies and TV penetrate our consciousness to such a degree that it affects our whole attitude to life. I began to see now how important it was for the media to be responsible as well as entertaining. I know we have to show the dark as well as the light side of life but we were totally out of balance.

I needed to take a step back and find my true values. What did I really want from life? I remembered once accompanying my father to a psychiatrist. He would become hyper and obsessed when business was good, or vegetable-like and depressed when it was bad. The psychiatrist asked him: 'Mr Franks, are you telling me that if you had fifty butcher shops and a Rolls-Royce you'd be really happy?' 'Sure I would,' my father answered in surprise. 'Wouldn't you?' I thought of him now, a sad, shambling wreck of a man, too ill with Alzheimer's to be looked after by my mother. I wanted to say to him: 'See, Dad, the fifty shops wouldn't have made much difference after all. Why didn't you just learn to relax and enjoy your life?'

I wanted to get out of London and start spending time in a more natural environment. I had fallen in love with the village of Deia in Mallorca earlier that summer. I thought it was the most beautiful place I'd ever seen. Ancient stone terraces, a legacy from the Moorish inhabitants nearly a thousand years ago, were covered in olive trees in unworldly shapes that were nearly as old. Magical mountains – which I later discovered had inspired the writer Robert Graves, a local resident – fell straight into the sea and the colourful wild flowers and purple bougainvillaea brought the landscape to life. The biblical sound of sheep's bells and donkeys' braying lent a pastoral air to the scene. Stone-clad houses and a small village street that hadn't changed in a hundred years convinced me I had found my paradise.

Most days in Deia there is a clean, clear Mediterranean sea and matching clear blue sky with awe-inspiring sunsets. From my terrace I can watch the sun sink into the sea while the sky is shot through with blue and pink and the moon rises over a night sky soon full of stars. I often joked that the Jews had somehow got lost on their way to the Promised Land and ended up in the arid desert of Palestine instead of my village in Mallorca where oranges and lemons, carob pods and olives were so abundant that they spilled from the trees. Through a friend of Katharine Hamnett I found my ideal home, a traditional small house on the side of a mountain overlooking the sea.

Since the turn of the century Deia has been a meeting place for artists, writers and musicians who co-exist happily with the friendly Mallorcans. They look on us eccentric foreigners with tolerance. Robert Graves died in 1985 but his presence continues to be felt everywhere. It's as if you can see his tall figure still walking through the village. His small stone amphitheatre is used for poetry readings by the locals as well as by visiting friends like Liverpool poets Brian Patten and Roger McGough. In the summer the young members of the Graves family often entertain us there with the rest of the local teenagers. The local Deia primary school is called after Robert and during his centenary in August 1995, the whole island celebrated his life with exhibitions and events. I feel as if I knew him personally and consider it another part of life's wonderful synergy that I should end up living in the village where he wrote such visionary books and poetry. Robert respected and acknowledged the power of the White Goddess, the magic of Celtic spirituality, the wonder of Sufism, and indeed the connection with moon worship and Mother Earth herself.

I was told by locals that marriages often break up when couples come to Deia. As Gertrude Stein said to Robert Graves fifty years ago, 'It's paradise if you can stand it.' For Deia has its dark side. The village is built like a spiral coiling up to the little church at the top of the steep hill called Es Puig and curving down towards the sea through the part of the village known as Es Clot. Legends abound amongst my friends from the foreign community of crazy parties they were at in the 1960s and 1970s, particularly in the Clot, where families split, children were conceived and sexual diseases were shared. It's certainly much tamer now but for some of those marooned here all through the winter it can get depressing.

Inevitably as Deia has become more popular – with the success of Richard Branson's picturesque hotel, La Residencia, and its role in a popular German soap – the price of houses has risen and for many of the local artist community it has become an expensive place to live.

When I first came to Deia I was intoxicated by the place and determined to spend as much time there as possible, children and work permitting. I was like a woman starving for peace and seclusion. I hungered after long solitary walks, longing to integrate with mother nature. It was in Deia that I began to relax into a different pace of life. I saw clearly that I had always lived at a manic speed, constantly striving to drive others along with me. I assumed everyone's mind worked like mine, and if they didn't keep up then I'd put it down to inefficiency or laziness.

For twenty years my mind hadn't worked like normal minds. It was constantly racing and searching for solutions to problems. I was always looking into the future: while dealing with the business of one meeting I was already planning two meetings ahead. It was a source of fun to those around me that I was able to be on the telephone, watch television, read a newspaper and have a conversation with someone else all at the same time. I never let people end their sentences because I knew what they were going to say before they finished. I never thought that you could operate just as effectively at a slower speed.

Once I'd found my home in Deia I knew it was time to get out of my contract at Lynne Franks PR. So, after one glorious holiday, I went back to London and told the directors that it was time for me to resign. I was amazed at the reaction from the British press. Several papers ran the story as front-page news, surprised that a woman at the height of her so-called success should choose to step off the merry-go-round.

One of my last assignments nearly went disastrously wrong because I was already thinking in such a different way. We had just been approached by the supermarket chain Asda, which would be a huge account for us. As I was officially still chair of the company I was told it was essential I should give a presentation to the board personally. We'd prepared a chart and presentations, as PR agencies do, and arrived to see Archie Norman, the chief executive of Asda, and his marketing team. But when I was in there I spontaneously found myself saying, 'Come on, we don't need to go along this conventional route, do we? Let's just talk about the company's needs and how we can best serve you. We can look at all these documents later.' Judging by their faces they weren't too happy about this approach and later we got a phone call saying they really wanted us to work for them but had been put off by my informal manner. They said they'd give us another chance but only if they met a more responsible director, such as Paul.

A few years later I was astonished when a head-hunter told me she'd heard from a former senior executive of Asda how refreshing my approach had been. I certainly didn't get that reaction at the time.

I was spending more and more time in Deia now. My family came over with some friends for my forty-fourth birthday. It was Easter Sunday in 1992 and somehow I knew it was a great turning point. Nothing would ever be the same again. And the next stage of my life was about to begin.

I was told about crystal healer Katrina Raphaell by Linda Penny, then the marketing director of the *Mail on Sunday*'s 'You' magazine who had trained with her in America. Although both Linda and I came from the cynical world of media we recognised each other's quest for knowledge in the areas of alternative healing.

Linda rang me one day to tell me excitedly that Katrina Raphaell, the doyenne of crystal healing who had not appeared or taught anywhere for more than two years, had decided to come to London and teach a small workshop in a few weeks' time at the Amadeus Centre in Maida Vale.

'I can't believe it,' I said. 'That's round the corner from where I live and I'm actually free that weekend.'

'Put it in your diary,' she instructed me. 'And I promise – it'll be an extraordinary experience.'

I walked into the basement room of the small healing and spiritual centre to see Linda and about forty other people, some of whom I knew, and tables full of enormous crystals of every colour, shape and size. Katrina Raphaell looked like a crystal herself. Her opaque grey eyes seemed to emit an unearthly energy that made my whole body vibrate. She asked if some of the big crystals could be taken out of the room as she was too sensitive to be surrounded with such intense energy. She told us that the power of the light forces within the mineral kingdom can bring benefit to ourselves and others if we know how to use them, and that this sacred knowledge which goes back to the beginning of time is part of the planetary transformation.

'If you think about it,' she said, 'different cultures and peoples have utilised the power within crystals and stones for as long as humans have inhabited the earth. Today, with the rapid advancement of technology, crystals are being used to transmit and magnify energies in many different ways. Ruby crystals, both naturally formed and man-made, are being used in lasers for microscopic surgery. Each year thousands of pounds of quartz crystals are being mined and crushed to be used for technological purposes. Quartz crystals are used in ultrasound devices, in watches, as memory chips in computers and for controlling radio frequencies in electronic equipment.'

She went on to explain that on a more esoteric level, stones and crystals can be used in meditation, placed under the pillow at night to induce clear thinking, held in labour and during the birth process for added strength, and used in the healing arts to stabilise mood swings and soothe troubled minds. In her workshops Katrina would warn people to use the power of crystals and stones ethically and consciously. She said the intention must be humanitarian and pure or the power could be severely turned against the abuser.

Katrina is considered one of the world's most expert

exponents of the power of crystals and how to use them for healing. Her background in the healing arts includes running a natural drug and alcohol rehabilitation centre, as well as nursing, teaching, massage therapies and other related healing practices. Through meditation she started understanding how to use the energies of crystals which contain their own light forces to rebalance mental, emotional and physical disease.

She and her assistant, Teddy, took us through a variety of simple processes and explanations on the power of crystals until the afternoon of the second day of the workshop. She then created an altar in one corner of the room and distributed tiny quartz crystals to all of us. 'I want you to decide what you really want out of life right now, focus on it and then bring that intention with your small crystal to lay on the altar.' I thought hard and decided that what I really wanted was happiness, honesty and clarity in my life.

I was still living with Paul in our big house on the canal in Maida Vale and working in the PR industry but I knew that there had to be major changes or I wouldn't survive. After I laid my crystal on the altar we were told to form two big circles, sitting on chairs with our eyes closed.

Teddy said: 'I have to warn you: something very major could happen in your life after this process and if you want to drop out now you should do so. I found myself divorced after I did it. Not that I regret it.'

Divorce was far from my mind and I felt eager anticipation rather than fear. To my surprise about half a dozen more cautious souls decided to leave the circle. I don't really know what happened then. I just know that at one point I felt hands on me and the touch of crystals on my third eye – the point in the middle of the forehead said to be the doorway to the soul.

Ever since working with Katrina I've had crystals around me. I use my intuitive sense of what to have near me, and on the altars in my London bedroom and my Deia home there is a strong presence of beautiful coloured stones and minerals. Some I have found in shops all over the world and some I have come across when walking or meditating in sacred places in Deia, India, Israel and even Stockholm.

Teddy was right: two weeks after doing Katrina's crystals workshop my life was turned on its head. 'I've got something to tell you,' Paul said sheepishly one day in the office. Somehow I knew what he was going to say.

'You're having an affair, aren't you?' I said.

He looked ashen. 'How did you know?' he asked.

I couldn't answer, but it was as if lots of missing pieces of the puzzle had suddenly fallen into place. I'd been going to Deia at every opportunity and Paul and I seemed to have been drawing further and further apart. All I could feel was a great sense of relief as if I now had justification for getting out of a marriage I was no longer happy in. We'd been together for more than twenty years but I felt it was time for both of us to move on, however painful that would be.

Once I'd made that decision, leaving Lynne Franks PR was easy. Letting go of so many aspects of my life seemed essential to my growth – and even my survival. Paul and I chose Samantha Royston, who had joined us in her early twenties, to be our successor. She was bright, highly intelligent, charming, a good strategist, hard-working, and understood business. Although still under thirty we felt she would be a dynamic leader for the enthusiastic, highly trained team we were leaving behind. Susanna Flynn had been my super-efficient and loving assistant for some years ever since living in my house as the children's nanny. I was desolate at the thought of not working with her any more but was promised access both to her and to my office at any time. Perhaps things wouldn't be as difficult as I thought.

Despite guidance from our Buddhist leader to stay together and see it through, neither Paul nor I considered going to a marriage guidance counsellor or therapist for help. We'd never been able to communicate about our relationship problems during the marriage and missed the opportunity of doing so now.

Our friends seemed even more depressed than we were about us splitting up. I think it made a lot of them look at their own relationships. When a couple decides to split after a long time together, everyone close also feels displaced and uncomfortable.

Our son was in the middle of his GCSEs and so we decided not to tell him we were separating until the exams were over. Finally at the end of term we told both our children and I took them off to Deia for the summer. It is heartbreaking when a family breaks up and although we felt we'd reached the end of our particular road together, I would always recommend to others to try and work it through with the therapist before making any final decisions.

It was at about this time that I decided to give up Buddhism. The previous Christmas I'd had to have an operation for nodules growing on my vocal cords. The doctors said it had to do with my chanting and I was told to stop for a few weeks. My throat had always been my weak point and they warned me that if it kept happening they wouldn't be able to heal me. According to Eastern philosophy the throat is the communication chakra, one of the body's energy points, and the weakness was indicative of some kind of blockage based on fear. As a communicator it was crucial that I didn't lose my voice.

I was feeling disillusioned because there had been a serious falling out between the Buddhist priests in Japan and the laity. I'd always been taught that this practice was the way to create world peace but if they couldn't find peace within their own organisation, how could I accept their philosophy?

I'd learnt a great deal from the Japanese Buddhism that had started me off on my spiritual journey. For ten years I had been trying to change my basic patterns and habits by chanting the morning and evening prayers, no matter where I was. I chanted about success at work, personal happiness, world peace and the health of my family, but I'd done it without allowing the space to change within myself. I now saw that it was only by stopping the habit of this practice too that my life could move on.

And so in one week in June 1992 I let go of everything I had always thought mattered – material wealth, successful career, a high profile, a long-term marriage and my religious practice. I needed to be on my own, become friends with my children and learn new values. It was a slow, painful process during those summer months. Some of the most generous people I met were the ones who had nothing. I realised that the wealthy people I'd known in the past were often the ones who felt they never had enough. I had to learn to trust myself and others and to enjoy a simple life.

The three months the children and I spent in Deia alternated between highs and lows. I cried a lot, drank sangria with friends at the Deia beach cafés, danced the salsa in local bars, made new friends, bumped into old ones and talked to the children into the early hours. We got tanned and started getting used to being a new family unit of three.

As a single parent I felt a new kind of connection with Josh and Jess. At fourteen and sixteen they were too young to have to see their mother collapsing but together we struggled through. Good friends from London, including Alan Rickman and his partner Reima Horton, followed by Ruby Wax, came to stay. We entertained each other and the summer started to mellow out.

I was with Alan and Reima watching folk dancing in the square of the nearby town of Soller one night when I met the woman who became my closest Deia friend. Frances Graves. She was a vibrant red-headed Australian the same age as me who had arrived in Deia some twenty years earlier with two small sons. She had married Juan, Robert Graves's middle son, and they had one child together, Llewelyn. Frances always dressed like an exotic Australian cowgirl, and spent whatever time she had left over from looking after her family painting and playing the guitar and running around looking after the rest of us. In my darkest, as well as my happiest moments in Deia, she has always been there for me.

The Graves clan, headed by Beryl, Robert's widow, were always friendly and hospitable. Juan Graves and his younger brother Tomas were in a rock 'n' roll band called Pa Amb Oli together with their friend, artist David Templeton, and other assorted local musicians. Pa Amb Oli is the name of the Mallorcan local dish of bread

43

soaked in olive oil with tomatoes rubbed on top. The English members of the Pa Amb Oli band, all in their mid-forties to early fifties, loved to sing 1960s rhythm and blues and were generous in letting other frustrated rock 'n' roll singers jam with them. They played regularly through the summer at Deia festivals and bars, as well as other hot spots around the island, and had a huge following.

When we first came to Deia, Alan Parker's film *The Commitments*, about a Dublin soul band, had just been released. Joshua was converted. He started singing sixties R&B numbers all over the house. Much to his joy the Graves brothers got him to join them on stage, where he energetically performed his two specialities, 'Mustang Sally' and 'Sittin' on the Dock of the Bay'. I was so proud of my sixteen-year-old son. After all, I'd grown up on this music. I got so excited during one fiesta, dancing around in the village square feeling like a proud Jewish mother, that I fell over and twisted my ankle. I woke up in the middle of the night with my ankle like a balloon and spent most of the rest of the summer on crutches. The children and I felt that our real story was much funnier than *Ab Fab*.

Once the summer was over I took the children back to London for the start of the school year and wondered what I was going to do with myself. I wasn't used to having time on my hands and there was quite a long adjustment period. I stayed in the large house which had been our marital home for another year or so but simplified my life in stages. I now entertained around the kitchen table, cooking bowls of pasta myself. I shopped at Sainsbury's, flew economy class and started using the Tube. I stopped shopping at Harvey Nichols and instead opened an account at Marks & Spencer's. But after my first visit to M&S I realised I wasn't taking my new budget entirely seriously: I had spent so much money on underwear and bits and pieces for myself and the children that their accounts office rang to say that someone must have stolen my card because such a high bill had been run up so quickly.

Slowly I became used to reality and even started to enjoy it. I held lots of parties and hung out with young hippie musicians who seemed to have more of a spiritual focus than my fashion friends. Eventually I put the house on the market and started looking for something much simpler. I sold it the following summer and to mark the end of the six years in what I'd thought of as my dream house, I held a huge Rites of Passage party. I invited my former staff, Buddhist friends, some former clients, and even my ex-husband. We all celebrated the end of an era together.

I literally closed the door for the last time on my dream palace in Maida Vale and started my journey to find a new kind of dream in reflective ritual in the undulating green Italian countryside. With a group of close friends I was visiting our friend Anthony at his remote country house in Umbria to take some ayahuasca – a gentle South American hallucinogenic tea.

Anthony, a quietly spoken half-English, half-Italian property developer, had recently changed his rustic home into a yoga retreat centre and had invited us to join him to experience the ayahuasca that he had encountered while in Brazil earlier that year. He had been travelling with his teenage son Damian through the Amazon basin and they had explored the effect of the tea on a number of occasions. Like all new converts, he was enthusiastic for his friends to share this new knowledge.

I was full of trepidation. I'd never taken hallucinogenics before, even in the acid days of the sixties. After hearing about friends' nightmarish trips I'd been too scared of the demons I felt lurked in the depths of my unconscious – but now it was time to face more of my fears. I was assured by my friends that the Brazilian organisation who were providing the ayahuasca for us would make sure the experience was safe.

I woke the first day feeling rested and ready for whatever life had in store. I felt my period about to start, as it always seemed to every time something significant was about to happen. We spent the day doing yoga, lying in the sun, massaging each other and eating light food. Then at 8 p.m. we were asked to join the two Brazilian maestros of the Union Vegetal Church to take the tea.

Made from an intricate mix of bark and roots from the ayahuasca tree found in the Amazon jungle, the tea had been used in ritual for centuries but had been taken up by modern Brazilian culture and had now become the centre of a religion. Members of the legal Union Vegetal Church met at least once a week and honoured Christian and humanistic principles. All the family including small children took the tea in a controlled situation. Apart from sometimes causing people to vomit or have diarrhoea, ayahuasca would give deep insight through visions and had also been shown to provide tremendous positive health benefits. It had immediately healed Anthony's third-degree burns when his car had blown up and was known to rid the body of toxins and build up the immune system.

We sat on cushions and sofas in a circle in Anthony's sitting room and the Brazilians started playing a tape of Amazon pipe music. We were then given a cup of the tea and made to answer some questions in Portuguese, which I didn't understand. It was now time to settle back and experience the ride.

It started very gently and I found myself thinking of my eighteen-year-old son, Joshua, who had just left home to go travelling for a year and was then off to university. I found myself grieving for him and for the loss of our home and family. A powerful piece of South American music set me off on to images of vibrant lights and dancing shapes. Then I imagined I was disappearing into one of Joshua's colourful abstract paintings which he'd done as part of his International Baccalaureate exams. I found myself communicating and relating to him through the painting and ended in floods of tears. I was completely unaware of my surroundings; I was a mother grieving the loss of her son to adulthood.

Throughout this experience I was rushing to the loo with stomach cramps. This, combined with my heavy period, made me start to come down to earth and I had difficulty rediscovering the deep space I'd found, even with a top-up of the tea. The next day my stomach felt as if it had been kicked by a mule, but I decided to take the tea one more time. This time I was careful to fast and meditate beforehand and had a far more positive experience. I saw myself cutting through a Technicolor jungle of huge curling telephone wires with the bright sword of a warrior in my hand. I heard an inner voice say, 'The sword is always there any time you need it. You never have to be scared again.' I came back to reality feeling strong and powerful and knowing that I would always be able to call on my sword for strength.

Shortly afterwards, back in London, I had another intense experience during a Denise Linn workshop. She had put the hundred or so people in the room into an altered state of deep relaxation to look at some of our past lives. As I lay down with my mind relinquishing control, images appeared and in front of me I saw a Madonna with a beautiful smile on her face. As a Jew I'd never identified with the Virgin Mary but I felt an incredible love going between us. 'I am always there for you,' she seemed to say, 'but you have a hard task ahead.'

As Denise brought us back to normality I talked to the few people sitting around me about their experiences. I was near a few Buddhist friends – a couple of whom were also born Jews – and they told me they too had seen Christian images. When I shared this with the rest of the room, a few other people, including a Japanese girl, volunteered that they had just had Christ experiences and even Denise couldn't explain what had happened. When the unconscious mind takes over, group energy can release deep archetypal experiences. Or is there a more mystical explanation which our minds are too closed to grasp?

My new flat, in the less grand but far livelier Maida Vale Avenue, was crumbling to pieces when I bought it. At the age of forty-five I finally had my own London home, albeit sharing it with Jessica, and with Joshua when he came back from his travels. I rebuilt and decorated it with the help of my brilliant designer friend, Yvonne Gold. She forced me to give or throw away at least half of the possessions I'd salvaged from the big house and then tortured me over my wardrobe. I'd loved clothes and fashion with a passion ever since I could remember. She made me go through every single garment I owned, shouting at me, 'You know you'll never wear that again. You know that colour looks dreadful on you. What on earth do you want that horrible outfit for?' until I gave in and put them in a charity pile.

I was still left with more clothes than most people would have in a lifetime and I saw that any time I was tempted to go shopping I just had to look through the beautiful Donna Karan or Ghost clothes hanging in my wardrobe, some of which I had never even worn, and pretend I was shopping in Harvey Nichols.

I still had a lot of old patterns to let go of. Filling my life with noise was certainly one of them. I returned to Deia that autumn to attend a Vispassana silent meditation retreat held at a convent in the town of Santa Maria. Vispassana or 'insight meditation' comes from the Theravadan Buddhist tradition and involves breathing techniques. The aim is to become detached from thoughts as they pass, to still the mind and bring about insight into reality. Being aware of the minutiae of a situation brings awareness on a large scale and out of this develops panoramic awareness. In other words rather than focusing your attention on detail you begin to see the overall pattern.

I'd heard about the retreat from an artist friend in Deia and didn't know what to expect. I found out that for five days I would be sitting or walking in meditation and eating my meals in silence. Talking was only allowed during a brief group discussion once a day led by the course master Christopher Titmus, an ex-Buddhist monk from Devon. Most of the other twenty-odd people on the course were Spanish but as we weren't allowed to speak, language was pretty incidental. I learnt the importance of going within myself, connecting with God through silence and enjoying the power of stillness.

I took the strength of the meditation process back with me to London, determined to keep the connection with my inner space.

One of the hardest experiences of letting go was the first Christmas the children spent with their father in Australia, where he was living part of the year. Christmas was an important family holiday for us wherever we were in the world, particularly Deia. I'd always prepared a traditional Christmas dinner and all the trappings that go

48

with it. I decided Deia would be too sad without Josh and Jess.

I took up a young friend's invitation to join her in St Bart's in the Caribbean. We were staying as guests of an older very wealthy friend of hers in an exclusive hotel on the beach. I hadn't appreciated that St Bart's was probably the most fashionable place in the world to spend Christmas and kept bumping into people I thought I'd left behind in my past life. Fashion editors, designers and photographers were everywhere. I wasn't feeling very stylish and just wanted to swim in the sea and lie in the sun. I missed my children terribly on Christmas Day and my elderly host was a megalomaniac who played constant power games on his guests, goading them and pushing boundaries.

The next day I started hanging out with a nice Jewish lawyer from London whose number had been given to me by mutual friends. Stuart took me for long walks and introduced me to his yoga teacher. He'd been living there for a few months on a sabbatical from the business world and appreciated how I was feeling.

A miracle occurred when I bumped into my late friend Kezia's teenage daughter, Cayli, on the beach. She was there with other old friends of Kezia's, fashion stylist Nian Fish and her model teenage daughter, Natané. I'd known Cailly since she was a baby and it was like finding members of my own family. If I couldn't be with my children, Cayli and the others were the next best thing. They had been staying in Rudolf Nureyev's isolated wooden house overlooking the sea. It didn't have a proper kitchen, was very basic but had a huge wooden deck where he was said to dance to the sunset every night.

'We're leaving soon, Lynne,' Nian told me. 'It's really cheap here. Why don't you take over the rental of the house?'

Yet again, I felt I was being protected by a greater power and I gratefully accepted, thanked God and moved in as quickly as possible.

Another bonus was that Nureyev's old masseur, Alain, still lived in the basement. In between walks along the seashore and dancing on the deck I got him to give me some incredible body work. I'd lie on his massage table, much as Nureyev must have done, listening to the sounds of the sea as the knots in my shoulders were pummelled away.

That New Year's Eve I was invited to the trendiest party in town but decided not to go. I asked my new friend Stuart Carroll to join me for a simple supper. At midnight we lay outside on the deck stating our affirmations and hopes for the next year. As I saw the fireworks go off on the neighbouring islands, one single shooting star came down from the heavens and soared directly over me. I knew it was a sign from God to remind me I was never alone.

Letting go and changing the direction of my life could not be done overnight. It would be a slow process of learning to stay in the present, understanding about relationships and how I wanted to live and work. It would be painful: often it felt like two steps forward and one step back. But I had my ayahuasca sword in my right hand and the beautiful smile of Mary the Mother to inspire me. I was ready to face my fears and begin my journey.

3

Learning about Sex and Relationships

I could hear a clear voice inside me saying 'trust and receive'. I was trekking through the undergrowth towards a magical waterfall on the Big Island of Hawaii with my friend John. It was our first day off during an intense three-week workshop on relationships with para-psychologist Chuck Spezzano.

I'd met John – a tall, rangy Californian osteopath – through friends a year or so earlier and had gone to see him whenever my back got too painful. We'd become close friends during the breakdown of my marriage although we'd never had a sexual relationship. I'd always found him attractive but perhaps I was too scared of getting rejected. We were interested in the same areas of spiritual healing and dancing and had often taken each other to hear different teachers or bands. He seemed the ideal uncomplicated companion.

It was John who had originally told me about Chuck Spezzano, a relationships psychologist based in Hawaii who fuses science with spirituality. We'd been to hear him speak in London and now, some six months after I'd split up with Paul, here we were in Hawaii working with him.

John and I had been expressing a lot of anger, as well as love, during the workshop, as if we needed to play out our patterns in order to see them. We'd already been arguing so much that day that I'd been crying hysterically and at times felt almost suicidal. I knew deep down that it was nothing to do with John, for I was learning that both the love and hate we feel for another person is just a projection of how we feel about ourselves. Up to that point we'd both been in denial about our past relationship blockages but as a result of the intense processes Chuck had been guiding us through we'd managed to open up.

It was through opening up to this vulnerability that for the first time I was able to hear the voice of my higher self. 'You are in this world to learn two lessons – to trust and receive,' I seemed to hear.

I don't know from what level of consciousness that voice came but it resonated somewhere deep inside me and has stayed with me ever since. In this materialistic secular age it's easy not to hear our higher self. Instead we allow all the little ego voices in our head to do the talking. It wasn't until this intuitive thought came into my consciousness that I realised I had begun to let go of my fortified mind and learnt to trust my deeper instincts. I had always done this in business, so why not in my personal life as well?

Only in a place of such natural wild beauty and at such a low emotional ebb was I able to open up to this message. It was as if I was surrounded by the devas and spirits peeking up from the wild flowers all around me trying to help me understand my own pain. After an hour of trekking we reached the waterfall. I climbed under the cleansing water which seemed to transform all the old fears into hope and optimism for the future.

The Spezzano course took place in a modern fantasy-style hotel on the beach. We got around the huge complex in small motorised boats steered on an artificial river by beautiful young Hawaiian girls in captain's uniforms. We ate in themed restaurants and, if we had the energy, danced out our changing emotions at the hotel disco at night. There was an inside lagoon with dolphins: we could swim with them, be photographed and videoed with them and even have dolphins printed on customised T-shirts. All of which I did, of course.

However, most of the day and night we spent behind closed doors projecting our blockages and patterns on each other, carefully guided by Chuck and his wife, Lency.

Having grown up watching my parents' marriage and listening to my formidable grandmother, I believed that women had to be much stronger than men, taking responsibility for the family. Certainly that's what had happened in my marriage; maybe I'd been to blame for creating the very situation I was trying to avoid. Perhaps if I hadn't been so controlling and had been better able to receive, Paul would have taken more responsibility. I'd also got the impression from the women in my family that married sex was a chore. Although that wasn't how my relationship with Paul had started it had eventually fallen into this pattern. By working with Chuck I started to change.

There were thirty of us on the course – ten Caucasians, ten Chinese and ten Japanese – some of whom had done the work before and some of whom hadn't. Initially I thought the language differences would cause complications and slow down the process. I very quickly understood, however, what Chuck meant when he said that only 7 per cent of communication is spoken word while 35 per cent is tone and the rest is body language and vibration. After a few days we all seemed to understand each other without any translation.

It was an intense time of healing and transformation for me, not least because Lency Spezzano's extraordinary gift of compassion enables her to release other people's inner pain. During her sessions she put on rather corny mood music and would go round the room looking deeply into our eyes. When it was my turn I felt as if she could see straight into my soul. I knew she could feel my pain, and through focusing her energy on me I was able to let out suppressed emotions and tears. I recognised the build-up of sadness I'd been holding inside me since my childhood and I was gradually able to release it. At last I was in a safe place where I knew I could let go of my pain and I found myself crying uncontrollably. There are very few people who don't give way under Lency Spezzano's stare.

I also began to recognise the destructive pattern of my relationships, to understand my fear of intimacy and see how I had been rooted in competitive masculine energy throughout my working life. Independent women are very strong in this type of energy and I was always very independent, scared of being hurt or rejected, and unable to receive anything from others, including intimacy.

Later on, when working with women's groups, I found that fear of rejection by men, often for a younger, newer model, is a far too common female trait and is inevitably brought about by lack of self-esteem. This is the pay-off for living in a culture that worships youth and beauty. It's only when we women can appreciate our own beauty and strength that we can expect men to worship us for the goddesses we are.

Men too of course have their fears and the most common one I've come across is what I call the Black Widow syndrome. On a deep level of their unconscious many men fear that women will eat them up live after receiving their seed, using them just as the Black Widow spider uses her mate. This can even be seen to go back to the biblical story of Eve leading Adam into temptation and ruin by eating the apple from the tree of knowledge. In ancient pre-Christian culture the serpent was often seen as a symbol of wisdom working with the Goddess or female deities for the good of all mankind. It is only by working through out deepest fears, by acknowledging and communicating them, that men and women can successfully cross over to a new place of true partnership.

In the intimate, safe environment that had been created in Hawaii, people could discover and examine their innermost feelings. There was a real sharing of the heart, mind and energy. At this point I hadn't slept with anyone since splitting up with my husband. I didn't feel very good about myself or my body and I couldn't imagine anyone finding me attractive. But by the last day of the course I felt so happy after clearing out so many tears that I was giving out a completely different kind of energy. When you feel good about yourself, it's easy to attract men. During our farewell party a young, attractive

Japanese man started dancing with me. We spent an affectionate, sweet night together and I felt I'd received a wonderful gift. After twenty-two years of being with Paul, it was a little like losing my virginity all over again.

But the next day, of course, I wanted the relationship to carry on and naturally it wasn't going to. All my neediness and expectations reappeared – but at least now I could recognise them for what they were. How could the relationship continue with this man in Japan and me in England? We may have connected in a very intimate way in Hawaii, but we knew nothing of each other's lives. I didn't understand at the time that spending a loving night with someone doesn't necessarily mean you're going to spend the rest of your life together.

'I have a girlfriend in Tokyo,' he told me as I sadly said goodbye. 'We've had a nice time together based on mutual attraction in the moment. And now it's time to go back to our lives.'

According to Chuck, all relationships go through three distinct stages – romance, power struggle and dead zone. He believes relationships get stuck because at the start of a relationship adrenalin gets confused with happiness and then communication breaks down as you begin to compete with each other. In the course of the power struggle your partner seems to manifest your worst fears and you move into a pattern of the dependent and the independent – the independent open to temptations, the dependent displaying needs. Normally the male is independent and the female dependent but it may change and shift within a relationship. In dead zone love seems to die and you feel sexual indifference to your partner.

Paul and I had talked a lot but never on a deep level and hardly ever about our relationship. We moved into power struggle because we were trying to change each other, whereas really what we should have been doing was changing ourselves. Although sometimes I felt smug if I was winning the battle, deep down I knew I was losing the war because I was pushing Paul away and diminishing his attractiveness in my eyes. In these power struggles the loser, feeling alienated, either gives up or seeks revenge. But revenge in this case is far from sweet and every time we seek it the only person we're truly hurting is ourselves.

The romance period with Paul had been volatile. Smashed plates and one or other of us storming out of a party was a regular occurrence. Both of us strong characters, we went quickly into our power struggle. We must have loved each other, though, because we stayed together. Unknown to me Paul was embarking on a series of affairs.

One exercise Chuck set us was to go to the telephone, phone up someone we were angry with and say we were sorry to them. So I called Paul to tell him I was sorry for what I'd done in the course of the marriage and that I forgave him for what he'd done. By holding grievances we are harbouring hidden fears based on our own lack of self-esteem, but by forgiving someone we free and forgive ourselves.

Equally, if two people are committed to communicating, their relationship is redeemable and they can graduate from competitiveness to partnership if they're prepared to work at it. Commitment will always move you forward from dead zone and you will be able to achieve a respectful and mutually sustaining relationship through what Chuck calls the three stages of co-creativity, tantra and unity.

My escape from commitment had been my work. Needless to say I carried on working through both pregnancies, right until the day I went into hospital, and then returned to work two weeks after the birth. I made no attempt to slow down the pace of my life and would carry on in the evenings and weekends, going out to functions or unwinding with friends in restaurants. Not surprisingly, I'd usually end up slumped over the dinner table exhausted.

I wish now that I hadn't handed my children over quite so readily to nannies, some of whom were pretty unreliable. I cared deeply about my children but I was so involved with work that I couldn't be around as much as I should have been. I still feel guilty about having left Jessica when she was a few weeks old to go and visit Paul's family in Australia. It seems almost inconceivable today that any parent would do such a thing, but in the mid-1970s attitudes to child-rearing were very different and everything was geared towards the mother's convenience. Young babies weren't taken on long journeys, there wasn't the emphasis on breastfeeding there is today and no one talked much about bonding with your baby in the early stages of its life.

I continued to neglect my relationship with Paul when the children were babies. Guilty at being out all day, I'd make sure I was the one to get up and do the feeds at night. Inevitably, sexual passion became my last priority. Never for a moment did I imagine that Paul might be seeking sexual gratification elsewhere because I really believed that if you were married you stayed faithful. I remember once going to a party when Paul was away on business and meeting an extremely attractive man who made an intense pass at me. I'd just lost weight after having the babies and was looking good again but it never occurred to me to take him up on the offer. After all, I was married and a mother. How naive!

One reason why breaking out of my marriage proved to be such a wrench was that I was scared of being on my own. Now I know that although I was never alone when I was married I experienced tremendous feelings of loneliness. At the time I may not have been prepared to acknowledge these feelings, being under the illusion that a busy life and lots of friends meant you couldn't possible be lonely. But actually nothing can make you feel lonelier than being in a relationship where there is no real communication.

Now I know how vital it is to express how you feel in a relationship. It's such a simple lesson to learn but if you say to your partner, 'I am feeling hurt because . . .', and then try to explain why, rather than accusing him or her of having done something wrong, all the anger and pain will dissolve. I was forty-four years old when I discovered this and it signified a big shift in my life.

A psychologist once told me that I had an orphan pattern because on a deep level I felt rejected by both my father and my mother. I knew my mother had desperately wanted a child and despite the fact that her domineering mother lived with my parents in the marital home she had assumed that once I was born I would be hers. But she was wrong, and from the moment I came along my grandmother took me over.

Of course from a child's perspective I didn't understand that my grandmother was blocking my relationship with my mother. I just knew that when I got up in the middle of the night to crawl into my mother's bed my grandmother would stop me on the landing, tell me my mother was too tired to be disturbed and take me into hers. I'm sure she meant well but it left me feeling cut off from my parents.

It is said that a woman should never be with a man who hates his mother because if he's angry with his mother, then he'll be angry with all women. Similarly, if as a woman you never get the attention you need from your father, then you'll always be out there looking for attention. My father didn't get the attention he needed from his mother and she didn't get the attention she needed from her father, and so it went on. Like so many families, ours had a series of dysfunctional generations.

My father didn't know how to be loving or physically affectionate to his wife or two daughters. He had always wanted a son so I felt a deep sense of inadequacy which I was constantly trying to make up for. It's quite clear to me now that one of the reasons I put so much energy into my business was to get his attention and approval.

A *Sunday Times* photographer once came to the house to take a photograph of me and my father for the 'Relatives Values' series, at the end of which he admitted that he had never in his life photographed two people who had such a problem hugging each other. My father was never really able to show how he felt until just before he got Alzheimer's Disease when at last he started to allow me to hug and kiss him, massage his neck and hold his hand. The sadness is that although our relationship was eventually healed through this physical affection, it could happen only when he'd started to become senile.

These days I'd describe myself as a very affectionate and tactile person but I haven't always been like that. I used to feel very awkward kissing and hugging the fashion crowd I hung around with in the seventies and eighties. It all seemed so insincere. After having my children I got over that and nowadays I love being physically affectionate with my friends and loved ones.

It was my children who introduced me to an entirely new dimension of love – the kind of love which is unconditional, without demands or preconditions. Nowadays in my life I strive to find unconditional love in every one of my relationships – although there's little doubt that it is far easier to achieve with friends than lovers.

In my teens and early twenties I'd had close girlfriends but never thought of friendship as love. Later, in my thirties, I definitely felt love for friends but wasn't able to express it. My American friend, PR Kezia Keeble, was the first friend I was able to acknowledge love to – but that was only after she was diagnosed with cancer and I knew she was going to die. With death staring me in the face, the embarrassment of expressing my emotions evaporated and I wanted the people I loved to know that I loved them. Affirming the people you love allows you to reach the point where you can affirm that you love yourself.

One of the things that has totally changed in my life during the past four years is that many of my closest friends are now heterosexual men. Before that, the only men I was able to have intimate friendships with were gay. I just didn't know how to communicate with heterosexual men. Now I spend so much time with women, both in work and play, that my close friendships with men have given me a balanced and healthy perspective. I'm very fortunate because my male friends are a diverse bunch, from hippie musicians to entrepreneurial businessmen aged between twenty-five and fifty-five. The one thing they have in common is they all have open minds and are as comfortable in their feminine energy as they are in their masculine. Some have been my lovers, but most have not. As the film *When Harry Met Sally* says, there can never be a platonic relationship between men and women without some form of sexual energy and this just adds to the chemistry of the friendship.

Getting to know myself and exploring my relationships with

men has inevitably led to exploring my sexuality. I had been vaguely aware of the Indian system of tantric yoga without really ever understanding it, until my friend and yoga teacher, Caroline Aldred, explained how the disciplines of tantric yoga together with those of the Chinese teachings of the Tao could be used to enhance sexual pleasure.

Sacred sex teaches that if a man can hold back from ejaculating, through visualisation techniques and muscle control, then both the man and woman will receive maximum sexual satisfaction. It is a far more erotic, ritualistic form of lovemaking involving oils, candles, music and games. One very powerful meditation before you make love is to sit opposite each other with a candle in between you, close your eyes, then open them and look into each other's left eye (the left eye being the window of the soul) for as long as you feel comfortable, with your hand on your partner's heart. This is an extraordinarily powerful way of becoming intimate with another person and doesn't necessarily have to end in lovemaking.

Sacred sex works much better if you're in a monogamous relationship because it requires a growing together and understanding of your partner's needs which is much more difficult to develop with casual lovers. You have to be in a space where you both feel safe with each other.

I believe women's and men's attitudes to lovemaking need freeing up. Despite being a part of this instant gratification generation – whether it's using a credit card to go shopping, or slipping a penis inside a vagina – we don't seem to be able to say what we want. In reality there's a lot of self-consciousness around the subject of sex in the Western world, particularly among women. One of the exercises Caroline Aldred used at her women's sexuality workshop at the 1995 What Women Want festival was getting women to express what they wanted from their partners while making love. We were told to partner up with someone in the room and then in turn to tell each other how we best liked making love. A first articulation for most of us!

I met Caroline's friend Jahnet at that workshop: she explained how to bring the mistress out in us. She showed us her collection of sexy underwear and bedroom clothes. 'Men love a feminine sexy woman inside the bedroom, however independent you are outside,' she told us. Jahnet was an expert and worked as a 'sacred' hooker. She considered her job to be as much healer as provider of sexual relief and taught both men and women how to express themselves in an open and trusting way during lovemaking.

I grew up as part of the pre-AIDS pill generation but for most of my teens I was influenced by my parents' views and believed in remaining a virgin until I was married. But at the age of nineteen the spirit of the age suddenly took hold of me and I knew the time had come to get rid of my virginity. It was the generation of free love and I wouldn't think twice about meeting someone in a club and ending up in bed with them. The only pitfall was pregnancy, and since we were all on the pill anyway that hardly mattered. We didn't think about cervical cancer or venereal disease, and condoms were used only by married men for illicit sex.

Then, after the initial passion with Paul had waned, I shut down my sexuality for many years. It was only after splitting up that I began to discover my patterns and preferences. As I gained more confidence as a single woman I would meet desirable men who were attracted to my strength and inevitably I would take on the 'mother' role. But as soon as we became lovers I would disempower myself. I would go from being what Chuck Spezzano calls the rock – the dependable strong one in the partnership – to the swamp, when I'd lose my power and become emotionally sucked in.

My own theory is that in relationships every woman and man can swing between two roles – either the little girl or the mother, or in the case of the man, the little boy or the father. Often these roles are reversed or alternated. I love men who look after me in a fatherly way because I certainly have that little girl in me who is looking for a father, but I also find it very easy to slip into the mother role. I think the answer is learning to be our own mothers and fathers internally and being supportive and nurturing to each other.

One of the most nurturing relationships I had was with Gerry

Beeby – still one of my closest friends. We met during some of the worst days of my marriage, when I was feeling lonely and insecure. Gerry, a very good-looking man who was a couple of years younger than me, had been gay all of his adult life. Because I felt so safe with him I was able to open up in a way that I never had before. Like many of my friends he'd started practising Buddhism. He was working as Katharine Hamnett's managing director and loved to go dancing and have fun like I did. We spent major amounts of our time talking on the phone or being together, giving each other all the love and nurturing for which we were both so hungry.

Because he was gay we could openly travel together without too much gossip, yet our relationship was more intense and loving than many heterosexual affairs. Inevitably it took me even further away from Paul, who didn't seem to notice. Having someone to love and spoil me, someone who saw through my defences and vulnerabilities, gave me the strength to handle many of the other pressures in my life. However, no matter how much Gerry and I loved each other in our minds and in our hearts I had to accept the existence of the young lovers in his life.

I'm certainly not the first woman who thought she'd fallen in love with a gay man, but this kind of physical rejection is ultimately one of the most painful. Our commitment to each other remained strong for many years and through many changes, including my divorce and after Gerry tragically developed full-blown AIDS. But however much we loved each other, a relationship can only be complete when one mind, heart and body can embrace another.

The difference between being in love, loving someone and just being infatuated is something I've put a lot of personal research into. I am a great romantic and once separated from Paul looked forward to falling in love – whatever that meant. Being a naturally warm person I often did feel great affection for my lover of the moment and would express it but knew inside that this was never the great romance – that was to come. I had a checklist of what I expected from my next partner which would be added to after my regular sessions with psychics on both sides of the Atlantic.

I was impatient for Mr Right to arrive and so would often try to make various Mr Wrongs fit the bill. Even if I could get them past the critical test of meeting my children, the final day of reckoning would come when they met my psychic-sensitive mother . . .

'Very nice, dear, but definitely not for you,' she'd say as I paraded Bruce, Carlo, Nigel, *et al.* in front of her.

Being in love has to be two adults in a mutual flow of love, commitment and chemistry who are ready to become each other's teachers and healers through developing a relationship based on communication and integrity. That's what I was looking for – someone I could grow with who was my equal in every way. I opened myself to God and the universe and determined that my future partner would be everything that I wanted and more, and that we'd find each other at the right time.

Meanwhile I had relationships with men of various nationalities, races and ages. I learnt something from all of them but tended to have more in common with ones with similar experiences.

The age difference in relationships seems to have become more diverse in the 1990s. Although there's always been a pattern of older men getting together with younger women, in recent years I've noticed a lot of my women friends taking the priestess's path of having young men as lovers, or in some cases even husbands. Whatever the gender mix there is definitely an energy exchange between younger and older lovers that can be very intense.

I experienced it myself one summer in Deia with a young German fire-eater in his early twenties. Although at first I didn't appreciate how young he was, when he told me it didn't seem to make a lot of difference. He was interested in the same things as I was, sex was great, and my friends accepted him. I remember one party at my house to celebrate a night of shooting stars. The guests included many celebrity friends who were passing through Deia for the summer, and Michael spent that night entertaining them with his circus tricks.

But as one Deia friend said: 'What is glamorous in the summer doesn't always stand up in the winter,' and Michael and I eventually went our separate ways.

Naomi Dean and George Kedourie, Mallorcan friends originally from London, have the longest-running 'age gap' relationship I know. When I first met them they'd been together for about twenty years. They'd met when George was a precocious young man of nineteen and Naomi an exotic fifty-year-old painter, well known in the markets of Camden Town for her colourful sartorial sense and tribe of young fans. Sharing the Libra star sign, they had an immediate soul connection and set off travelling the world on many adventures. Eventually they settled in Mallorca where they set up home together. Naomi continued her career as an artist and George ran his own business importing furniture from Indonesia. As time passed George had relationships with younger women and eventually a daughter called Zelda. Although Naomi says she wants George to get married and be happy, their connection is so deep he can't envisage them ever separating. Contrary to expectations, George often seems to take the older, more responsible role and they have a friendship and understanding that many couples would envy.

As I travel across the world I find that most women I meet and some of the men, whatever their backgrounds, are still holding on to the dream of a Prince or Princess Charming, the perfect soul partner. Compromise is less of an option as more and more people are choosing to be on their own rather than risk being in the wrong relationship.

It is possible to meet the ideal partner, whether a prince on a white horse or a woman with the brain of Einstein and the body of Pamela Anderson, but it is important not to be blinded by illusion or disappointed by unrealistic expectations. It is essential to stay in the moment, taking one step at a time while being prepared to commit to the honest communication that will take you through to the next stage.

People have told me how damaged I was when I came out of my marriage; I thought I was doing just fine. Often you don't acknowledge the pain you're in when you're living through it and I hadn't appreciated how long it would take to get over the break-up. I was impatient to get on with the next relationship, not understanding that I had a lot of healing to do. It can easily take between two and five years to get over the break-up of a long-term marriage and it's very easy to rush headlong into a second relationship before you've actually healed. Little wonder that statistics show second marriages to be even less likely to succeed than first. I've so often heard of people getting married on the rebound and then after a short time, or even after a baby or two, it starts to go wrong, usually because they're carrying too much excess baggage from the past relationship. Very often it isn't until they move on to their third partner that they find a relationship that really works.

This seems to be an especially common pattern among men. Men find it much harder than women to be on their own even though for centuries single women have been described in deeply insulting terms – 'on the shelf' or old maids, for example. But now women are beginning to acknowledge that they don't need to be in a partnership to be seen as sexually desirable. Far from it – in fact some of the sexiest women I know are single.

Letting go of your partner when a marriage or relationship comes to an end is crucial if you ever want to find mutual happiness. Chuck Spezzano told me that you can always find what you're looking for in the future in your current partner, but I believe there are times when letting go is the only way to achieve individual growth. There can be a sell-by date on a relationship, and although I know that Paul and I could have stayed together for many more years if we'd worked at it, I wouldn't have grown and changed in a positive way if we had. He too is now much more fulfilled – settled in a happy relationship which suits him, his partner and his lifestyle. When we decided to break up, we were conscious of the importance of remaining friends both for ourselves but more importantly for our two children.

I've noticed that this is the exception rather than the rule. There is usually so much anger and guilt that invisible hooks are kept in on both sides leaving neither party completely ready for a new commitment even though they often go through the motions. This can be true even if the couple don't speak to each other. Angry silence can sometimes be more damaging than noisy arguments particularly if children are involved. I can't say I was completely innocent on this score. I held a lot of anger towards Paul and even though I didn't express it to him, my children certainly knew how I felt. Perhaps some form of counselling might have helped.

Peter Gabriel told me that he had been in therapy with his ex-wife for some time after they broke up and this allowed them both to close the relationship in a healthy and meaningful way. When Paul and I split up Peter advised me to do the same thing, but because I was desperate to put the past behind me, I decided to deal with it alone. Exploring my own personal growth was my form of therapy, and that in turn certainly helped my children, particularly my daughter who was going through her own deep sense of rejection by her father. By opening myself up I was able to communicate with my daughter in many painful areas that would have been difficult before. When I talked to her about my experiences they became lessons for both of us.

Perhaps, if I'd done as Peter suggested, it would have helped the four of us heal as a family. In the end it was really just a question of time and I hope no long-term damage has been done. Our children have an equally good relationship with both myself and Paul and most importantly we can now all communicate honestly.

I've always tried to end a relationship in a loving way, whether it has lasted for ten days or ten months. It's so important that there should be an *acknowledged* end to a relationship: only then will two people be able to move forward in a positive way leaving the past behind them. I'm certain this is why I have managed to remain friends with my ex-husband and ex-lovers. And in every relationship I've had since splitting up with Paul I've learnt something new about myself.

Sadly, some women never recover from the break-up of a marriage because their sense of hurt and loss automatically casts them in the victim role and once they've taken up this passive and retrograde position it's very difficult to shake it off. A lot of women don't realise what they have inside them and think they will only find happiness again if they find another man.

Even though my husband was the one who had affairs, I never felt like a victim, perhaps because I have always believed that, as the Hindus say, we write our own drama. Technically speaking I may have been the injured party but I too had to take responsibility for what had happened. After all, I had never put enough time or energy into our relationship so how could I possibly expect it to work? When a relationship ends we have to let go of the anger and blame. Even those who have been abused and abandoned must take 50 per cent responsibility.

Ending in love and friendship can only be done without the presence of guilt. The Buddhists say you shouldn't feel guilt. I believe this is true. I have met men who have been separated from their wives and long-term partners for up to ten years and who still go around feeling guilty and unable to move on. This feeling of responsibility they have is of no service to either. If a relationship built on dependency continues when the couple are separated, the dependent partner will never be able to take their own power.

Obviously if a man walks out on a wife who has several small children and no means of income he does have a financial responsibility. Nevertheless there should still be an unknotting of the emotional ties and a clear friendship developed by honest communicating.

I have known a variety of perfectly capable and intelligent women who – rather like the women in the harems of the sultans of old – don't know how to use their power to step back into the world once the door of their gilded cage is open. As long as the men stay guilty the women will never be able to move forward. And women can always find the support they need from other women. We are much stronger and more resilient than men give us credit for. That halfway limbo of not being together and not being apart is getting more and more common as couples realise that, unlike their parents' generation, marriage isn't necessarily for ever.

So much of this is based on the physical. Men, during their mid-life crisis, may often decide they want a younger woman for image and sex but can't let go of the in-depth relationship they've had with their partner of many years. This does not help the women left behind to move on and themselves find new partners. It is very hard in relationships not to have hidden agendas even on the unconscious level but if clarity, integrity, love and friendship can be the foundation stones of the closure of a partnership, as well as the opening of a new one, there will be less pain for all.

I was shown a very simple exercise for unhooking emotionally by my friend Ann-Marie Woodall, a trained relationship therapist who specialises in divorce and separation. The previous summer I had met a Swedish photographer in Deia and we had had a very intense relationship both there and later in London. However, the timing wasn't great, as he had separated from his wife only a few weeks earlier. Both of us ended up having other relationships but still keeping a very deep connection. I was worried that I could get hurt once I saw him again and was nervous about seeing him on a forthcoming business trip to Sweden.

Ann-Marie came round to my flat and using several simple exercises helped me clear away my hooks. 'Close your eyes and first make sure you're in your centre,' she said. 'If I asked you how far off your centre you are right now, what would you say?'

'About 30 per cent,' I replied and then visualised myself upright and centred.

'Now how much out of his centre is he?' she continued.

'About 60 per cent,' I said, sending him love and visualising him becoming strong and centred. I was now ready to unhook.

'Imagine an invisible line going from your body and ending up in a hook in his. Now visualise where that hook is in his body, extract it, and pull it back gently towards you until it disappears.'

I did this slowly and after completion felt a great sense of release. While I was doing it, I thought I might as well take some hooks out of some of the other men I'd been close to, including my ex-husband, and repeated the exercise several times. I was now ready to have friendships with these men based on unconditional love and knew that we would not hurt each other any more.

After the session with Ann-Marie I was able to go to Sweden and spend time with my former lover, meeting his ex-wife and children and becoming friends with them all.

During the following two weeks it seemed as if all of the others I had unhooked myself from were reappearing in my life. Visitors from Paris, Australia, New York, LA and King's Cross came round to see me and I was able to complete with all of them. People might think this was a coincidence but I felt sure that this was God's way of telling me that I'd learnt another lesson.

I believe that it is possible to create unity through duality and connect with God through the sacred love a man and woman can feel for each other. I also know that it is necessary to learn through experience the importance of true communication in partnership. I learnt that I would only be ready to receive my partner with unconditional love when I truly felt love for myself.

4

Getting in Touch with my Body

I looked around nervously as I slipped the towel away from me and gingerly stepped naked into the hot tubs. 'Are they hot?' I muttered unnecessarily, ignored by the super-cool men and women stretched out in front of me. The baths were *piping* hot. After I got over my excruciating British self-consciousness I started to relax and look out at the scene of the sea lions and whales gambolling several hundred feet below me along the Californian coast.

I was in the infamous hot tubs at Esalen in Big Sur, the Californian New Age centre that inspired the sixties comedy *Bob & Carol & Ted & Alice*, where Robert Culp and Natalie Wood were transformed from hyper LA types to free-thinking, free-loving swingers. Esalen had changed since the sixties but it was still a pretty way-out place.

Esalen is a teaching and healing community, similar in some ways to Findhorn in Scotland. The members of the community live there or nearby, tending the organic garden, the art centre, the playschool, the huge vegetarian kitchens, dining room and comfortable guest cottages.

During the Easter holidays in 1991 I was driving through Big

Sur on my way from LA to San Francisco enjoying the views from Highway One with my husband Paul and our friend Johnny Rozsa.

Johnny is an extraordinary character whom I have known since we were both in our early twenties. The flamboyant son of Jewish Hungarian parents he was brought up in Kenya before coming to London to study architecture. He'd ended up selling second-hand clothes and even working for me for a few weeks in the early days of my agency before starting a successful career as a fashion photographer. He'd become a Buddhist while visiting his family, now based in California, and we'd practised together when he came back to London. He loved to dress up in exotic frocks, high heels and wigs, miming to his favourite singers, and after eventually moving to the States he combined his photographer's career with that of a successful nightclub drag hostess. He managed to sustain a sincere committed Buddhist practice, loyalty and kindness to his many friends with two successful high-profile professions.

Paul and I were having a last stab at bringing some romance back into our marriage and were staying at the idyllic Ventana Inn, a few miles away from Esalen. Ruby Wax had been over recently making her Californian New Age spoof TV show and had told me that although Esalen was generally closed to people who weren't there on a workshop, you could get in on a day's pass if you rang at the right time and held on until they gave in.

Ruby and I had become friends when she interviewed me for her very first TV series in the mid-eighties. I found her very bright and very funny and we recognised each other's vulnerability as two high-achieving Jewish Aries women looking for 'Daddy's' approval. At first she had shown a lot of cynicism about anything spiritual but went through a genuine shift after filming her Vision Quest for her New Age TV show. She has a voracious curiosity about people and life: getting paid to ask people intensely personal questions on television is a job made in heaven for her.

If Ruby had got in to Esalen I was determined I would too. After a variety of desperate phone calls and messages I was allocated a masseur and a pass. I had no idea what to expect and the gate man didn't instil confidence when he curtly directed me to wait in the tubs before I was called by my body worker.

So here I was. I took my clothes off and slipped unnoticed into the hot tubs. Afterwards I was pummelled by Bill, who was almost naked himself, while I was stretched out on a stone slab in the sun. The masseur at the next table had decided halfway through her session to sit down and play the flute and I was charmed.

Being an inveterate shopper, I had to hit the little New Age store before leaving the complex. After buying the Esalen T-shirt and bag to show that I'd braved it, I started looking at the books and tapes. I was attracted straight away to the title of a book called *Maps to Ecstasy: Teachings of an Urban Shaman* by Gabrielle Roth. I loved the idea of an urban shaman, whatever it meant, and I was then drawn to several tapes bearing her name.

Back in London, I started reading the book and found to my delight that Gabrielle was a teacher of ecstatic dance. I'd loved dancing from my days as a teenage mod and when I played her wild, drum-driven tapes I found myself spinning round the room. Then I found out through fellow dance lover and shiatsu massage practitioner, Hilary Totah, that Gabrielle occasionally came to London to teach – and was due in a few months' time. In fact it was nearly a year before she came, by which time my life had already started on its transformational path. Hilary and I signed up early to ensure places at the workshop held in dingy rooms at the YMCA off Tottenham Court Road. As this thin, bird-like woman in black, looking like a cross between Patti Smith and Chrissie Hynde, started talking with her melodic voice and her body, I was enthralled.

Gabrielle taught us about the five rhythms – the 'Maps of Ecstasy' that she had devised and taught at Esalen some twenty years earlier. It took the mind, body and soul through rhythm to a point of ecstasy and then back to a place of inner stillness and prayer. Accompanied by her percussionist using African rhythms on his big African drum Gabrielle showed us her Wave. First of all she moved us through our body parts showing us how to loosen up and let the attention focus on our head, neck, shoulders, elbows, spine, hips, knees, feet and hands, all the time moving to the sound of the drums.

'Now,' she said, 'move into the first rhythm – the flowing rhythm, the feminine energy, and be aware of your "in" breath.' I moved around the room feeling the feminine side of my inner self emerging through the dance using circular movements in a natural way as I followed the beat. 'Take a partner,' she said and to my embarrassment we had to dance opposite the nearest person, keeping eye contact. I loved dancing on my own, often facing the wall to avoid intimacy with others, and this was a full-on way of facing that fear. The overseas visitors from Germany and Holland had far less trouble than us Brits in keeping eye contact but I persevered, knowing it was something I had to do.

'Now staccato,' she said, concentrating on the exhale breath and making short, sharp gestures. It was bit like going from the balletic shapes of t'ai chi to the more angular karate. The music quickened and I found myself naturally moving into what felt like the masculine rhythm. I felt competitive in this rhythm when I was partnered with a man and consequently put my energy out in such stabbing movements that he nervously backed away. I calmed down as the staccato continued, getting in touch with a softer but still masculine energy.

We moved on to the faster rhythm of chaos. When the music speeded up we let our heads loll like rag dolls spinning round in the rhythm of puberty. I went faster and faster round the room letting go so much of my tension that I could feel the bile rising. Just the idea of letting my head and my neck go was as if I was letting go of controlling my life. I felt a huge weight lift off me as my dance became wilder to the fast rhythm of the drums. I felt myself move into a trance state, although at the same time my body was totally connected with the floor we were dancing on. The rhythm grew more gentle and although my body screamed at me to sit down and rest, Gabrielle talked us through to the next rhythm – lyrical.

'Imagine yourself like a leaf in the breeze gently spinning,' she said and I became airy and light. 'Imagine you're the dancing fool. Be playful and effortless.' I found a grace I didn't know existed.

Gabrielle brought us back to our centre, slowing us down. 'Move as though you're moving through honey, gathering your energy inward,' she told us.

I could feel my energy coming back inside as I disappeared into the dance. Ancient archetypal shapes moved through my unconscious into the physical as I went into slow motion. I danced to the floor and naturally went into shapes of prayer. I felt the inner dance as I relaxed into stillness. I closed my eyes and focused on my breath and the space between breaths. I felt I was in my centre for the first time in my life, not noticing or caring about the sweat pouring down my face and body.

As the weekend progressed we did a workshop called Cycles, where through dance, theatre and mime Gabrielle took us from birth to death. I'd never play-acted my emotions before in public and once I got over my embarrassment I started to enjoy it. I realised that all those years as a high-profile assertive PR woman were just a sham. I was so self-conscious that I had covered up my shyness with noise and high energy. I wondered how many of my seemingly confident contemporaries felt the same. I'd created the outer persona of Lynne Franks as an armour to conceal my vulnerability.

Through Gabrielle's work, and the experiences I'd had with Denise Linn and Chuck Spezzano, I got in touch with who I really was and was no longer scared to be seen.

I sometimes read poems by Ben Okri at Gabrielle's workshops and they really came alive to the sound of drums. It was Ben who had advised me to start writing a journal and I still never fail to record the experiences and emotions of every day. I rarely look back at them, but writing them daily means I'm able to integrate them into my life and move on. I got closer to poetry through working with Gabrielle, particularly the inspiring Sufi poet, Rumi. I even started writing a little poetry myself.

Later I attended a Gabrielle Roth workshop in an old wooden health spa in northern California. Set in the redwoods in the Napa Valley wine-growing region, it was said to be an ancient gathering place of the American Indians. Amongst the natural healing sulphur springs and round clearings in the towering trees, our tribe of 'tantric warriors' – as Gabrielle called us – seemed to take on the role of 'The Ancestors'. I felt shy and nervous when I arrived, not knowing anyone except Gabrielle. I was sharing a small log cabin with a stranger and had to use communal showers and toilets. My Jewish princess instincts flared up and I rushed to find the organisers, Cathy and Laurie, who were patiently making sure we settled in comfortably.

'Do I have to stay where I'm allocated?' I protested. 'Surely there's not nearly enough showers and loos for all the people here?'

Laurie looked at me shrewdly. She too had been a Jewish princess before settling down with her partner Cathy. 'It'll be fine, just relax, and trust,' she said. Reluctantly I went back to my cabin to unpack my two huge suitcases into a tiny space.

Of course she was right and my room-mate was a delightful woman from Canada. I had plenty of space and there was never any-one else in the showers when I wanted to use them.

When we gathered for the first dance session I immediately felt intimidated by all the beautiful young women and men. There were in fact women and men of all shapes, ages and sizes but my insecurity didn't let me see that until the drummer started beating his magic, the rhythm took over and I relaxed. The workshop was called Mirrors and for a week I examined my emotions through the dance, culminating in acting out different aspects of my personality in front of the others. Gabrielle called them our ego characters and showed us how to give them names. I acknowledged Polly Planner, always with Filofax in her hand, Nancy New Age sitting 'omming' in front of her crystals and Olivia Overpack with her endless luggage.

It was the first time I had performed in front of other people and I found it liberating. We behaved like a group of children in dressing-up clothes and silly props. A lot of the men put on sexy women's clothes and a lot of the women took their clothes off altogether. I was a lot tamer but it was still an intense experience coming out from behind the shield of my PR role and laughing at myself.

The hardest part of the course was the repetition exercise. We sat across the couch from a random partner in front of the rest of our group and alternated repetition of the same word or phrase over and over again, changing emphasis by tone and taking the communication as far as we could before shifting to another phrase. The phrase could be as simple as 'you're wearing a pink T-shirt' and it's amazing how alternately aggressive and friendly it can sound if it's repeated endlessly with different tones and emphasis.

We had to stay conscious and present with our partner, regardless of the twenty-five sets of eyes on us, and try to communicate our feelings, frustrations and attitudes in that moment in a very focused way. You could tell that no one wanted to do this from the way some people would rush up to get it over with and others, like me, would sit at the back hoping we'd be overlooked.

Gabrielle guided us through this tortuous exercise and it had such a powerful effect that people would start crying, hugging or in some cases getting angry with one another. It taught me more about listening and staying present with the person you're communicating with than twenty years of PR.

My daughter Jessica came with me several times to work with Gabrielle at Esalen. No longer scared of the hot tubs, I've had some of my happiest moments in the beautiful grounds there. By now I was no more self-conscious about taking my clothes off in public than in my bedroom at home and I had some great conversations about life, death and the universe while sitting in the tubs by the light of the moon and the surrounding candles.

This was California so we sat on wooden decks in the evening amongst the bougainvillaea and sweet-smelling jasmine. We swam naked in the swimming pool and we meditated in the beautiful sanctuary in the middle of the woods.

I love Esalen, particularly celebrating the Fourth of July there to the rhythmical beat of Baba Olatunji and his band. The famous Nigerian king of drums has influenced many American bands including Santana and the Grateful Dead. If you're in America on the Fourth of July, there is no better place to be than at the Esalen barbecue, dancing to Baba.

We started connecting with some of the Esalen tribe too. The Heran family became our Big Sur extended family. Dick Heran the original Nordic Californian woodman was the father of Gabrielle's beautiful twenty-six-year-old son Jonathan. Gabrielle and her husband Robert had raised Jonathan on the East Coast for half the year while Dick and his wife Peggy had raised him on the West Coast the rest of the time and he combined his New York street savvy with laid-back California surfer-speak. Peggy Heran, an East Coast Jewish girl who went West in her early twenties and met Dick, is a beautiful woman full of warmth and grace who runs the massage department at Esalen. She and Dick live in a large eco-friendly house further down the coast on a mountain overlooking the sea.

Big Sur is the only place in the world that reminds me of Deia and I have the same sense of feeling at home in Dick and Peggy's sprawling house full of Dick's drums and family pictures as I do in my house in Deia. Their daughters, Lucia and Jasmine, are blonde, beautiful Big Sur young women. Jasmine, Jessie and I have done many workshops together and Peggy and Jasmine have stayed with us in London too. We are family even if we don't see or speak to each other for months.

This tribal way of living is something that we've sadly lost in the West. I feel so fortunate that Jessica, Joshua and I have both Deia and California tribes as our extended family. I am a tribal person and as much as I sometimes love my own space, I also like the sense of belonging to inter-generational families with whom I can laugh, cry and love.

Esalen too was the place where Jessie and I received intense healing one summer from a Native American shaman, or medicine man. I was going through painful feelings of self-doubt and Jessie was subdued, also suffering from a lack of confidence.

On the last day of another Gabrielle course, as people were beginning to leave, I tried to interview Gabrielle for a radio programme. We'd been putting it off all week and the DAT machine kept malfunctioning. When I finally got it working we couldn't find a quiet spot. There always seemed to be some problem or other and while she was patiently waiting, she started talking to the Indian shaman who had been at Esalen for a sweat lodge ritual the night before.

He certainly looked authentic enough in his fringed Indian clothes; with his imposing build and strong chiselled face he had the confidence and charisma of a spiritual chief. As he sat patiently outside the Esalen dining room with his teenage son it was as if he was waiting for us. Gabrielle asked if he would do some healing on those of us who were left. He agreed and friends from the workshop started appearing from all over the estate, gathering on the central lawn outside the main building.

He put us in a circle and with his teenage son laid out his medicine man tools. A bearskin was placed in the centre surrounded by ritual instruments including rattles and some other, strange-shaped objects.

'What we're now going to do is part of our ancient tribal magic,' he said. 'Our family has lived here in California for many generations and we work with our ancestors and the spirits of the mountains and the forest in our ancient ways.' I flinched as his son cut some skin off the chief's chest and back with a scalpel. There were scars on the bodies of both father and son and the younger man explained to me later that it had been part of his initiation to endure this process.

The skin was wrapped carefully into a small tin which was placed in the centre of our circle to add to the power of the shaman. He lit some sage which he waved around all of us so that its pungent smoke would clear away bad spirits and welcome in the good ones. The bearskin's head in front of us had a lit cigarette propped in its mouth to make sure there was always burning tobacco, another important part of Native American ritual. His son started to chant songs that were as old as the land we stood on and as these extraordinary sounds filled the air, I could feel the hairs on the back of my neck rise in anticipation. He got two young South American girls to be his assistants, shaking the rattles and using their fresh energy to support him.

Gabrielle was the first person to enter the circle. He whispered in her ear and laid her gently down on the bearskin. As I watched she seemed to become a black raven, her animal totem and symbol. Although a strong-willed woman, she seemed to float off under the shaman's magical hand and loving gaze into a restful trance. He laid his hands on and off her, moving tired energy out and good energy in. Jonathan was next: he too was put in a trance with just a light touch and a few whispered words. Jonathan's six-foot frame and long blond hair gave him the look of a Nordic tribesman but he seemed to take on the nature of a young Native American warrior. As he relaxed into trance he started laughing from a deep place inside and whoops of joy came out of him.

I lay on the bearskin. I found myself unable to move or talk although I was aware in one part of my brain what was happening. I completely trusted the shaman as he touched me. It was as if he was going into my deepest being and pulling out my inner ghosts. I felt myself shaking and starting to sob. After what seemed like for ever, but was really just a few moments, he brought me back up and whispered in my ear, 'You are beautiful, you have to understand not all physical relationships between men and women can last, but always know how beautiful you are.'

I heard these words in the depths of my soul and it was as if he knew the insecurity I was feeling after the end of a recent love affair. I rejoined the circle shaking and sobbing quietly but knowing that I'd undergone a deep change. I then watched him heal Jessie and went through it with her, feeling my beautiful daughter's own lack of confidence and sense of self. I watched him shift something deep inside her so that she too recognised her inner and outer beauty. Shudders and sobs tore through me as I felt Jessie's pain, and later she told me she had the same experience as she'd watched me.

He went round the circle all afternoon healing my friends and companions and I watched the tears of sadness and joy as this extraordinary process worked on us all. Ruth, my lively Brazilian masseuse friend, had been seriously ill during the whole workshop. We discovered later that she'd had pneumonia and we watched this magician take out all her sickness until she was able to sleep peacefully. After three hours or so he'd finished and slumped to the ground, having given all the energy he had to give. He went down to the hot tubs with the two beautiful young South American girls and in the tradition of all shamans had them massage him back to full strength. He told me later he'd only recently got over cancer and was no longer at his full power.

When we finally left later that afternoon Jessie and I knew that something had healed inside us and we hoped it would last for ever. We realised we were strong, beautiful women who no longer needed to look for outside approval to feel good about ourselves.

5

On a Health Trip

Warm feelings and wholesome smells comforted my senses as I walked into the isolated Welsh cottage belonging to earth mother and health guru Leslie Kenton.

Standing in her spacious kitchen, surrounded by her American imported giant stainless-steel food mixers, piles of organic bananas ready for freezing and a strong sense of healthy nurturing energy, I felt I never wanted to go home. I wanted to be wrapped in the soft cocooned world of Leslie Kenton and be made healthy and whole like her.

Leslie has long been a source of inspiration to me. Since her days as beauty editor on *Harpers & Queen* magazine, this Californian-born independent woman has been the first to bring to public attention much knowledge about the toxins we're putting into our bodies and the positive aids to healing. She taught us about aromatherapy; the energy you receive from raw foods and juices; the importance of fish oil and sea vegetable algae as food for the body, skin and hair; how exercise, nutrition and fresh air can create 'ageless ageing', and many other methods of staying healthy.

She and I became friends over a period of years and I found her a constant source of new information and ideas on healthy living. I'd interviewed her for the radio on natural menopause after her revolutionary book *Passage to Power* was published in 1995 and she'd invited me to visit her in Wales.

'I think I've got candida,' I told her when I arrived. 'I've certainly got all the symptoms and although doctors don't take it very seriously I'm sure I should be eating different kinds of foods.'

Leslie generously gave me the answers to all my questions on what I should be eating, the supplements I should be taking and the way I should be living. Leslie too has the power of the shaman or wise woman and we acknowledged feeling the same powerful kinship with each other as I have felt with Gabrielle Roth, Denise Linn and other powerful sisters living in their full energy as healers and teachers.

She'd invited me to visit her for a Native American soul retrieval and I was taking full advantage of the nurturing atmosphere of her home. According to shamans one common cause of emotional and physical disease is soul loss – the concept of losing vital, energy-giving parts of ourselves through trauma. This trauma remains with the child inside us, and soul retrieval is an ancient technique that can coax out the misplaced souls in a person's body and bring the child 'home'. It involves taking the light and life of the child, with its curiosity and imagination, and allowing the adult to see through the child's eyes.

In order to bring back what is missing the shaman must leave everyday consciousness and enter into the spirit world. The drum – and occasionally percussion instruments such as rattles or sticks – enables the shaman to enter into other worlds, track the errant soul of the client and remove it by trickery, sacred tools or gentle negotiation.

It was time for my soul retrieval. Leslie took me upstairs to a comfortable bedroom where I lay on a warm rug surrounded by symbols of tribal magic and large, ornate Native American style dream catchers she had made. Shaped like a spider's web using wood and thread and dressed with feathers, beads and shells, dream catchers were traditionally hung over babies' beds to keep the bad dreams out and only let in the good ones. She told me to relax as I matched my deep breathing to the rhythmical sound of Indian drums on the sound system and she too lay very still in a form of trance. Later she told me she felt herself journey to a different level of consciousness where she was guided to various representations of parts of my lost soul. She told me of one that looked like a small, fat girl child whom she coaxed back to my centre.

Healing using imagery and visualisation from the unconscious can be very soothing. I came out of my trance feeling nurtured and complete and Leslie gave me more advice on how to keep this feeling of wholeness. I left her house in the late afternoon feeling healed on all levels of mind, body and spirit and was determined to adapt Leslie's ideas on health to my own lifestyle. Through her contacts I found a great American food mixer and started making my own organic vegetable and fruit drinks, which I take in the morning.

Part of the territory of PR during the 1980s was being a party animal and for years I neglected my body, ignoring the need for relaxation, exercise and good nutrition. I was permanently on some diet or other or trying yet another alternative therapy without taking responsibility for my body myself. I'd hated exercise since school but now through dancing I found a way of getting fit which I really enjoyed. And I hadn't been breathing properly for years. The tension I had created in my life meant my back and neck were always stiff and my breath very shallow. I was learning to breathe through my diaphragm and found that dancing combined with yoga was starting a slow change in my unhealthy body.

It wasn't just the lack of exercise that made me feel sluggish and unhealthy. It took me years to understand that my stressful life combined with eating erratically and greedily to fill the emotional hole inside had resulted in tremendous strain on some of my vital organs. I would ignore my full bladder if I was in a meeting or on the phone and obviously this had taken its toll on my kidneys. Nor did I drink enough water – you should have at least a pint or more each day – fortunately I had dropped coffee and tea from my diet many years before. My habit of taking herbal tea bags to all my meetings caused great mirth amongst my clients until many of them too realised the danger of constantly ingesting caffeine or tannin. The growth in herb tea departments in supermarkets all over the world shows how much attitudes have changed, although filtered or bottled still water is even healthier.

Some years earlier, while I still worked in PR, I'd tried being macrobiotic at the suggestion of Kezia Keeble. She had remarried a good-looking journalist called John Ducka after an amicable divorce from Paul Cavoco, and they had been eating that way for a while although I hadn't appreciated that it was because they already knew how seriously ill they were. Sadly, John died from AIDS a year before Kezia died from cancer. Losing so many friends at such a young age from these diseases made me even more aware of the importance of healthy living, although it took me a few years to be consistent.

Macrobiotic cooking was brought to the West by Japanese-born Michio and Aveline Kushi who had studied the teachings of George Ohsawa and wanted to spread them widely. The diet is based on organic grains and brown rice, soya-based products and vegetables. Although it can be extreme, organic brown rice and vegetables have always been my favourite meal and I pursued this path during some of my busiest time at Lynne Franks PR. Taking bags of organic brown rice into London's top restaurants and asking the chefs to heat it as part of my meal was considered a little eccentric, but Jeremy King and Chris Corbin, owners of the Caprice and The Ivy restaurants, were always patient with me. In fact The Ivy now has an excellent vegan menu. Whenever I could, I would persuade journalists to come to the East West Centre in Old Street where you used to be able to get a delicious healthy and balanced macrobiotic meal cooked on the Far Eastern principles of a balance of yin and yang ingredients. Traditional Chinese philosophy tells us that yin and yang are the two great complementary principles on whose interaction the whole of the manifest universe depends. Yin is defined as dark, passive and feminine; yang as light, active and masculine, and achievement of a balance of the two is the aim of medicine, divination and nutrition.

The Japanese and the Chinese have one of the healthiest soya-based diets in the world, supplemented by sea vegetables and fish. It was only after the Second World War that the bad eating habits of the West started to creep in, including dairy products, red meat, sugar, chemicals and artificial preservatives and Japan and China started to have a higher incidence of breast and prostate cancer.

It's not just what you eat but how you eat that's important. I used to bolt my food on the run or between talking almost non-stop over a business lunch. Eating macrobiotic food also showed me that it's far healthier to eat slowly; chewing food instead of swallowing it creates enzymes that take away my incessant hunger. Through different teachers I was introduced to the concept of blessing my food and giving thanks to God before eating. This in itself brought a consciousness and stillness into mealtimes leading to better digestion and a keener sense of taste.

While still at Lynne Franks PR I was told by several of my holistic therapists that I had candida, a yeast infection usually caused by stress and the use of antibiotics. I was advised to drop bread, fruit, chocolate, alcohol and fermented foods. I'd already stopped eating red meat, at the same time as I'd stopped drinking tea and coffee. I was also advised to combine my foods so that protein and carbohydrates were not eaten together as this would cause fermentation in the intestines.

But I would go on huge bread, chocolate and dairy binges when I felt stressed or depressed. Years later, I bought a book on candida from my local health food shop. As I read it, I recognised symptoms – bloating, energy swings, back and neck pain, digestive problems, foggy brain, thrush, PMT, heavy menstruation cramps, food cravings, and not being able to lose weight. I seemed to have had the lot at one time or another. I filled in the symptom chart in the book to see how I scored. It said that if I got 180 I was almost certain to have yeast-connected problems. I got 350 and started to panic.

Candida seems to create cravings for the very foods you should avoid and I realised that I'd been encouraging the nasty little parasites for years. I read the book from cover to cover and discovered how even amalgam – mercury and silver fillings – was thought to encourage candida as well as depression, mood swings and headaches. The book was written by Jane McWhirter who had opened a multidisciplinary complementary clinic, All Hallows House, in the City of London. I read that people who had been breastfed for less than six months were more likely to have candida and I knew that my mother had had a problem with her milk. GPs do not generally recognise the serious nature of candida, although recent scientific studies have shown that it can lead to cystitis, depression, eating disorders, infertility and more painful menopause, and that it causes a variety of intestinal diseases. It also looks as if it could be a contributory factor in ME and MS.

Jane's book even suggests that alcoholism could be created by candida, which actually causes the craving for alcohol in the first place. After my healing session with Leslie Kenton I went for an appointment at All Hallows, a small converted church. I saw their nutritionist, Gillian Hamer, who gave me some more good advice on supplements to take which would help heal the damage done by the candida as well as more details of the sort of food I should and shouldn't eat. I realised how lucky I was to have stopped eating bread six months earlier.

Meditation was also strongly recommended as part of the cure since that in itself eliminates a lot of stress. I saw and felt in my body tremendous changes almost immediately. By cutting out sugar, wheat, dairy and refined products I found the bloating went, I had far more energy and clarity of mind and felt years younger. My weight started to drop too and my periods became much lighter and less painful. My skin, which I now regularly brushed before showering, felt soft and healthy and people would remark on how my face had started to glow and look younger since I'd changed my diet and started meditating. Colonic therapy too is particularly important for candida sufferers. As you detox and clean out it's usually a good idea to have regular colonics or enemas to make sure the old toxins and waste matter are cleared from your intestines.

People with candida – and it can just as easily be men too – are often super-sensitive to cigarettes and toxins in the air and I found that I was starting to become allergic to big cities, including London. As this was my base, where my children and parents lived, I could not avoid being there to some extent. Whenever I'm in London now I make sure I eat healthy food, avoid smoky environments and make a point at least once a day of either having a long walk on Hampstead Heath, a yoga lesson or doing Gabrielle's Wave.

In Deia I become very healthy with a combination of pure air, healthy water, mountain walks and swimming. The constant travelling my work now requires has meant being very cautious about how to handle being on an aeroplane. I drink lots of water during the flight, stick to vegetarian food, and try to get as much sleep as possible so my body clock will adjust.

In America, Japan and Scandinavia nutritional supplements extracted from algae have been discovered which can counterbalance the toxins in the air we breathe, the food we eat and the water we drink. The assortment of supplements I take daily include blue-green algae, vitamin C and newly recognised American supplements such as DHEA and melatonin, minerals including magnesium and zinc tablets, antioxidants, Co Q10, digestive enzymes and Biodophilus.

Melatonin is viewed in the US as nature's answer to insomnia, depression and jet lag. It is produced naturally by the brain's pineal gland in response to sunlight and helps to regulate sleep and other bodily processes. Taking the pills helps my body clock to adapt to new time zones when I'm travelling. Research also suggests that melatonin may have anti-ageing and anti-carcinogenic properties. DHEA is being hailed in the States as the new super-supplement, the hormone that does it all. Produced by the adrenal glands DHEA can be converted into other hormones in order to compensate for any imbalance in the body. It appears to be remarkably efficient in all areas of disease: it builds up the immune system, increasing energy levels and a sustained feeling of well-being.

Natural creams such as progesterone for premenstrual

problems and tri-estrogen cream with progesterone as an effective replacement for hormone replacement therapy during menopause are now available in the US, although they are harder to find in the UK. There are even natural supplements for pets in America, as they too can get addicted to junk food causing degenerative illness and premature ageing!

This is not excessive when you consider the amount of chemicals now being discovered in our food, our air and our water. Although I try and eat organic vegetables when I'm in London or Deia, it's not always possible and as we saw from the hysterical reaction to BSE (mad cow disease) consumers are often ill-informed about what they put in their bodies. All I can say is that since I have watched my diet, exercised regularly and taken supplements I have never felt or looked better. Taking time out for simple exercise is essential for everyone, even it it's only for ten minutes.

One of the most effective natural medicines that both Leslie Kenton and the All Hallows Clinic told me about was *pau d'arco* tea. In Portuguese, *pau d'arco* means 'wood of bow' and the Europeans learnt about this tree from the Inca Indians in southern Peru. In addition to making bows, the Incas drank tea from the bark of the tree and claimed it worked miracles. *Pau d'arco* also comes from south Argentina, the southernmost region of the old Inca empire and the Andes.

The *pau d'arco* tea I drink is produced by Natural Flow and comes from Argentina where the trees are grown in unsprayed plantations, thus preserving the forest. *Pau d'arco* is said to have complex biochemical properties from the Lapachol it contains. It works as a general nutritional supplement and is particularly helpful in clearing up candida.

The nuts, seeds and trees of the South American jungle contain many special healing properties which we are only just hearing about in the West. *Guarana* comes from the legendary seed of the rain forest where they call it the life force of the Amazon. It can give natural energy when it is taken in the form of drink, pills or chewing gum without the bad effects of coffee or other stimulants. However, like all stimulants it does cause an increase in adrenalin, which is not helpful when healing candida. The secret of healing candida is to stay calm, not hype yourself up.

I've always found regular massage and body work important. My favourite body worker of all is the star of the Esalen massage team, Cee Cee. Sadly he's in California and I'm not there very often but I try to get some kind of body work including shiatsu, lymph drainage, reflexology and aromatherapy pretty regularly. The success of aromatherapy oils and flower remedies in the mass market is indicative of the new awareness of the natural healing properties of plants and herbs.

The chemicals in the dye we put in our hair, the creams we put on our face, the ingredients of toothpaste and the soap we use, and for women the bleach and bacteria in cotton used for tampons, and the damage they can do is starting to be taken seriously. The increase and importance to us of natural products, whether they go on the body or in the mouth, is part of a huge awareness shift by the consumer.

Leslie Kenton also alerted me to the changes in our bodies caused by the hormones we ingest through our drinking water. I was horrified. A Finnish study published in the *British Medical Journal* in January 1997 showed that between 1981 and 1991 the sperm count of a sample of middle-aged men had decreased by more than half. A similar report from the Medical Research Council Reproductive Biology Unit in Edinburgh states that men born after 1970 have a sperm count 25 per cent lower than those born before 1959, and that fish and whales are frequently found with both male and female sexual organs. This is mostly due to hormones getting into our water system, from the contraceptive pill or from environmental chemicals, particularly weedkillers, and through the foodstuff of chicken and animals.

We humans have not only done our best to ruin nature and the animal kingdom through our ignorance in playing with chemicals in the name of business; we have also gone a long way down the line in destroying our own bodies. In many places throughout the world it will take years to get natural non-toxic fruits and vegetables to grow again.

Amalgam tooth fillings have been proved to have a detrimental effect on our body, although frighteningly this is still denied by many dentists. It's expensive to get such fillings changed but gradually I've been removing mine over the past few years and have now almost got rid of them all. I'm quite sure that this has helped with my general health improvement. As my homeopathic dentist, Vicky Lee, says, 'We spend the second part of our lives making good all the damage we've done in the first half.'

I'm encouraged that what was once seen as alternative therapies, particularly the Eastern healing arts of acupuncture, Chinese herbs and Ayurvedic medicines from India, are starting to be taken seriously by Western doctors. I believe modern medicine has a long way to go in really understanding how the body works and what makes it sick. We are capable of avoiding many diseases through the use of preventive measures including positive mental attitudes, healthy nutrition and disciplines like yoga and meditation.

The overuse of antibiotics, radiation treatment and inoculation has already been proven to have done far greater harm than good to the human race. As a result of chemical additives in food, plus the damage from cigarettes, alcohol, air pollution and day-to-day stress, it's not surprising we get sick.

I envisage that this initial shift in consumer attitudes to health will continue to grow. We will want to know exactly what we are putting into our bodies and how it can affect us. This will include foods as well as medicine, and the demand for organic produce will increase.

There is already a return to people growing their own fruit and vegetables wherever there's a garden or allotment available and organic supermarkets are opening up across Europe as well as the States. Thirty per cent of adults in the United States now take vitamins and supplements daily and their European counterparts are catching up rapidly. People want to live longer and live healthier, and disillusionment with the existing sources of food and accompanying information will result in experimentation with new nutritional sources. There's a new infrastructure of network marketing to distribute the latest natural wonder drugs. It's a hungry market. Obviously some are more effective than others and they are all fairly expensive. It's important to find out what suits you best by consulting alternative health therapists you trust, reading up about the various products – they can all be traced on the Internet – and trying them out for yourself.

The wise women and wise men of indigenous native tribes have always known the secrets of natural herbs: many of our modern medicines were originally based on this information. Homeopathy is the modern form of a traditional healing art which was practised by midwives and shamans for centuries. These natural remedies for most illnesses can now be obtained, packaged in little white pills from specialist pharmacists. I carry my travelling homeopathy kit covering everything from colds and sprains to travel sickness everywhere I go. I prefer homeopathic anti-malaria pills to hospital-prescribed ones, although there is no proof that they are as effective.

We are going through a major consciousness shift in how we view our bodies and our health. We will take the best of natural medicines and preventive cures from the East and other indigenous peoples, and combine them with the best of Western science. We will be far more cautious about what we put into our bodies and we will try to de-stress our lives to a point of general wellbeing. This in turn will affect our entire lifestyle and have major repercussions on how we live and work.

6

Tribal Quest

I'd always fantasised that visiting the spiritual community of Findhorn in Scotland would be similar to a visit to the ancient mystic Isle of Avalon. There, so legend has it, you would wait by the lake of King Arthur for the mists to clear and the boat to transport you, manned by Druid priests and priestesses, would appear.

Ironically I'd first heard of Findhorn while on the West Coast of America. You tend to have to go a long way to find out what's close at home. The Findhorn community was founded by Peter and Eileen Caddy and their Canadian friend Dorothy Maclean in the sixties on a barren caravan site situated on unfriendly and windswept sand dunes on the west coast of Scotland. Findhorn has its legends too and Dorothy Maclean's powerful silent communication with plants is said to have soon transformed what had been inhospitable terrain, good for only spiky grass and pine trees, into a thriving vegetable garden. Judging from the giant lettuces and cabbages that grew there it was clear that the nature spirits – or devas – were working in co-operation with the community to nourish the soil, turn deserts into flourishing gardens and purify contaminated soil.

Following instructions, through the guiding inner voice of

Eileen Caddy, a community centre and garden were created that began to attract interest and visitors from all over the world. Almost overnight, it seemed, word of what they were doing in this tiny corner of Scotland had spread and all sorts of people, young and old, began to arrive on their doorstep, drawn by the magnetic spiritual power generated by the three founder members. Peter and Dorothy had absolute faith in Eileen's inner voice and would follow the guidance to the letter as it was written down. In one message to the community it was stated that 'one garden can save a world'.

Although based on spiritual principles of love and service the Findhorn Foundation today is very much on the cutting edge of technology and ecology. It was the place where I first heard about the Internet, and the Foundation's solar energy panel business run by my friend George Gouldschmidt exports all over the world.

It is a centre for sustainable innovation and has been a source of light and inspiration for literally thousands of people all over the world. It was at Findhorn that I first saw a huge modern windmill on the beach creating wind energy and first stayed in an ecologically friendly house. Like a giant Meccano kit the wooden houses are imported in bits from Finland and are made from strictly non-toxic material. I was able to breathe so comfortably at night through the naturally clad walls that it made me appreciate just how congested I got in London.

The first time I visited I signed up for what they call an 'Experience Week' – a kind of induction course. I stayed in Cluny College, a former 1930s hotel managed at one time by the Caddys before they got the sack for their 'avant-garde' spiritual ideas. Now owned by the Foundation, it is kept constantly busy by the visitors who come every year to try out the Findhorn magic for themselves.

Although it wasn't my first experience of living in a community – I'd been several times to the Nichiren Shoshu Buddhist centre in the South of France – it was certainly the first time that I didn't know anybody and indeed didn't know what to expect. I met the other members of my group, mostly European and English, some men but more women, aged from around twenty to forty-five. They included a doctor, a young Scottish writer and his artist girlfriend, a couple of social workers, a Danish engineer and some members of a French commune. They too were all here for the first time and most of them were just as nervous as me.

We were introduced to each other by two attractive forty-something Findhorn residents. They lit a candle, asked us to hold hands – the left hand receiving, the right hand giving – and invoked a blessing for our week together. We were all self-conscious but it certainly eased our nervousness. It is said that there are angels at Findhorn and I, for one, believe it. When a large group of people are together with the same intention of service and love it creates an energy which you can feel all around you.

That is not to say that there aren't problems. As I got to know the Foundation better I saw it was just a microcosm in many ways of many problems in the outside world – ego, jealousy, ambition – but at Findhorn the intention is to heal these problems by sharing how you feel and communicate from a soul-to-soul basis. It doesn't mean that everything becomes perfect again. Even the Caddys eventually split up when Eileen was told by her inner voice not to pass on any more guidance. Dorothy Maclean went back to North America.

We were told that we could volunteer for three different areas of service during our Experience Week – helping in the laundry, in the garden, or with general cleaning. I knew the last of these included the bathrooms and toilets and I was determined that I wouldn't end up doing that – after all, hadn't I worked for twenty-five years to be able to afford to pay other people to clear up my family's mess? Why should I pay to clean up other people's?

But Findhorn works in mysterious ways and after a suitable amount of meditation and reflection I heard myself say, 'I'll do the bathrooms.'

My experience at Findhorn was a lot more comfortable than it would have been for Eileen Caddy in the early days when she wanted to meditate and listen to her inner voice. She shared a caravan with her

94

husband, their three sons and Dorothy Maclean, and had no personal space. Eileen prayed in desperation to know how to meditate with so much going on in such a confined area.

The answer came back: 'Why don't you go down to the public toilets? You will find perfect peace there.' Although at first she was horrified at the idea of sitting in a public toilet to listen for the voice of God, she soon realised that, however unorthodox, it was the perfect solution. It was there that much of the inspiration for Findhorn was imparted.

The week passed pleasantly enough. We were taken out to see the magic of the beautiful countryside, the rivers, and twisted oak forest. In the main caravan site we saw for ourselves the eco-village, user-friendly houses and buildings with turf roofs. The large and impressive Universal Hall was built on love and trust by members of the community for conferences and debates. I saw the cluster of eco-homes made from giant whisky barrels cut in two, the famous gardens still yielding perhaps not enormous vegetables but beautiful organic fresh produce and colourful flowers, and of course the sanctuaries or meditation centres where collectively or individually we could go inwards and connect with the divine source.

The Findhorn community believe that eco-villages provide 'a guide and model for finding the balance in human systems – social, spiritual, cultural, economic and physical – that can work within the natural system of nature'. I watched the kitchen crew prepare delicious vegetarian food, peeling the potatoes after strong group meditation, and appreciated how we can change the energy of work situations by such simple means – lighting a candle, coming together holding hands in silence for a few moments and then sharing what is going on inside. It opens the way to far more creativity and harmony in the workplace. I observed the long-term residents of Findhorn planning their life as a community while still respecting the rights of the individual. I saw that group decision making, although sometimes frustrating for my impatient mind, at least enabled the genuine participation of all those involved.

Business meetings too would benefit from starting with a small meditation or moment of silence to rebalance the individual's energy to the group's before important decisions are made. I've tried it myself before in meetings and found it effective.

I've never worked out quite how to travel light and as usual I came to Findhorn with far too much baggage. One of the most frequent arguments I'd had with Paul was about the amount of luggage I would take. On one trip to India I took a huge bag of special macrobiotic food including organic rice. 'You're not serious,' said Paul when he saw me unpack. 'You must be the first person I know who takes rice on holiday to India.'

I still hadn't learnt my lesson and although I didn't take brown rice to Findhorn I did have a huge heavy bag full of tapes, books, clothes, a sound system, crystals . . . you name it, I had it.

I think it must have to do with insecurity of some sort. This time when I arrived I had to ask for help from one of the men to get my bag upstairs – not the kind of practice encouraged in a democratic community. I'd been told I had to share a bedroom but was thankful when I saw I'd been allocated a large room with three beds just for me. The angels of Findhorn were kind and there was enough room for me, my bag, my books and all my other madnesses. But I seldom listened to the music, read only one book and wore jeans and sweatshirt plus my thick coat the whole time I was there. I never learn. I must have been a possessionless beggar in a past life and have tried to make up for it ever since. But it's one of the patterns I'm trying to change.

The dozen or so of us on the Experience Week were mostly newcomers to many of the concepts of community life, and some of us, including me, really had to struggle with opening up. I always wanted to be the carer, pushing my own problems aside to try and help others in pain. It was only towards the end of my week that I became aware that this was just my way of escaping from the truth and there was no way I could help anyone else until I learnt to help myself.

After dancing together, praying together, hugging, crying and connecting, my group went through its final ritual of saying goodbye and turning our backs on the circle. I felt as if I was leaving my family and I think, like the others who had come such a long way during the week, I was full of fear. Looking back I can see that in a way I'd temporarily replaced my former safe family of Buddhists with a new family. I knew I needed to go back into the world while keeping the connection and learn to step forward on my own.

This was the first of several trips to Findhorn and the start of a long association. One one occasion I was honoured to be present when the fourteen-year-old daughter of some community friends along with other young girls were celebrating the rites of passage for their menstruation and puberty. The girls received presents from their fathers and were then adorned with flowers by the women, who took them to the sanctuary and offered prayers of thanks.

Rather than being sheepish or embarrassed, these young girls shone with pride and happiness at being part of the ritual of entering into womanhood. It was important too that the men as well as the women of their family celebrated with them instead of adhering to our Western customs of never mentioning such a significant and wonderful experience in mixed company.

I looked back at my puberty years. I'd been very late to start menstruating and my body had been almost anorexic as if denying my womanhood. I was about to go into hospital at seventeen for a dreaded internal examination when my period unexpectedly started literally the day before. There was great relief among the female members of my family that I was normal. I was given some sanitary towels and told to hide them from my father. Certainly not the joyful occasion I witnessed in Findhorn.

I started hearing of more and more people, particularly in communities, bringing back rites of passage to mark significant milestones in people's lives, or indeed in nature itself. Harvest, moon, birth, death and marriage rituals are a vital part of human culture.

We should use ritual in many areas of our lives. A former husband and wife could mark their divorce by a loving cutting-of-the-ties ritual instead of an angry exchange of lawyers' letters. And other emotional situations, such as a miscarriage or moving house, could be softened by symbolic ritual and nurturing support.

The Findhorn Foundation opened a Steiner School for their children, and subsequently for children from neighbouring villages. It was the first time I'd come across this innovative teaching concept by Austrian social philosopher, Rudolph Steiner. His method of teaching respects the essential nature of childhood and enables each pupil to develop the abilities and confidence needed for life. All subjects are taught in an interdisciplinary way according to the individual child's development. The method includes a comprehensive balance of practical life skills, such as gardening, crafts, technology and design complemented by a wide range of artistic activities. In Steiner schools young people are encouraged to develop qualities such as trust, compassion, an inner moral sense and the ability to discriminate between good and evil. It is a teaching method which leads the pupils to 'know and love the world' and their fellow human beings. As a reaction to mechanistic formula teaching, Steiner's approach is still popular all over the world today – an effective antidote to the kind of schooling which Steiner himself called a process of 'planned amnesia'.

Another time I went to Findhorn I stayed in the main caravan park in the eco-friendly B&B and took Ruby Wax with me. At the time there was an exhibition of finalists in an architectural competition for the Holy Island multi-faith retreat centre belonging to Samye Ling, a Tibetan Buddhist community outside Glasgow. The affable Tibetan Lama Yeshi, the abbot of Samye Ling, was there with his team creating interest in their project.

Findhorn, one of the exhibition's sponsors, and other friends had offered to host the launch of this exhibition. They needed a celebrity to open it and I thought Ruby would be just the job. She had started on her own spiritual search and loved Findhorn and Lama Yeshi. She made a very moving opening speech. Subsequently Ruby became a friend of the Foundation, taking her whole family back there on several occasions.

I saw a scene in a later edition of *Ab Fab*, of which Ruby is the script editor, based on a New Age retreat with people hugging trees, 'omming' and chanting. I pointed out a possible physical similarity to Findhorn to Ruby but she assured me it was just a coincidence!

I volunteered to advise Findhorn on their PR and marketing. I would regularly get worried phone calls or faxes from them asking for help on negative editorials being encouraged in the Scottish press by local residents. I think the words 'New Age cult' were used on several occasions, which was absurd. Theirs was an open-door policy. There was no sinister hidden agenda: they saw themselves as part of the local community and aimed to serve it and the rest of the world. Personally I always found the proximity of the local RAF base with its low-flying war jets far more sinister.

After meeting the Samye Ling contingent at Findhorn I was invited to head up a weekend conference at their Tibetan monastery outside Glasgow on how to work with media and spirituality. I arrived by car from Glasgow airport in a blizzard. It was an out-of-world experience before I got there – blinding white snow in front of our headlights until suddenly out of the whiteness I saw a vibrantly coloured exotic temple from another place and another time. It is the only authentic temple built outside Tibet and the dream come true of two Tibetan brothers Lama Yeshi and Akong Tulku Rinpoche.

Samye Ling is unique in its method of working with troubled youngsters from Scotland and England. They often arrive with drug or alcohol problems and parents at the end of their tether. These tough young people in their teens and early twenties from the streets, some adorned with tattoos, would agree to shave their heads and take on the robes of Tibetan monks and nuns. They live a life of austerity and service within the community for one year and are shown love and how to find self-esteem, whether learning how to build brick walls or creating delicious concoctions in the kitchens. They rarely want to leave but are encouraged to go back into the world so as not to replace one dependency with another. Some still choose to return and together with other committed European Buddhists often go into silent retreat in a special enclosed building for three years, three months, three weeks and three days. There they find the silence inside and time for pure contemplation. Lama Yeshi himself has been in silent secluded retreat for a total period of more than twelve years of his life, although he always seems jovial and social when I meet him. Samye Ling also teaches in the style of the old Tibetan masters how to paint traditional mandalas on fabric and keeps the many traditions of Tibetan Buddhism alive.

The various participants in the media and spirituality conference ranged from representatives of charities, international publishers and Buddhist groups, to journalists and PRs. We all agreed that the British media seemed fairly cynical about beliefs not based on traditional Judaeo-Christian religions. It really was a question of getting past the fear barrier using language that created trust. It was also a matter of timing. I noticed over the next few years many positive spiritual articles in the media, particularly on Buddhism and often featuring the Samye Ling community. The enormous worldwide success of James Redfield's New Age adventure book *The Celestine Prophecy*, the high profile of teachers like Deepak Chopra and Denise Linn, the endorsement by many showbiz personalities who had undertaken their own spiritual journeys plus regular alternative health and healing pages in the middle-class *Daily Mail* and *Daily Express* had slowly brought about a softening in attitudes.

It was at Findhorn that I first met singer Mike Scott. He'd been spending time there after leaving New York when his band the Waterboys split. He also met his future partner, Janette, there, one of the facilitators from my Experience Week. Later I saw Mike perform material from his new album at the Hackney Empire. The crowded audience cheered as he appeared on the stage with just a simple lit candle and an acoustic guitar and sang his songs of light and love, many of which had been written at and inspired by Findhorn.

Saturday morning, Experience Week
I'm so nervous I can hardly speak
Arrive at Cluny Hill, half past ten
Almost turned and went home again

My focaliser showed me my room
Like she was consigning me to my doom

What am I doing here? What's going on?
Who are these people? What are they on?

Here comes my room-mate, he sure looks weird
Wild black hair and a big fuzzy beard
Met the rest of the group after lunch
What a strange and motley bunch

Sunday morning, I'm feeling bad
Enjoyed the dancing but now I'm sad
Things feel different, I don't know why
Feelin' lonely, wanna cry

Monday afternoon, I've learned everybody's names
We go down to the ballroom to play some games
Something happened I can hardly describe
Changed my feelings, changed my life

Tuesday morning, with a hoover in my hand
Cleaning out the dining room, beginning to understand
Tuning in, tuning out
Startin' to see what Findhorn is all about

Wednesday morning in the winter sunshine
Down at Cullerne garden everybody's feeling fine
In this wonderful place, as smooth as a dream
Eleven strangers have become a team

Thursday morning, at a quarter past three
I'm wide awake in the Sanctuary
Opening myself to the love and the light
Thanking God for steering me right

So now it's Friday, almost time to go home

And back into the big wide world I must roam
But I'll take it with me, every single thing
Send it out with every song I sing

So that's the tale of my Experience Week.
It was beautiful. It was unique.
It made me friends and it opened my heart.
This isn't the end, it's just the start.

'Experience Week' by Mike Scott,
reproduced by permission of Sony/ATV Music

Mike, Janette and I hung out together at another interesting gathering – the twenty-fifth Glastonbury Festival. Created by farmer Michael Eavis, Glastonbury Festival was the grandaddy of a more transient type of community – the British summer rock festivals and raves. This was the first time I'd made it to Glastonbury and by 1995 it was already a temporary city with more than 100,000 people, mostly under twenty-five, living under miles of big and small tents stretched out in every direction. The festival was divided into a range of musical areas, including the enormous main pyramid stage, acoustic stages, dance tents and many smaller venues. The rest of the festival was arranged around different themes including a children's area, theatre area, healing field, green field, and green futures field. It was like a giant psychedelic theme park for adults, with temporary gardens, huge vegetarian restaurants and disgusting-smelling Portaloos.

I was there to do a talk during the Saturday afternoon on women's roles and the consciousness shift of the planet. Although willing to be a Glastonbury 'raver' I was still hesitant about letting go of my creature comforts. I'd booked a room in a small hotel nearby and planned to end each day with a good night's sleep and a hot bath!

The first afternoon I listened to Sinead O'Connor do a great set and hung out with her and her family before continuing to play groupie watching Mike Scott. He was one of the earliest Glastonbury regulars when still in the Waterboys; afterwards I stood with him and

Janette watching Oasis. They dropped me off in their car at my hotel in the small hours and I decided to spend the next day doing Glastonbury in a more grassroots style.

I walked the two miles down country lanes to get back to the festival early next morning with a different plan in view. I was wandering around the children's playground trying to get my bearings when I sensed there was someone nearby whom I knew. I felt if I stood still they'd find me. Sure enough after a few minutes I heard my name being called: 'Lynne, I thought it was you,' said the breathless voice of beautiful Kari-Ann Jagger, one of my closest girlfriends, who is married to musician Chris, Mick's younger brother.

Kari-Ann was a successful model in the sixties and despite having four grown-up sons still looks much the same as she did when featured on the cover of Roxy Music's first album back in the early seventies. An old hand at Glastonbury, she took me off to her friend Hal's Turkish bath complex on the green futures field. It really was something to see. Out of one tap Hal and his team had created a miracle. A tented Turkish bath, sauna bath, vegetarian kitchen and restaurant, massage tents, a beautifully decorated Tibetan yurt tent with an elaborate altar. Various Hari Krishnas and other devotees of Eastern religions came to sing and dance during the day. There was even a clean, perma-culture toilet dug out of the ground. I decided I'd found my base.

I hung out there for most of the next two days with an assortment of close friends and their children and ventured out to dance and hear music, as well as visit the healing fields. I was fascinated by one tent whose stage was lit up by electricity generated by several people madly pedalling away on stationary bicycles. I saw windmill power light up the giant pyramid stage, displays and demonstrations on the versatility of hemp, perma-culture gardens and different ways of recycling rubbish.

I did a trance dance workshop with my friend Ya'Acov Darling Khan, tried different forms of healing and saw an illuminating exhibition of paintings of the sacred wise women of the earth. I was pleasantly surprised when I got such a positive response from the young men in the crowd who attended my Saturday afternoon talk on women's empowerment in a changing world.

Celtic legends were re-enacted by dance and theatre groups, continuing the tradition of the travelling storytellers from centuries before. I was told how theatre groups like this are increasingly being used as an alternative means of spreading eco-information, particularly in schools.

I saw thousands of young people happy and enjoying themselves on the beautiful June weekend, and were it not for commitments back in London, I would have stayed until I got thrown out.

Driving back to London in the summer heat made me sleepy and I wandered off the main road near Bath to park in a lay-by, then fell asleep for an hour in a yellow cornfield. I woke to find blood trickling down my leg, as if I too were one of the earth's wise women. I felt I was giving back my sacred blood to the ground in acknowledgement and thanks for the positive energy I'd just experienced.

I got a similar feeling of this type of group energy and bonding when I went to one of the last Grateful Dead concerts in San Francisco the year before. Like the Glastonbury Festival crowd, the Dead Heads focused their tie-dyed veggieburger existence on music and followed the band from stadium to stadium across the country creating temporary psychedelic villages in the car parks. They would put up painted tents amongst their colourful trailers selling and trading everything they could, including drugs, hippie clothes and food.

Grateful Dead guitarist, Jerry Garcia, was an icon for millions in the United States for more than twenty years – he even has a Ben & Jerry ice-cream named after him – and his untimely death in 1995 resulted in national mourning. I was in Haight Ashbury in San Francisco – the centre of hippiedom – shortly after and saw a large street altar erected in his memory. The Grateful Dead were representative of a desire for a better world where love and peace would replace fear and greed. Although some sad victims, including Garcia himself, never managed to extract themselves fully from a damaging drug lifestyle, many of America's top entrepreneurial businessmen and women, academics and writers, look fondly back at their sixties acid flashes as a time of inspiration and connection with the universe.

Drugs too became a big part of the more recent British rave culture. It was in the summer of love in 1989 when young people high on dance energy and house music as well as tabs of Ecstasy and acid would dance their way through psychedelic nights surrounded by fluorescent banners and extraordinary light shows in isolated country spaces. I found raves of crucial importance in moulding many young people's attitudes. The mood was gentle and loving, the visuals highly creative and the music great to dance to. You could get high just on the atmosphere. There were cavalcades of car convoys, finding out the secret designation of the raves from mysterious phone boxes and garages on route. There was always plenty of water available to prevent dehydration – the main danger when taking Ecstasy and dancing for hours. There are arguments for and against the use of soft drugs but the reality is that cocktails of unknown chemicals can be dangerous.

The police and authorities were not happy and soon succeeded in making raves illegal. They were equally irritated by the young travellers who crossed the country in the summer months from sacred sites to festivals. Finally, the Conservative government decided all this fun and freedom had to stop and introduced plans for the Criminal Justice Bill. With a disappointing lack of opposition from the Labour Party, the bill was enacted in 1994. The Criminal Justice and Public Order Act gives police unprecedented powers to remove any persons attending or preparing for a rave, as well as supplementary powers of entry and seizure and powers to arrest without a warrant. Two or more people are subject to arrest if found preparing for such a gathering, groups of no more than ten people are permitted to dance in the street, live music without a licence is now banned in public places, as are large public gatherings, and much of the heart and soul of some of the summer of love was squeezed and bled till it was dry.

However, what the civil servants and politicians hadn't reckoned on was how a law like this could bond young people together.

For many thousands of young people, already disillusioned with party politics and an outdated system they couldn't relate to, the Act was the final straw. A whole spread of politically active groups outside the mainstream system started working together. Many communicated through flyers and noticeboards at London rave clubs like Megatripolis and started using camcorders to make videos of action protests to show inside the clubs. They protested against the Act itself, the exportation of young calves to turn into veal, they became surfers against sewage and most important of all they formed the nucleus of the tree protesters.

Horror stories of the ruination of beautiful British woodlands and the destruction of unspoilt countryside to make unnecessary bypasses and motorways had slowly been appearing in the *Guardian, Time Out,* and more left-wing publications. It wasn't until Bel Mooney and a few other media personalities committed themselves to taking a stand to protest at the destruction of the beautiful countryside on Salisbury Hill in Wiltshire that the mainstream TV channels and newspapers started taking note. Many protesters, mostly young men and women, went there and lived in communities, building tree houses or living under plastic 'bender' shelters or tents. They shared their food, learnt how to climb and bonded with the spirit of the trees.

Despite widespread media coverage and local sympathy, the authorities and bureaucrats had their way. The big machinery came, security men were sent to drag the young people off the trees and often arrest them, the trees were cut down and an irreplaceable area of British countryside was destroyed for ever.

I didn't make it to Salisbury Hill but I did visit the protesters at Newbury. Here too a bypass was being constructed by planners who later admitted it could have been put elsewhere and in the long term wouldn't really alleviate the town's traffic problem anyway. My friend, writer Alex Fisher, had written an article about the new politics and had herself decided to become a tree person. She showed me round the mother ship camp. Young people climbed up and down the trees and across from one towering giant to another on what seemed to be the thinnest of ropes with their belt, pulleys and hooks keeping them upright.

I was welcomed with a cup of tea from a kettle on the camp-fire and shown the altar to the trees and Mother Earth made from symbolic artefacts including knives and spoons. It reminded me of the Afro-Caribbean plate and cutlery altars I'd seen in an exhibition in New York some years earlier. A variety of tree houses had been created with love by the inhabitants and there was even a functioning stove in one of them. I talked to several of the predominantly young men present who ranged from environmental students to angry drop-outs. They all seemed united in their disappointment with authority and with what the adult world had to offer.

'I was reading environmental studies at university,' one of them told me. 'I needed to get out into the action and live with nature myself before I settled into a job. I want to know where I can really make a difference.' Not all were so committed. I met another young guy who just ranted about how he hated all forms of authority. Alex shrugged and said the protesters attracted all types and the older activists encouraged the more militant to keep to the spirit of non-violent confrontation.

I revisited Newbury for a major protest with thousands of others another weekend with Kari-Ann and an assortment of our children and friends. I found Alex decorated with leaves and body paint looking like a tree elf dancing to drums by one of the camps. What amazed me was that amongst the thousands of protesters there were so many middle-aged and elderly good upstanding British citizens who had probably never been on a protest march in their life before. They wore their green huskies and wellies and were united with the brightly coloured and dreadlocked young travellers in their horror that once again another part of a beautiful area of British countryside was about to be covered in tarmac. There was a feeling of unity and bonding between everyone. Later in the day tears were spilt when the speeches reminded us that the beautiful environment we'd been enjoying all day was about to be destroyed.

The next time I met some of the demonstrators was at an empty building site in Wandsworth. The nucleus of the tree protesters of Newbury decided to turn their attention to urban wasteland. They had made a list of more than ten huge empty sites across London which they wanted to show could be transformed into sustainable communities for some of London's many homeless. I'd been overseas and as soon as I got back Kari-Ann took me down there to show me what was happening. They had only been there two days and already temporary dwellings, organic gardens, and perma-culture loos had been installed. There was community cooking, a beautiful mosaic on the wall facing the River Thames and again a feeling of joy and commitment.

Phoenix, a highly intelligent young man in his twenties, who had been a founder of the Rainbow Arts Centre created in an abandoned church in Kentish Town, showed me around. I met Suzanne, a woman of my age and a friend of Kari-Ann's, who had become the 'wise woman' at Newbury. She had moved to the Wandsworth site, named Pure Genius by the residents, with her two teenage daughters and twelve-year-old son who seemed single-handedly to be doing the cooking for the 150 or so inhabitants.

People were playing music by candlelight on my first visit as the sun went down over the Thames, creating a glorious sunset. I could see the beginnings of the gardens and pathways already put down with so much love. Phoenix explained that the space belonged to Guinness, who were hoping to sell it to a supermarket chain. Wandsworth Council had decided there were too many already in the area so the space was in limbo. The police told the squatters they'd be left alone if they behaved themselves. Both Guinness and Wandsworth Council also seemed content to leave them there for the time being. Phoenix told me there had been loads of press already. Tony Benn had popped in at seven o'clock that morning and offered some intelligent support, and CNN were due the next day. Their spokesperson George Monbiot, who had previously been with Friends of the Earth, was becoming quite a media personality but I was assured that the community made all their decisions by democratic committee.

Sadly some months later the authorities moved the community out. By then the vegetables and plants had grown to full size but the utopian dream of Pure Genius had dissolved into harsh reality when social care agencies sent many of the area's displaced individuals to join them. They were not equipped to deal with some of the schizophrenic and aggressive characters who moved in.

George Monbiot was quoted as saying: 'Eco-villagers made the mistake of trying to solve all the world's problems at once, to take on the entire burden of dispossession and alienation so starkly displayed in the shattered borough of Wandsworth. They tried to reconcile a host of communities of interest, with the result that none was served well. Next time we – people who seek to alter the way the world sees itself – must define the limits of exploitation our social commons can support.'

The concept had reminded me of a dream I'd been told about by dreadlocked Afro-American church minister, Ted Hayes, whom I'd met several years earlier in Los Angeles. He had left his family home to join the homeless on the streets of downtown LA and create a series of temporary housing made out of Perspex geodesic domes, originally inspired by inventor Buckminster Fuller. His vision was for the homeless and other displaced people to be given empty sites such as disused army bases where they could become self-sufficient, growing their own vegetables and learning simple skills. 'I know my dream works but I've yet to convince the authorities,' he told me. 'I want to come to England and show my dome to Prince Charles. If I can get him photographed endorsing the idea I can get the people of LA to listen to me.'

I later heard that the dynamism of his personality was such that despite having no money or resources he got both Prince Charles and Prince Edward to visit the Californian site where he'd erected several domes and, as he predicted, the LA authorities were backing his scheme.

I witnessed another extraordinary success story based on initiative and sheer determination on another visit to LA. I was taken by associates who were members of the Liberty Hill Foundation to visit Skid Row Access Inc., a non-profit artisans' co-op founded by former homeless men and women together with local architect, Charles

McClain. They produced wooden toys, greetings cards, art prints and many other decorative products. In five years the business had grown and was now selling thousands of items. These former Skid Row residents were running a constantly expanding, successful business as well as employing and training other homeless people.

While I was visiting Pure Genius in the early days, Phoenix, who'd first shown me around the site, showed me his exhibition on Agenda 21. He was holding a workshop the next day for members of the public who, like me, were not sure what it was all about. Agenda 21 had arisen from the United Nations Conference on Environment and Development held in Rio de Janeiro in June 1992. It was one of three documents approved at the conference and is a comprehensive plan to guide national and international action towards sustainable development. Signed by all the member states it seeks to hand the power of the local environment back to the community who live and work there.

The problem in the UK, as in many countries, was that local governments and councils had very little money. I believe Agenda 21 could be the beginning of community power in its truest sense. The message of the old bumper sticker THINK GLOBAL, ACT LOCAL that I'd had on my fridge for the past few years was finally being heard.

As I travelled round the world I could see how communities wanted to become more responsible in working together to make the decisions that affect their lives. Whether squatters on a piece of wasteland in Wandsworth, residents of an eco-village on the coast of Scotland, the homeless in LA, or villagers in southern India, people want to rediscover how to support and empower each other.

We need to find our sense of community and bring it into our day-to-day lives. Western society has lost the whole concept of extended family. The wisdom of the elders is no longer valued. We must learn from the positive aspects of the tribal life of people in developing countries instead of teaching them the bad habits of isolated urban existence.

7

Plugging into the Future

'Lynne, it's Beth,' the young American voice said down the line. 'I've been meditating today and heard a voice telling me that I must introduce you to Jay Levin. He's an old boss of mine in LA and is working on an idea for a conscious TV channel called Planet Central. I really think you should go over and see him.' I'd met Beth some months earlier on my Experience Week at Findhorn and I was just planning a trip to LA.

At about the same time I got the call from Beth I also heard from my friend, director Kevin Godley. 'Lynne, I think you should go and see Dave Stewart,' he said. 'A funny thing happened the other day. I got a message that he'd rung me, although when I rang him back he said he hadn't. He started telling me about an idea for a healing TV channel he was working on with Deepak Chopra. I thought it sounded your kind of thing and told him he should have a chat with you.'

Getting these two phone calls in the same week in spring 1994 was obviously no coincidence. There was lots of talk about the growth of cable and TV, which would give us access to hundreds of channels via satellite technology. It would make sense for several of them to cover healing, environment and human potential.

I went to see former Eurythmic Dave Stewart in his high-tech Covent Garden offices. The navy carpet contained luminous fibres that gave the impression of a night sky full of stars. Small TV monitors and the latest technology gave me the feeling of being somewhere in the future. Dave Stewart, apart from being a very talented musician and record producer, is also a visionary and has more creative ideas in a week than some people have in a lifetime. He suggested we got together with his new friend Charles Saatchi.

A few weeks later we met for dinner at Charles and his wife Kay's art-filled Chelsea house along with Dave and Rita Clifton, the Saatchi director responsible for the project. Although Charles seemed keen, it became clear that a healing channel would be a new departure for the advertising magnate, who sat puffing cigarettes and drinking cans of Coke constantly through dinner. We discussed at length the biggest problem of the channel – the question of which companies would be considered clean enough to have as advertisers. Charles and Dave said they'd take the money from anyone willing to give it but I had my doubts. This was the first time I'd thought about what made business ethical and it was a topic which would recur in many future conversations.

Shortly after this, I started my journey across North America. I was on my way to find out what was happening at the cutting edge of the communications business and whether I had a role to play.

I first went to Los Angeles and met up with Beth's friend Jay Levin, a small but very affable and hospitable man. On my first night Jay took me to a gala dinner to celebrate an 'Oscar type' event for TV shows and movies featuring animals. We sat on a table with a group of wealthy Beverly Hills people who voluntarily looked after unwanted rabbits, some of whom had offered to invest in Jay's station – the volunteers, not the bunnies. It could only happen in America, and we sat for hours through a major awards ceremony.

I spent some time with Jay over the next few days and he explained that Planet Central had started as an environmental cable station but the concept was rapidly growing into something bigger which would feature healing and New Age personalities. I told him about Dave Stewart's idea and his access to so many top world musicians (Bob Dylan and George Harrison are amongst his close friends) and I offered to get them together. 'Meditation music by Bob Dylan,' I enthused. 'Can't you just see it?'

He was full of ideas but was learning about the industry as he went along. It's a long, expensive process setting up a new TV channel, particularly one with global potential, and Jay had his work cut out. We talked about my possible involvement and he suggested that some kind of international ambassadorial and presenting role might suit my roving personality.

In the meantime I was full of creative ideas about how television could start to become a medium for positive messages and healing information, instead of the violent tabloid sensationalism and endless, mostly inane, chat shows that monopolise particularly American TV.

I met other interesting players in the TV arena during the next few months. These included Tom Rautenburg, a delightful investment banker with a rabbinical business wisdom who became a close friend; and Bill Gray, a committed, sincere man based in Colorado. I hoped they all made it.

By the twenty-first century healing channels as well as other speciality areas such as cooking, fishing, motorcycle maintenance and numerous shopping channels will be part of our daily life. The name of the game will be narrowcasting not broadcasting, and whatever our interest we'll find it on our TV sets.

The new digital technology means that we could soon have literally hundreds of TV channels to choose from, both in the States and in Europe. Of course many won't survive. The technical standard of programmes could be seriously affected as budgets take a nose-dive but the development of computer graphics and virtual reality could also mean a new form of visual art. Instead of seeing a film of an explorer going up the Amazon, there would be a simulation of the scene by computer which we could enter and experience.

Even more diverse will be the enormous amount of information coming over the Internet. To a large degree the beginning of the 1990s saw the hype of new technology take over reality. So many people started surfing the Net that the system went into overload and getting any information became a slow, laborious process.

The other problem has been that the democracy of the Internet means a lack of control over the information available. Communication has no boundaries on the Internet and anybody can set up their own web site putting out endless misinformation on poor-quality Internet magazines. There are no entry requirements: all you need is a computer and the technical know-how. Conspiracy theories abound, particularly about the powers of the CIA, and you can receive propaganda from right-wing fundamentalist groups as well as daily reports from left-wing guerrilla groups from the jungles of South America.

Although initially a toy for white middle-class men from the ages of twelve to forty, the Internet has gradually gained ground with women too. The UK is running behind the United States with regard to Internet gender balance but the signs are that worldwide women are becoming aware of the importance of understanding the new technology. Sadly it is a tool mainly used by the middle classes, while the urban poor, particularly the black and Hispanic communities, have not had the opportunity to learn how to use computers.

Although we talk of ourselves as a global village, 50 per cent of the world have never used or even had access to a telephone, never mind Internet and cable TV.

Of course, some may consider it a relief to have no access to cyberspace. We're an information overload society with our TVs, newspapers, radios, e-mails and faxes bombarding us daily. If you add billboards, sides of buses, shop windows, magazines, unsolicited direct mail through our door and even literature in doctors' and dentists' waiting rooms, it's surprising we ever have time to talk to each other. I once saw a report in the *Wall Street Journal* that said Americans receive 3,000 marketing messages a day seeping into their brains: that's three a minute.

In Western society, children are facing an illiteracy problem; Oprah Winfrey has started a book club on her TV programme to encourage us back to quality reading.

We can now use our credit cards on the Internet and for many people it will be a resource for acquiring even more material goods. Anyone can set up a shop on the Internet advertising their wares for instant purchase and many see its future as a kind of Yellow Pages.

Having an e-mail address which is your own personal computer mailbox can be an efficient way of communicating if you're travelling around. However, it also means that anyone can contact you with an endless stream of garbage. Not even presidents of countries and companies can escape this.

I had been computer illiterate for years, despite running a communications agency that was one of the UK's most advanced in its use of the new technology. I understood what it could do but had a block about using it myself. I think, like many women, I have a dislike of machines but I've finally come to terms with my computer – even making friends with it. I have taken my e-mail address off my business cards for the time being due to my own personal information overload and I'm trying to come to grips with an efficient lightweight personal organiser instead of my jumbo-sized diary and separate address book full of endless little bits of paper with phone numbers scribbled on them. Changing the habits of a lifetime doesn't come easy!

The new technology also gives people the opportunity to work in a different way. People wanting a quality of life that includes spending more time with their children and working from home now have the tools. More and more individuals, especially women, will be starting small entrepreneurial businesses from home, doing network marketing, teleworking or becoming freelance consultants servicing the many large companies who have chosen to downsize.

Communication skills are about more than learning how to use a computer. Interpersonal skills and learning to dialogue can help us live our lives in a far more satisfying way. Through many of the so-called New Age workshops I did, especially with Gabrielle Roth, Denise Linn and Chuck Spezzano, I learnt to stay in the present when I was talking to someone, instead of drifting off somewhere into the future. I also learnt to listen properly, which is just as important as getting my own message over. Many of society's problems could be alleviated by clear and open communication, particularly in relationships. And inter-generational dialogue is something we've forgotten how to do. The frustration of youth has done much to exacerbate teenage violence, and if young people are unable to talk to their parents about their problems, experienced counsellors could be of far more constructive help than locking them away in prison.

Teaching communication skills is fortunately now being considered a worthwhile aim of many national educational curriculums. One of the most impressive schemes I came across was when I visited a small church-run youth empowerment project in South Central LA – right in the middle of gangland. Here I saw a mixture of Hispanic and black young men and women teaching each other how to communicate with the business world. They were shown how to find what they were good at – including home skills – and then how to write a résumé, practise job interviews, express themselves, use computers and, most of all, find their self-esteem.

I met sixteen-year-old Rosa who left school at 4 p.m. every afternoon to teach other teenagers from her area how to find their sense of self. Brought up in a poor Hispanic ghetto she had no doubt that she was going to college and on to an executive career. 'I get phone calls day and night from other kids wanting to know when I can get them a job and I just tell them I'm doing my best. I've been on the phone repeatedly to the human resource department of a supermarket who are opening a big branch down the road explaining that we have the skills they need if we just get given the chance. So far they don't seem to want to know.'

I watched her teach computer skills to a group of other young women, several of whom were single mothers with small children playing nearby. They wanted to change their lives if they could just be given a chance and were prepared to work hard, whatever it took.

Many of the neighbourhood's young men were being shown by nineteen-year-old Mark how to create organic gardens on urban wasteland and paint murals for the local school. I was moved to tears and thought of the irony of the millions of dollars being spent by the movie and TV industries just a few miles away making films and programmes glamorising the violence and lifestyle that these kids were trying to get away from.

Violence on television was a major point of concern at a conference on the future of media and communications I attended in Los Angeles in 1996. Futurists, media specialists and grassroots watchdog organisations discussed the crisis in the United States, where children from pre-school age upwards are bombarded with violent imagery. The public in both the UK and the United States not only get fed an endless fare of mindless titillation and celebrity-led culture but seem to thrive on it. Tabloid newspapers, television and even computer games know that their audiences shoot up when violence, sex and scandals dominate the news.

Adam Clayton-Powell from the Freedom Forum at Columbia University told me that foreign news bureaux could seldom get their stories on American network news any more. His research has shown, for example, that in Orlando, Florida, O. J. Simpson's trial was watched by 90 per cent of local viewers, while stories on Bosnia got only 4–6 per cent of the potential audience. He said the future outlets in the US for most foreign news will be specially created pay-as-you-use news tiers, sending out the stories on-line where there is an almost insatiable appetite for them, and of course the specialist cable news services such as CNN and Fox.

Demands for change in media literacy have to come from the public. Parents and children need to be educated about the impact the entertainment industry has on our behaviour, and an alliance of grassroots networks is already working together in the States towards this. I heard about one such initiative at the conference from Lois Salisbury, executive director of Children Now, an organisation which acts as a

117

voice for the millions of children who cannot speak for themselves in the mass media and the community.

She told me they sought to accomplish their goals through independent research, media industry outreach and public policy development. 'Each year we organise a large international conference of major industry leaders, bringing them together with children's advocates and academic experts to help them better understand the impact their work has on children. We've had conference participants including First Lady Hillary Clinton, NBC news anchor Tom Brokaw, television pioneer Norman Lear and many others.'

The tremendous increase of violence on television and in movies seemed to me directly connected to the increasing violence amongst young people in both the UK and the United States. It doesn't take long for frustrated, angry teenagers to assume that violence and aggression is the only way to deal with their lives. After all, it's what they're shown on their TV sets every day.

The other major point of discussion at the conference was media democracy. The entertainment industry in the United States, the largest producer of electronic culture in the world, is owned by a handful of companies many of whom have interests in other areas as diverse as nuclear power plants and radioactive waste disposal. After the Disney Corporation merged with ABC I made and saw a variety of jokes and cartoons about Mickey Mouse reading the news. But there was genuine concern that the level of news information available would become even more sanitised and celebrity led. We live in a culture where Princess Diana or Madonna influence the way people think more than statesmen and politicians – a culture that I am, in part, responsible for creating.

At least in the UK we have one of the world's most independent broadcasting networks, the good old BBC, and commercial TV and radio stations that, although reliant on advertising revenue, are not influenced by their advertisers' or their owners' political beliefs. In America advertisers have become adept at blocking certain subjects. Right-wing politician, Newt Gingrich, has urged advertisers to boycott non-cooperating media and has calculated that the twenty biggest advertisers can silence opposing views.

Don Hazen was another of the conference's major speakers. Executive director of AlterNet, the electronic wire service, and the Institute for Alternative Journalism, he is a leading activist in the area of media democracy and has worked in politics, public affairs, think-tanks and publishing as well as being the author of several important books and articles on this subject.

He told us: 'People need ideas, information and inspiration in order to be fulfilled as active citizens. Societies thrive on a bubbling up of opinion and public debate in order to get closer to the truth and for people to be empowered. They have been encouraged to fear public life, to spend more of their time consuming, viewing TV and playing computer games. People are offered less and less information and more and more titillation. As more information is privatised, as more information is controlled by fewer and fewer global corporations, the national debate shrinks, and the dialogue disappears.'

I ran a session at the media conference with American PR David Fenton on socially responsible public relations, a title which I'm sure is an oxymoron to many people. Public relations has become a worldwide communications medium in its own right, often reshaping reality and altering perception. David and I agreed that this was an unhealthy state of affairs, especially in America, where 150,000 PR practitioners outnumber the country's 130,000 reporters and the gap is widening. With media becoming more dependent on PR for so much of its content I was the first to agree that public relations executives have become far too powerful.

David, a dapper Washington-based communications consultant, is very selective about the clients he represents. His company, Fenton Communications, consider themselves a socially committed public relations firm and believe it is their job to communicate truth and expose the corruption and lies that abound in industry and politics. David told us how the right wing in the United States had developed an immense propaganda network with their own radio stations, particularly those of fundamentalist religious organisations, television discussion programmes, foundations, think-tanks and of course the Internet. 'Sadly,' he added, 'the progressive left does not have the money or the foresight to do the same.'

He also told us how PR can negatively manipulate media and public opinion and cited the disaster of some half a million women who are suffering silicone poisoning from their implants. Dow Chemicals, manufacturer of the silicone, employed a PR company who circulated the story amongst journalists that the extent of the problem was being exaggerated.

We agreed that the very real situation of global warming has constantly been denied by scientists paid by petrol and chemical companies, and of course the tobacco industry has been supporting scientists for years who deny the dangers of personal or passive smoking.

I explained to the other delegates at our session that there were creative ways of putting business messages across to both the media and the consumer while maintaining integrity. I mentioned as examples using shop windows as The Body Shop do, working with schools on environmental messages, creating community-linked projects and sponsoring programmes on local radio.

There were also presentations on responsible advertising, an equally contentious area, and how companies can use attractive imagery and still put over ethical messages.

A constant thorn in the side of the American and Canadian advertising industry is the progressive Vancouver-based Media Foundation and its *Adbusters* magazine, founded by filmmaker Kalle Lasn.

'In '89,' he told us, 'I produced a 30-second TV spot about the disappearing old-growth forests of the Pacific Northwest, but to my dismay none of the commercial TV stations would sell me any air time. The Media Foundation, *Adbusters* magazine and Powershift Advertising Agency were born out of this incident and the realisation that there is no democracy on our airwaves. I've spent the last six years producing media campaigns and fighting the human rights battle of our information age – the battle for the "Right to Communicate".

'We in the First World are living in a media consumer trance. We are being urged to consume more and more. Waking up to reality is what the social activist movement of the future should be about.'

Kalle creates campaigns such as TV Turn-Off Day or Buy Nothing Day with strong accompanying TV ads. He believes in using conventional marketing tools such as commercials, posters, T-shirts and print ads to promote his sustainable society messages – but has great trouble in getting them placed. 'Big TV companies won't take our ads and yet the airwaves belong to us,' he said. 'We've become so disempowered and have no say on our own channels, public interest has eroded, corporate interest has taken over and the TV is the command centre for our consumer world.'

He added, 'The dilemma is how you can change society if you don't have access to air time. How can you bring a new vision of the future into people's consciousness?' He compared not being able to speak out against a sponsor in North America to the old days in the USSR when you couldn't speak out against the government.

I leant that North America contains 5 per cent of the world's population, consumes a third of its resources and creates about a third of its non-organic waste. Sadly, all the bad habits of consumerism are being taken up by much of the rest of the world, including many of the developing countries, the Far East and Eastern Europe. I agreed with Kalle that the planet cannot sustain this level of consumerism. We have to invent new ways of measuring progress, and redesign the American dream.

Adbusters were also responsible for creating specific campaigns against what they considered unethical or exploitative advertising. They have taken on multinationals including American Express and McDonald's and were responsible for stopping the Calvin Klein pre-pubescent underwear posters.

I have often quoted *Adbusters* when talking to the marketing industry. The grassroots and consumer backlash to the constant onslaught of hype and over-glamorised imagery to sell products is just starting. The public are beginning to realise how this affects their self-esteem and makes them insecure about their own appearance and lifestyle.

Western consumers – 80 per cent of whom are women – want to be told the truth in advertising and they want to be told it with wit and humour. The huge hype advertising and PR of the 1980s, in which I certainly played a part, is on the way out. Rather than present glamorous and stereotypical images through expensive TV ads, agencies are going to have to think of a more community-led strategy. Partnership between big brands and the people they are trying to sell to will be the most effective kind of communication as we move into the twenty-first century. After all, with the new technology we'll be able to zap the ad that we don't like off our screens anyway.

Sponsorship of childcare centres, libraries, school projects and sports training facilities could build up more brand loyalty in a town than spending equivalent money on an expensive TV campaign. It would create long-term rather than short-term awareness and would give a far greater sense of well-being to companies and the people who work in them.

Canada too has a progressive view of communication and social change and I learnt a lot on a visit there. The city of Vancouver, where *Adbusters* is based, is somewhere I'd wanted to visit for a long time. I'd heard it was beautiful, set amid rain forests, mountains and sea with easy access to the unspoiled islands of British Columbia.

My guide to the city was Raffi, North America's top children's entertainer. A charming and sincere man in his mid-forties, of Armenian descent, he came to meet me at Vancouver airport and put himself at my disposal during my two-day visit. 'Vancouver is a hotbed of new thinking in conscious communication,' he told me and explained he was committed to promoting positive messages on the environment and nature to children through his bestselling records and shows.

I visited the newly renovated area of Gastown which as well as being the 'in' place to live had become a permanent film location site for hundreds of American TV shows and movies. Vancouver had the technology of LA but was a lot cheaper, and big American studios were opening up there all the time.

I wondered if I should come and live here as it seemed to have everything I wanted – fresh air, nice people and a booming communications industry. I'd felt the same in San Francisco but knew it was premature to make any decisions about the future.

Raffi took me to one of the area's many organic healthy supermarkets to get some food for supper one night and I found the huge selection of products enticing after such a restrictive choice in the UK. I went on the ferry to Granville Island where I saw the stunning and vast daily selection of fresh fish, fruit and vegetables.

It was harvesting time in British Columbia for their famous local crop of marijuana. Big smoke-ins were advertised, with invitations to people to come and try out this year's vintage much like a Beaujolais Nouveau tasting back in Europe. It was tempting but I had to move on to the next part of my journey.

While in Toronto visiting my sister Sue and her family I went to the City TV studios. City TV are considered innovators in community television. They'd been the first studio to use their street window for live TV shows as a way of gaining public involvement and interest long before any of the New-York-based stations. Half a car was suspended from the City TV building and the young staff and high energy spilled out on to the streets.

I was made welcome by the producers and shown round the studio. One of the other good community ideas that I took back with me was a video sounding-off box in their reception. For a few dollars, which went to charity, anyone off the streets could air their views for a few minutes on any subject and the best were put together in a programme. City TV shows how inexpensive broadcasting can be exciting and creative. Although much of their work is aimed at the Toronto community many of their ideas and their programmes are sold round the world.

Before I left Toronto, I took Sue and her family to see Raffi's stage show. I was moved by the hundreds of tots singing along to his songs accompanied by their parents. Songs like 'Baby Beluga' and 'C-A-N-A-D-A' brought the house down. Raffi's simple lyrics and presentation, putting over the message to children about the importance of saving our planet, have affected the culture of the nation for nearly twenty years. It made me realise how vital it is to communicate environmental messages to young children so that they will grow up understanding the importance of saving the planet rather than destroying it.

When I said goodbye to Raffi he told me he was shortly due to attend a meeting of Social Venture Network, a group of ethical entrepreneurs in Boston. I arranged to see him there.

I thought of all the different ways that we receive information and how crucial communication is to our everyday life. If we can create an honest and clear exchange, whether using the new technology, broadcasting, printed media or even in our one-to-one dialogues, we can co-operate and co-exist in a productive, fulfilled way.

We need to filter out misinformation and negative imagery by using our internal zap machine and be open to the messages that can bring a positive consciousness into society.

8

Ethical Business

I thought back to when I'd first heard of Social Venture Network.

'Why don't you come to our next meeting of SVN in Europe?' asked the fast-talking American I was seated next to at the traditionally Jewish wedding of our mutual friends Sam and Francine Rosen. The elaborately decorated rooms in the London hotel were full of good will as the bride and groom led the guests in lively dancing.

In between enjoying ourselves on the dance floor, my neighbour explained he was one of the founders of this progressive business organisation together with Anita and Gordon Roddick of The Body Shop and Ben Cohen of Ben & Jerry's home-made ice-cream.

His name was Joshua Mailman, and he is an extraordinary young man who has dedicated his life to creating powerful networks of wealthy investors and businesspeople across America committed to making a positive difference to the future of the world through their wealth and their businesses. He originally set up a group called the Donuts comprising a number of wealthy young Americans like himself who were interested in investing their inherited wealth only in companies with an ethical trading policy.

That group was the forerunner of many of the green

investment groups across the States and in Europe and now has substantial influence on the White House and the stock market. Josh then went on to form Social Venture Network in 1987 in Boulder, Colorado, with a group of investors, venture capitalists, non-profit organisations and businesspeople including The Body Shop and Ben & Jerry's. The aim then as now was to bring together people from the business world who are committed to changing the way that business works to help build a just and sustainable society.

I explained to Josh that I couldn't go to the next meeting in Geneva because I would be attending a conference in Ireland. However, I knew the right time would come for me to join these forward-thinking entrepreneurs. As on so many other stages of my journey, coincidences kept happening until I accepted them as signposts indicting my next direction.

During the months after I met Josh I met several people in Europe and the United States who were members of SVN; they too encouraged me to go to a meeting. Raffi seemed the last link in the chain when he told me about the next meeting in Boston. Finally I was able to go.

I later found out that SVN has twice-yearly meetings in the States although the smaller European branch of the organisation only meets annually. SVN brings together not only entrepreneurial business people but opinion leaders, philosophers and futurists to discuss how business can progressively lead the way with social values. They share information and support and inspire each other. They advocate business standards that will enhance relationships between business activity and social good and their main mission is to see their businesses as tools for ecological and social change.

They are not the only business network initiated in the States who are dedicated to making a difference. World Business Academy, with which I was later to become involved, and Global Business Network have also worked extensively on getting enterprise to be in partnership with community and the planet.

SVN has grown until it now has some 500 members in the

States and spawned other organisations such as Business for Social Responsibility which has less stringent membership rules and a far bigger membership, and Students for Socially Responsible Business. SVN Europe was formed in 1992 but it has taken much longer to get off the ground, particularly in the UK. At its annual meetings there is a strong presence of Dutch, Scandinavian and German members.

Amongst the British members of SVN Europe other than The Body Shop, are Josephine Fairley and Craig Sams of Green and Black's Chocolate, Romy Fraser of Neal's Yard and Terry Thomas of the Co-Op Bank. The Co-Op Bank is tiny compared to the huge clearing banks, but in terms of ethical investment it has had a tremendous influence on the way the public view how banks and building societies use the money entrusted to them.

When I arrived at the meeting at Boston I was delighted to see spiritual teacher Ram Dass, there to hold the spiritual energy for SVN. Ram Dass, originally a Jewish academic from Harvard called Richard Alpert, had gone to India in the 1960s in pursuit of spiritual truth. He had met his guru, changed his named and dedicated his life to service. He has written several world bestsellers including *Be Here Now*, which has become a bible for many young people. Ram Dass told me that although he was in the midst of writing a book on conscious ageing, he felt it was important to work with SVN to help remind them of the importance of spirituality in business.

The SVN meeting in Boston was where I became acquainted with Gordon Roddick. I had known Anita for a while but Gordon was a bit more of an enigma. He is, as I know Anita will agree, the backbone of The Body Shop and has always been there supporting Anita's creative ideas and radical activism.

I'd first met Anita some years earlier when we shared a platform on an early conference on women entrepreneurs. I was immediately impressed by her dynamism and focus. She is an expert communicator and her passion ignites all those around her. We immediately felt a rapport and found that our views coincided. She spends much of her time travelling around the world, sharing her vision for a better world with business groups, students and the many members of the public she comes into contact with through The Body Shop. Sadly our schedules rarely coincide but when they do, sparks fly. Gordon Roddick thinks we are very alike, and says he can never get a word in edgeways when he's with the two of us.

The fact that the Roddicks, and Anita particularly, can be such activists for human and planetary rights, and run a successful multinational ethically intentioned business, never ceases to inspire me.

Anita, like me, believes in the feminine way to do business. We've both run our businesses in a nurturing, intuitive manner showing that creativity and enthusiasm grow through teamwork. Although as our businesses grew we had tremendous help and support from our husbands, neither of us seemed to have any fears about starting a business we loved, feeding it with our passion and still taking the responsibility for a family. After all, as children and grandchildren of immigrants – her roots Italian, mine East European Jewish – we had both seen our mothers and grandmothers do it too.

In the UK The Body Shop was the first retailer to promote green ideas. From 1976, when Anita Roddick opened the first branch, she has been conscious of the difference that business can make to society. Campaigns against animal testing and acid rain, in support of the environment and recycling, human rights, women's rights, and opposing French nuclear testing in the Pacific are just some of the major issues that The Body Shop has confronted in the last ten years. The Body Shop considers campaigning as important to their business as successfully selling toiletries and cosmetics. Yet, like all companies who set themselves up as 'caring', they have been hounded by the media as if they are the ones who are trying to damage the society they live in. As Alan Reder says in his book about SVN members *75 Best Business Practices for Socially Responsible Companies*, 'The downside of being considered socially responsible in any area is that the public and the media tend to place you on a pedestal from where you have nowhere to go but down.'

If you're a woman and you're seen to cock a snook at the

establishment, you're automatically inviting criticism. The media like everyone in their own neat little boxes. Anita has certainly found this to be true.

Of course companies have to be profit orientated to stay in business and none of them can be 100 per cent perfect in their social or environmental practices. They are made up of human beings with human frailties and no successful company can be free of blame. The important thing now is that these socially aware companies are admitting they may not always have got it right but are prepared to constantly look at themselves and make changes.

Motivated by major criticism about some of their methods of working, by both UK and US media, The Body Shop commissioned a self-audit to collect the views of key stake-holders and to find out for themselves how integral the company's values were to their business. The report and the processes leading to it were subjected to external independent validation and in 1995 *The Values Report* was published and put out on the Internet as an enterprising exercise in openness.

This was the first time The Body Shop had taken such a courageous step to really look at itself, leaving no stones unturned, and to use its findings for change. I'm sure there was quite a lot of pain within the company when they discovered how they were perceived internally by their staff and franchisees. But at least they went forward positively, with Anita continuing at full strength her one-woman global campaigning for social justice.

One of The Body Shop's most high-profile campaigns was mounted on behalf of Ken Saro-Wiwa and the Ogoni people of Nigeria. The first I knew of Ken Saro-Wiwa was seeing petitions to free him in the reception of The Body Shop head office in 1993 when I was advising Anita on external communication.

The company informed their customers what was going on in Nigeria through their shops and by sending petitions to the Nigerian government. They also pressed Shell to release information about their environmental policies, practises and performance in Ogoniland and urged them to use their influence with the Nigerian dictatorship to achieve justice for Ken Saro-Wiwa and the Ogoni people. Ken Saro-Wiwa was a martyr to the Ogoni people and to the whole of the global environment effort, and what happened in Nigeria is a potent example of how a powerful multinational can, by doing nothing, appear to support a corrupt regime, as it rides rough-shod over the wishes of millions of people.

In the case of Shell, the Nigerian situation created tremendous internal and external dialogue, eventually resulting in a radical new human rights policy.

The Body Shop very strongly led the way with this campaign and they stuck with it until finally the whole world was in uproar. It was a formidable example of a retailer having a political voice. After the brutal execution of Ken Saro-Wiwa and eight other innocent Ogoni leaders by the Nigerian military authorities in November 1995 The Body Shop brought his brother and family over to England, put them in safe houses and arranged for them to have access to the European Parliament and Commission. This clearly goes far beyond the realms of what we expect business to do. It had a key role in raising public awareness and is a good example of how businesses and consumers can become a powerful campaigning force.

Thankfully, not all companies have adopted a myopic vision when it comes to environmental matters and human rights. Though many consumers may still be unaware of it, there is a progressive business movement slowly but surely gaining ground which is showing how the same inventiveness used to create wealth can also be applied to social concerns.

For example, the dynamic British fast food chain Prêt-à-Manger have actively campaigned in their shops and raised a lot of awareness when the French government insisted on testing nuclear weapons in the Pacific in the mid-1990s.

Ben Cohen of Ben & Jerry's is another flamboyant character who throws himself into SVN social life as much as he does into the more serious aspects of the organisation. He's like a big cuddly teddy bear with his long hair, beard and oversized T-shirt and looks just like the co-founder of one of America's favourite ice-cream brands should look.

'Jerry and I were virtually unemployable in the late seventies and couldn't even get into college,' he once told me. 'We finally wrote away to do a mail-order course on making ice-cream and started a little operation from an abandoned gas station in Vermont. We were so surprised the business didn't collapse after just a few months that we celebrated our first anniversary by holding a big party in the town and giving away free ice-creams.' He spoke about the ethical dilemmas he faced: 'We weren't even sure that we wanted to keep going when we saw how easy it was for our ideals to be lost in the name of the business. Business, after all, is about the bottom line, and that bottom line usually has no concern for people or the planet.'

Thankfully Ben and Jerry didn't give up but dediced instead to grow the company 'into something we could respect ourselves for'. Their idea was to have a business which used a substantial percentage of its profits to promote progressive social concerns. They wanted to demonstrate to the mainstream business community that profits and the needs of the planet did not necessarily have to be contradictory.

Ben & Jerry's three-part mission is to produce the best ice-cream, to have a good return for shareholders, and to improve the quality of life in the community. They believe that business has a responsibility to give back to the community, which is why when the company went public they gave their community the opportunity to be owners of their business, allowing the stock office to operate only from Vermont and arranging for an extremely low minimum buy. As a result the flotation was opened up to almost everybody, and one in a hundred of every Vermont families bought shares.

Here is a business which has made an art form out of alternative marketing as well as creating a company where people love to work. Back in 1993 the directors did not want to look as if they were starting to run their business on a conventional basis and so when they were looking for a CEO, for fun they put out a poster mimicking the old UNCLE SAM NEEDS YOU war posters and displayed them in all Ben

131

& Jerry's outlets. The reaction in the US was 30,000 applications for the job and nine million press and media mentions over a few months, a PR success even I'd never heard matched before.

Ben & Jerry integrated social needs and business with their own source market. For instance their Rain Forest Crunch ice-cream can only be made from Brazilian nuts gathered by the local population from the floor of the rain forest. By establishing a demand for this flavour of ice-cream they helped to grow an economy other than tree felling for this particular area of the world. Also, the production of their Chocolate Fudge Brownie ice-cream depends on brownies purchased from a community baker's owned by a religious organization in New York which employs people who are trying to re-establish themselves in the community, such as the formerly homeless or ex-drug-users. And in many of Ben & Jerry's ice-cream booths during their campaign with the Children's Defence Funds they had a direct line to Congress which allowed their younger customers to get on the phone and give Congress a piece of their mind about the way children are being treated by government.

Ben Cohen has said: don't talk about what you're going to do, don't do PR or advertise, just *do* it and *be* it. What he means is, use the organisation to make a tradition because it costs the same as traditional advertising but actually works much better as a way of communicating with the market. Social actions have actually been responsible for Ben & Jerry's success and added value to their brand.

I met futurist economist Hazel Henderson and her partner Alan Kay at a subsequent SVN meeting at Colorado Springs. A warm, blonde British-born woman now living in Florida, Hazel is accepted as one of the leading-edge economists by the business, political and banking worlds. One of her gifts is to be able to talk about her vision for the future of money in accessible language that even I can understand. She explained to me that money was just energy and had no inherent value in itself. 'We take money far too seriously,' she said. Hazel and other SVN members like Ben Cohen 'believe in the double bottom line where companies can make profits while still giving back to the community they sell to, the community that works for them and the environment itself'.

Hazel also talks about the love economy where communities develop the LETS and barter systems, exchanging goods and services instead of money. Hazel believes it's only a matter of time before local communities have garage sales on the Internet and exchange babysitting sessions for driving lessons.

Hazel has continued to be a mentor of mine. She travels the world with Alan when she is not entertaining like-minded souls and creating new visions or writing books back home in Florida. She is consultant to investment groups but also spends a large amount of her time making speeches and giving advice for free. She told me it all balances out and there is always enough for her needs. Now a grandmother, Hazel's comparatively recent relationship with Alan – they travel and live together, supporting each other's joint and individual projects – has also been a great inspiration.

Another stalwart of SVN in the States is Alice Tepper Marlin, a wonderfully dignified articulate woman who founded the Council of Economic Priorities. In the early eighties she started publishing a list of America's major companies to send to the top 750 share brokers in America. The list indicated the social ethics of all the companies in detail, and which do or do not make their profit at society's expense. Although it took a while for Alice's list to be taken seriously, it has now become a major force in the business world and has significantly influenced the policy of a number of major companies. More and more businesses and manufacturers are showing how well-designed products and systems can both fulfil their primary function and make a profit, without sacrificing social issues.

Alice Tepper Marlin also produces an annual shopping book for the consumer called *Shopping for a Better World*. Described as the quick and easy guide to all your socially responsible shopping, the book gives detailed information on social issues grading over 200 companies with 2,000 brands over 17 different industries from snack foods and beverages to clothing and automobiles. It acts like an external audit and gives American consumers the power to go into any supermarket with their book in hand and vote with their purse.

The Council puts out a monthly research report covering everything from airline corporate responsibility to multinationals' policies on discrimination on the basis of sexual orientation. They have created the Corporate Conscious Awards – a kind of Oscars for the ethical business industry. Businesses are measured for their charitable contributions against the size of their profits as well as their attitude towards minorities, women, family benefits, community outreach and environmental stewardship. The vast amount of research necessary to produce this information has limited Alice's work to the United States, although it is only a matter of time before information like this becomes available in Europe and, hopefully, the rest of the world.

We've never been active enough in the UK on exploitative labour, so I was pleased when Oxfam came to see me in the spring of 1996 and asked me to become involved in the Sweatshirt Sweatshop campaign they were about to launch. They told me about Bangladesh where conditions were particularly bad for the women. I asked why the workers didn't leave and set up small co-operatives of their own? The girl from Oxfam looked at me in disbelief as I sat in my comfortable, spacious kitchen. 'They can get raped or murdered if they ask for a tea break,' she told me.

The textile, clothing and shoe industries are some of the worst perpetrators of child and women sweatshop labour and environmental exploitation. Small local contractors in the developing world are generally used by the big international brands and retailers. It is only by exposing human exploitation in the media through initiatives by Oxfam and other non-governmental organisations like Human Rights Watch that pressure for change can be applied.

SVN members Reebok and Levi-Strauss use contractors in other countries to manufacture their goods and are therefore totally reliant on businesses they cannot control except through purchase. Levi's have always been a socially conscious business and are one of the American companies to have set the position on child labour. They decided that to ensure there was no exploitation they would create a document setting out a code of conduct to which they expected their factories and subcontractors to comply. Within the framework of two ethical policies came the resolution that they would no longer work with any factories shown to be employing children aged fourteen or under. Much good will is behind companies' refusal to employ children, but the consequences can be disastrous, with children often turning to begging or prostitution instead. This is why Levi's have guaranteed that where children are forced out of factories they will ensure that these children receive a proper education.

Jimmy Carter, who does more for human rights than any other former President of the United States, was a member of the Amnesty International team concerned with this area and it was he who, in the early nineties, gave Reebok Levi's ethical guidelines for global business dealings, as a result of which Reebok have adopted a similar procedure. Reebok have also set up a Witness programme with Peter Gabriel whereby they give camcorders, computers and training facilities to local activist groups in Third World countries so that people at the grass roots of society have access to the world of communication.

The 'gotcha' press can potentially damage a brand personality in one scoop. For example, in 1994 an American TV news programme got hold of footage of a sweatshop in the Far East manufacturing jeans for most of the major US brands. Levi, being the market leaders, were the ones whose logo was constantly flashed up on people's television screens. Levi were appalled and immediately looked into the situation. Giving their supplier forty-eight hours to clean up their act or lose their account, they were instrumental in bringing about key changes in the industry. By immediately issuing a press statement which generated positive TV coverage, Levi were seen to have cared and acted, whereas most of the other brands quoted did not even respond.

Anita Roddick once said, 'Business has to move with the times and introduce feminine values into the workplace', and where better to incorporate this information than into the area of marketing?

Promoting positive product background information does not

have to be restricted to the media – Green and Black's Maya Gold chocolate success story shows there are alternative routes. Although Jo Fairley and Craig Sams are great friends of mine in London I didn't know much about their Green and Black's chocolate range. I went to hear Jo talk about her fair deal trading programme at one of the seminars in Boston and was very impressed. She explained how they were the first to be awarded the Fair Trade mark in the UK by the Fair Trade Foundation in 1995 when they launched their organic Maya Gold dark chocolate. Jo and her entrepreneurial husband Craig had such a success with their original Green and Black's chocolate that they ran out of the organically grown cocoa from the co-operative in Togo, West Africa, which had originally supplied them. When they wanted to add more products, they contacted Mayan farmers in Belize, Central America, whom they had met on a visit, and found that many of the young farmers had been put out of business by false promises from big corporations. Trading direct with the growers' organisation they offered a unique long-term contract and a far better price.

This was in line with strict guidelines, conditions and prices established by the British Fair Trade Foundation (FtF). FtF is an independent certification body supported by Christian Aid, Oxfam, the National Federation of Women's Institutes and others. Representatives of the FtF helped establish the basis for trade, have visited Belize, met the Mayan growers and satisfied themselves about the trading arrangements there.

FtF then organised a promotion for fair deal trade to coincide with the launch of the chocolate when 20,000 young Methodists embarked on a run across the country lasting for twelve weeks. The aim of the run was to raise awareness of fair trade issues and to try to persuade individual supermarket buyers in the towns they stopped at to stock fair trade products. The young Methodists handed out thousands of leaflets and samples. The BBC covered the story on three different news bulletins and even sent a film crew to Belize to photograph the local children eating the chocolate. Green and Black's received an enormous amount of support from religious communities because of their close links with the Third World – even to the extent that local vicars were holding tastings and calling up supermarket buyers. There was a large amount of other national press coverage and the chocolate is now stocked at all the major supermarket chains and health food stores in the UK as well as being exported to Europe with an imminent launch in the US and Japan.

'This was a campaign based on reality, not hype,' said Jo. 'The response from customers and press proved that these are all key issues for the caring nineties consumer. Through leaflets, press releases and on-pack information, including the details printed on the inside of our wrapper, we are committed to instilling a new awareness in today's – and tomorrow's – shopper, by bringing to their attention all these vital issues.'

In the Council on Economic Priorities book *Shopping for a Better World*, they quote a 1993 Cone/Roper Benchmark Survey on Cause-Related Marketing which found that more than 60 per cent of Americans indicated they would switch brands or stores to purchase from companies that support particular social causes and that 48 per cent would support companies that 'donate money to a cause through a foundation or nonprofit agency'. A Gallup poll in the UK some two years later showed almost the same results. When customers in large numbers start to use their shopping trolleys to bring about social change then we'll be looking at unshakable consumer power.

Yvon Chouinard, founder of Patagonia, the American outdoor clothing company, was one of the most inspiring speakers at a subsequent ethical business conference in Paris. I believe, and so does he, that it is the process that counts in business and not the bottom line.

When his company kept growing in size and profit he went to see a leading business consultant because he was unhappy about the direction his life was taking. All he'd ever really wanted to be was a mountain climber and now here he was running a multimillion-dollar business. The first thing the consultant said to him was that if he really didn't like the business he was in he would have sold it long ago, and so the really important thing was to stay where he was and use his position for change.

From there sprang his whole philosophy of business. He realised that his company didn't have to be profit driven and he could turn down business to keep the company a manageable size. Certainly he wanted his company to remain privately owned so he could have the freedom and flexibility to do as he wanted. 'Success is not about instant gratification, greed, and immediate growth,' he told me, 'and growth is not necessarily about being bigger and better. Never exceed your limits, be true to yourself and live below rather than above your means. Progress is about staying in business for the next hundred years with loyal – not necessarily new – customers.'

The staff at Patagonia seldom leave, there are excellent child-care facilities, mothers are allowed to bring their babies into the office and Yvon Chouinard casts himself in the role of the philosopher while his staff run the show. He has always given a large percentage of his profits back to environmental issues, and every employee pays what is known as an earth tax whereby they put back a percentage of their wages each year into the environment, supporting causes which the staff have voted for internally. He now only uses paper made from hemp and corn and recycles everything used in the business. He believes that the notion that business is made up of disposable assets is disastrous and what counts are people.

Comparing business to the Zen philosophy of archery he says, 'Forget about hitting the goal in Zen archery, it's about the preparation, the breathing, the aiming and it's when you perfect the elements of shooting an arrow that you can't help hitting the bull's-eye. The same is true of climbing mountains, and dealing with any huge and complex problems. Perfection is obtained not when there is anything to add but when there is nothing to take away.'

His ambitious goal is for the company to give back to the planet as much as it takes out. He only uses 100 per cent organic cotton because it is the least damaging fabric in the world, the most damaging being 100 per cent industrial cotton. He has also eliminated all unnecessary packaging from his products even though it was predicted that in getting rid of the packaging on thermal underwear he would lose 30 per cent of his sales. In fact sales increased by 25 per cent. This is a fine example of social concern reflecting profound business sense.

Chouinard has warned the clothing industry not to build in planned obsolescence by designing garments that will rapidly date – in other words, he is telling manufacturers to take the fashion out of design. That's a revolutionary thing for someone in the clothing industry to say and no doubt many top designers and department stores would be appalled at the idea because it is precisely in the fashion that they make their profits.

My trip round North America opened me up to many new ideas and friendships. Ideas like responsible marketing, conscious communications, ethical business practices, environmentally friendly industry, spirituality in business and many more. I had a feeling of coming home. Although the ideas I heard were such a contrast to many aspects of my former working life, in a way they were a natural development. I'd become increasingly uncomfortable with hyping up products that did not create any benefit to people's lives. I was now seeing the reality behind the illusion and meeting many people with the ideas and attitudes to life and business that had been surfacing in my mind over the past few years.

I could see I was at the beginning of an involvement with a new kind of win-win business world where consideration of human, environmental and ethical values is as important to a company's success as annual profits.

9

What Women Want

I led the dancing on the stage as the packed audience swayed to the rhythms of the tribal chant. World-famous Irish, African, American and English women singers blended their voices in a celebratory song containing elements from many cultures. It was the gala finale at the What Women Want event I'd put on at the Festival Hall in London in the summer of '95.

I looked out at the thousands of smiling faces and felt that a force larger than me had helped create this extraordinary weekend. What Women Want had been the culmination of many months' work based on a dream, a lot of support and no money. It was meant to happen.

A series of events had led to my becoming a spokesperson on women's issues that summer. It had started a year and a half earlier when I was approached to get involved with VIVA! Radio.

'We're thinking of starting a women's radio station and we'd like you to be chairman of the board,' said the dapper media executive sitting opposite me on the sofa in his comfortable Marble Arch office.

'Why me?' I asked, thinking surely it should be chair or chair-*woman* if this was to be a women's radio station. I'd been contacted by Katie Turner the marketing director of Golden Rose Radio the week before. It was just a short while after I'd decided to leave Lynne Franks PR and she asked me to come in for a meeting with her and her boss David Maker, a jovial Liverpudlian ex-journalist, to talk about some mysterious new project.

Golden Rose, the company behind Jazz FM, had decided to expand and apply for some of the new radio licences available. Katie had suggested a women's radio station and, seeing the commercial potential, her board had agreed to let her run with it. I thought the idea was brilliant. Radio had always been an underused but still popular medium for women and as a vehicle for community communications from a feminine perspective would appear to have great potential. David Maker explained that he saw my role as a kind of moral guardian, rather like Richard Attenborough when he was chair of Capital Radio in the early days.

What I didn't appreciate was that Golden Rose needed a high-profile figurehead who would help get them the licence and be a press spokesperson but who in reality had no true influence. I wrote to all my well-connected friends plus a lot of powerful women I didn't know personally asking for their support with the project. There was a tremendous response – from journalists, businesswomen, academics, entertainers, politicians and sports personalities. They were all positive and many offered their help. There was a lot of agonising over the name and finally David and Katie's idea of VIVA! 963AM was agreed on. It was never really my cup of tea but VIVA! we became.

With some group input Katie put a very professional package together to present to the radio authorities by June 1993. We spent all summer waiting to hear if the arbitrary decision would go our way but, despite getting loads of publicity, we were disappointed to hear we'd been turned down. Apparently they'd sought the opinion of one or two women journalists who felt that the concept was ghettoising women. I was incensed but David and Katie advised me to cool down and we put the application in again for the following year.

While waiting to hear if we'd got the VIVA! licence I'd

sacrificed my privacy to the cause and allowed numerous profiles to be written about me in the national press. Reading other people's projections of me had never been enjoyable. We always have a subjective view of ourselves which rarely resembles the way a journalist will sum us up after an hour's interview. Before they come to see you they get out all your old cuttings, pick up something that wasn't correct to start with, repeat it, and that's how legends are born. They've often written the articles in their minds before they even see you and project their prejudices on to you as they walk into the room.

Since *Ab Fab*, things had gone from silly to ridiculous. Journalists seemed to expect to meet Edina Monsoon and were quite disappointed to meet the far more sober Lynne Franks. On more than one occasion journalists told me how surprised they were to find that I was really quite a nice person with interesting views. However, regardless, they would still put in all the old *Ab Fab* projections, headlines and photographs and it was often only in the last two or three paragraphs of the article that you'd get any sense of what we had really talked about. As a PR I should have been used to this but it's very different when it's about yourself.

All this publicity intensified when we were granted a licence the second time round.

I was concerned that VIVA! would be transmitted on an AM frequency, which meant that people would have real trouble finding it on the radio. David explained it would cost a lot more money to apply for FM, and these licences weren't easily available. I felt we had to embark on a big education campaign to explain how to get 963AM on the radio dial, especially on car radios which were all knobs and buttons. I certainly needed lessons.

I started hosting breakfasts before the VIVA! launch, inviting some of my forward-thinking friends like Eve Pollard, Janet Street-Porter, Glenda Bailey of *Marie Claire*, politician Barbara Follett and publisher Gail Rebuck to air their views about how they saw a women's radio station developing. We asked experienced media mogul Linda Agram and literary agent Debbie Owen to join me on the board as non-executive directors. We had a tight team in place and some brilliant ideas were being thrown around. I was also impressed by the high calibre of journalists and celebrities who started contacting me, offering to present shows. They knew there wasn't much money in it but, like me, they believed in the concept of a women's radio station.

We all felt that we needed a radio station to present intelligent, articulate, as well as humorous views for women living in the London area. We didn't want to make it exclusionary either. *Cosmopolitan* has a huge male readership and we felt that if we got the bite right for women we could attract a good percentage of male listeners too. I'm sure men want to know what women really think, especially about sex and relationships.

Katie, who by now was managing director of VIVA!, went along with this but understandably her priority was to make it a commercially successful radio station. Her way of working was more in the traditional marketing style rather than focusing on programming development. She was also talking to advertising agencies about the station's potential, working on VIVA!'s own big spend campaign and falling in and out with different PR agencies. It was all far too much to do within the time frame allowed for a July 1995 start combined with floating the parent company on the stock market. I watched her get busier and busier while at the same time trying to handle the stress. Inevitably her body screamed *Stop* and Katie suffered a brain haemorrhage some three months before we were due on air.

Katie was seriously ill for some weeks but eventually made a complete recovery. She decided sensibly that her life was her priority and finally chose to leave Golden Rose for a saner job. She had left behind half-finished projects which were too late to change. In retrospect it's clear that the starting date should have been put back but money had been committed, ads had been booked and we seemed to be on some kind of merry-go-round that once started couldn't be stopped.

My role at this point had been very much that of spokesperson and provider of ideas which no one had any time to follow up. Chris Burns, a likeable young programmer from the BBC, had just been taken on and she was immediately thrown into the deep end to try and make some sense out of a programming schedule that had been badly neglected. David Maker took on a hands-on role as CEO. Although an experienced newsman his sensibilities regarding a women's radio station walked a fine line and his decision that the first voice to be heard on the station would be that of a male newsreader was picked up by much of the delighted media.

He had no presenter for the first week for the midday two-hour spot and put heavy pressure on me to do it. I was busy preparing a weekly interview show called *Frankly Speaking* and had no broadcasting experience. I didn't think it was a good idea but David seemed to have no option. With a sense of responsibility as well as foreboding I agreed to do it, getting great support from friends who came on the show. Ruby Wax, Uri Geller, hypnotist Paul McKenna, singer Chrissie Hynde, some politically active lesbians, tantric sex therapist Caroline Aldred, Janet Street-Porter, presenter and male chauvinist Paul Ross, news journalist and activist Sue Lloyd Roberts, homeless academic Chris Kitch and several live performers such as Chris Jagger and Sarah Jane Morris appeared in the first week.

Generally it went pretty well, as it was like chatting around my kitchen table. Although when I played the tapes back there were times that I could hear myself mumble or speak too fast, I was pleased with the outcome. Live radio was fun, I decided: at least you didn't have to worry about how you looked. At the same time as presenting the shows I was running round London going on other people's radio and TV shows and being interviewed by endless newspapers.

Unwittingly I had become the face and voice of VIVA! without any true say in its development. VIVA! was referred to as Lynne Franks's radio station, although I had been persuaded to buy a few shares at market value and had no ownership. I couldn't understand why we couldn't have themed programmes instead of huge chunks of the day being commandeered by specific presenters who would have guests covering a vast range of subjects. Nor could I understand why we had a male and female presenter on our breakfast show. Often the male presenter would be interviewing male guests without any pretence of a women's perspective and the banality of some of the subject matter made me cringe. Most of all I didn't understand why you couldn't hear VIVA! in so many parts of London. It appeared that the signal had never been tested properly and it should never have gone on air until that had been sorted out. As you couldn't hear it where most of the advertising agencies were based, inevitably the ads stopped rolling in.

I kept pushing ideas which to me seemed every obvious: an afternoon advice phone-in relationship and sex programme, a female version of *Loaded* magazine for Friday night, yoga on air, and different community-oriented promotions, but the powers that be were just bogged down in the daily grind of keeping on air and there seemed neither time nor budget to go forward. In retrospect everyone involved in VIVA! realised it would have been better to go on air at least six months later than it had so that teething problems wouldn't have been publicly aired. However, it's always easy to see things in hindsight. A bright American marketing director called Jeanie Bergin had been brought in to save the day but although she had lots of good ideas too there was no money left to develop them.

Golden Rose by now had a new smoothie CEO, Richard Wheatley, and he didn't seem too inclined to answer the press's queries when they rang. My home phone number seemed to be an open secret in Fleet Street and I was constantly being called on to defend the problems at VIVA! although I was frantically worried about them myself. I was starting to feel disillusioned with the whole VIVA! structure. Belatedly I realised that I would take the brunt of the bad press even though I had no executive power. It was a great lesson to me about lending my name and reputation to a project where I had no real influence. But it wasn't all bad. I had learnt a lot about broadcasting and radio and was sure that all this experience would be of great benefit, whatever path I was to take on my future journey.

After just nine months Golden Rose sold the VIVA! broadcasting licence for around £3 million to Liberty Publishing, the well-financed media arm of the Al Fayed brothers of Harrods fame. Ironic that Europe's only women's radio station should end up being sold to Arabs.

One of the most enjoyable aspects of VIVA! in the early days was the series of weekly interviews I did for my show, *Frankly Speaking*, produced by Chris Burns. They were more conversations than interviews and I'd managed to feature some of my greatest heroines – Gloria Steinem, Anita Roddick, Sinead O'Connor, futurist economist Hazel Henderson, Jo Brand and Labour Shadow Cabinet Minister Claire Short amongst others. I was particularly proud of an exclusive interview I did with my Deia friend Beryl Graves, the eighty-three-year-old widow of Robert, at the time of his centenary. She told me all sorts of stories about their life together in Mallorca. Gloria Steinem, a very youthful sixty-something, is a beautiful, articulate woman. She told me of the time she spent as a peace volunteer in India in the early sixties and the start of feminism in the States when she got back. It seemed extraordinary that such a seemingly confident woman could have ever written a book about her self-esteem problems. It made me appreciate how many women – me included – are perceived from the outside in such a different way than we see ourselves.

Self-esteem seems to be the recurring theme in conversations I have had with women all over the world. Over the last two thousand years or so we have allowed ourselves to take on an almost subservient role to our husbands, fathers and sons. We took on the myth that we were not as capable as men in making important decisions that would affect our lives. The men were the warriors, the hunters, providers and fathers and we women kept in our place as the mothers, nurturers, the home-keepers, and the healers. It is our own lack of confidence in ourselves and in our abilities that holds us back. In many cultures it is often the women who perpetuate this role by bringing up their sons as beings superior to their sisters. The sons get the education, inherit the family wealth and are even fed the choice food off the table.

The stereotypical image of the twentieth-century woman seen in advertising and fashion magazines has also done a lot to affect our self-esteem. The supermodel syndrome is coming to a timely end and women of all shapes and sizes are starting to understand the reality of inner beauty as opposed to an image of glamour and perfection that does not exist.

The early feminists of the 1960s and 1970s, particularly in North America and Scandinavia, overcompensated by becoming surrogate men. The media image of the bra-burning man-haters of the early days has been replaced by the new wave of 1990s feminists who, like Gloria Steinem, find strength in their femininity. I've had conversations with women of all ages across the world and invariably we end up talking about relationships with men. We're looking for the perfect balance, respect and communication in existing or future relationships that can bring about true partnership. We need to be in balance with the male and female inside ourselves, as well as in partnership with men who are comfortable with their own masculine and feminine energy.

In the business world too, women have often felt the need to use their male energy to compete and be successful. The eighties style of women power dressing with big shoulderpads was an indication of the 'surrogate men' syndrome and I always think of Mrs Thatcher when this kind of aggressive way of working comes to mind. When I look back to pictures of myself in the eighties with short hair and trouser-suits I see how I lost the plot too.

There is a different way of working – women can be successful and stay in their feminine, intuitive right-brain mode as opposed to the more intellectual, action-orientated male left brain. Of course there are times for men and women to use both aspects of their selves, but a more nurturing, less confrontational attitude in both business and personal lives has to be the way forward. In many ways it is not surprising that women have felt the need to be more assertive to get on; there is still an enormous glass ceiling in many corporations and even in the West women have never been given equal consideration in the worlds of business, politics or the media, although this is starting to change.

Before launching VIVA! radio as a women's network I'd never experienced sexual discrimination. However, even in my apparently modern Western world of marketing, I started to see that men had all the power. The decision makers in media were generally men, and most of our clients' senior management were men. Apart from small entrepreneurial PR companies like my own, most of the owners and board members in the advertising world were men. It had never bothered me before but now I was beginning to wake up to the lack of power so many women – more than 50 per cent of the population – had in deciding their future.

Why was it then, I wondered, that many of the women who had made it played such appalling power games with other women? My most difficult and in some cases quite impossible clients were always women and I noticed that most of the negative press articles about high-profile women (myself included) were written by women. Was it because women on the way up felt they had to be more aggressive than men to succeed? Or could it even be that high-powered women in corporate life use their aggression to overcompensate and cover up a lack of self-esteem?

I've often talked to my other high-profile women friends about why ambitious young women journalists seem to be the ones their editors choose to write hypercritical destructive articles about us. Women journalists are often the ones who delight in criticising the way we dress, the way we speak, the decorative style of our homes or offices and even the size of our bodies. And the language is different. If a businessman is seen as strong he's described in the newspapers as assertive; if a woman is seen as strong she's described as pushy and aggressive.

Of course, I have also come across businessmen who play power games but somehow it's less personal and doesn't get to you in the same way. If women want to play men's games let's at least do it from a place of understanding and respect instead of from the need to prove ourselves more critical and manipulative than men would ever dream of being.

Women's strength evokes a lot of fear in men, usually relating to their relationship with their mothers. I'm sure this is why I know so many strong women in their forties or fifties who are having relationships with younger men. Young men seem far more open to the power and wisdom of strong women instead of seeing it as competition.

Sinead O'Connor, one of my guests on *Frankly Speaking*, holds very strong views about the crucial importance of mother energy and female empowerment as we move towards the twenty-first century. She became a close friend after I approached her to appear in the What Women Want event held in London a few weeks after the VIVA! launch at the end of August 1995.

I first met her through her manager in a little café near where she lived in West London. I believed she was crucial to the What Women Want event and I was nervous. She has a reputation for being unpredictable and I wasn't sure how she would react to me. As soon as I saw this vulnerable, beautiful girl with her cropped head and big eyes I was overcome with a strong maternal feeling. I knew she'd had family problems and an abusive sick mother, and although she was a good mother herself she seemed just like a fragile child.

I told her of my idea and she started making suggestions in her soft Irish brogue. She told me about the Brigideen Sisters, the nun priestesses who are the guardians of the sacred flame of St Brigid, and about Noírín Ní Riain, a Gaelic singer of Celtic songs with the voice of an angel. I promised to follow up her ideas and find the money to invite these wonderful women over from Ireland. 'I want to be kept in touch,' she told me, promising that she would be there on the day with her band.

I decided to hold What Women Want as a prelude to the forthcoming UN conference for women due to be held in Beijing that September. I'd been aware of this major event for some months. It was the fourth of such conferences on women to be held by the UN since the 1960s and I felt it could have major global repercussions. I was concerned that there was so little awareness of it in the UK, which is still such a patriarchal society. I went to see the organisers of the NGO forum in New York that January. They represented the interests of all

149

the non-governmental organisations going to Beijing and I talked to them about holding high-profile women's concerts both there and elsewhere. We also discussed a whole awareness-raising campaign to be built up in the UK and possibly through Europe. They explained that they had little budget or resources themselves but would be happy to endorse any ideas I had.

I also went to see Bella Abzug, founder of WEDO (Women's Environment and Development Organisation), the *grande dame* of American women's politics. A lawyer and former Congresswoman, she was now in her early seventies and battling with ill health. She was still in the office every day when she wasn't travelling on some campaign or other and was full of fire and energy for improving the lives of the women of the world. I spoke to Bella about my plans and regretted that the UK was sadly bereft of high-profile active women campaigners or campaigns. I came back to London full of enthusiasm and after conversations with some of the women's groups here decided to see if I could pull off a major event in London, even with no budget and no organisation.

What was very clear to me in New York and then back in London was the amount of politics and competition between the women's groups themselves. Although appearing to pool resources, everyone wanted their slogan, their logo and their message to be the one to be taken seriously. I realised how naive I'd been about the 'Sisterhood'. In conversations I've had with early feminists like Gloria Steinem, Germaine Greer, Erica Jong and Bella Abzug, it became very obvious that competition between the groups had been one of the major weaknesses in the women's movement of the 1970s. Erica Jong told me she had writer's block for years because of the aggressive seventies American feminists who hated the fact she loved men and wore sexy underwear.

In the build-up to Beijing, everybody was trying to get funding from the same sources, the same celebrities were hounded for support and lobbying was aimed at the same governmental agencies. Yet it's only by pooling our energy and resources wherever possible, even within the context of our own individual agendas, that we can move forward and make positive change. I tried to sustain this attitude during What Women Want but here I too got involved in political skirmishes and ego battles.

What Women Want was the name of a report prepared by excellent journalist and women's campaigner Lesley Abdela for The Body Shop. Neither seemed to mind if we borrowed both the name and the graphics. I looked around London for locations and found that the Festival Hall on the South Bank was available for August bank holiday weekend. I'd spent some great evenings there recently watching and dancing to world music bands and the convivial management offered me free of charge lots of other spaces in the complex to hold different events during the weekend.

What Women Want was a combination of a concert featuring women artists and two days of workshops and seminars on many women's issues. Part of me didn't really want to organise this event at all and every time it looked impossible I would breathe with relief. Then almost as if I was being pushed by an invisible hand from behind I would be given the OK on another aspect and off I'd go again. The Body Shop agreed to pay for the graphics and decorations, Orange, the telecommunications company, agreed to be sponsors and the Co-Op Bank ended up agreeing to a small sponsorship involvement. With a total budget of £20,000 plus The Body Shop's commitment I set out to create the free day-time events which I knew by rights should cost more like £100,000. VIVA! Radio was in its early days and still had a respectable audience. They agreed to lots of free plugs in return for a free stand. John Bird, editor of the *Big Issue*, the large-circulation magazine sold by the homeless, offered to devote an issue exclusively to What Women Want and produce our official programme.

Bit by bit, with a small team of volunteers, consultants and my then secretary Miranda, I got it together. *Time Out*'s arts editor, Sarah Kent, agreed to create a women and video art exhibit, Romy Fraser of Neal's Yard Remedies took over the important area of women and natural health and mounted a beautiful display of healing products and some very effective seminars. Eva Pascoe of Cyberia, London's first cyber café, set up a techno room where women could learn to surf the Net. Linda Christmas of Women in Journalism arranged an excellent presentation by prominent women journalists and broadcasters on women's position in the media. The Body Shop agreed to do massages and facials. Financial consultant Fiona Price and the Co-Op Bank talked to women about finance and starting a business. Susannah Darling Khan taught a Gabrielle Roth workshop and Caroline Aldred presented one on tantric sex.

Inevitably our biggest publicity magnet, Caroline's was our only exclusively women's event. I attended this seminar myself and loved the way that Caroline and her friends had transferred a fifties Festival of Britain South Bank room into a temple of the Goddess. There was an altar with Goddess artefacts, flowers, fruit and candles, and smells of exotic incense wafted through the room. I remember learning to trust as we walked around with our eyes closed just gently touching each other and breathing in the atmosphere of female sensuality.

In the lobby of the Queen Elizabeth Hall there was a far more specific political agenda. We had displays and talking circles on subjects including women in the environment, women and domestic violence, women and homelessness, women and hunger and refugee women living in the Diaspora – several of which were suggested by Chrissie Hynde who'd also agreed to appear in the concert. We showed some of the results from the excellent accompanying What Women Want postcard campaign organised by Bernadette Vallely. This formed the basis of a book and various reports. We made some mistakes and we were under-resourced, but organisations that had helped us, including the British Council, Oxfam and the Equal Opportunities Commission together with the South Bank management themselves, felt it had been a highly successful start to what they saw as a regular event. Together with the concert, some 8–10,000 women, men and children visited What Women Want over the weekend.

The concert was a complete sellout. It was introduced by Jo Brand, Sinead O'Connor gave her first major London set for more than five years and Chrissie Hynde publicly launched her new Pretenders acoustic album. Zap Mama, the internationally acclaimed Zairean a cappella group, came over especially from their home in Belgium, top African singer Angélique Kidjo came from Paris and British jazz singer Sarah Jane Morris made one of her first public appearances since her son Otis was born.

The concert started off with a blessing and presentation from the Brigideen Sisters, the members of an Irish holy order. As Sinead had told me, the Brigideens are responsible for the holy flame of St Brigid, Ireland's patron saint. Like many saints Brigid had appeared in Celtic folklore years before the advent of Christianity to Ireland. Brigid is one of the names of the Goddess and she is represented as the crone or bringer of death and rebirth. She is also the goddess of learning who delights in knowledge of nature and the fruits of the earth. The sacred flame of Brigid had been blown out by the Catholic Church some five hundred years ago during the general religious unrest of that period when the Reformation cut ties with so many of the old traditions. The sisters had only recently been allowed to ceremoniously relight it. They brought the holy flame from their home in Kildare in Southern Ireland down to the Festival Hall in charcoal and symbolically carried it on to the stage in a lantern as part of a moving ritual. Appearing with them was Ireland's foremost sacred singer Noírín Ní Riain, who performed Brigid's prayer.

I'd sit with the men, the women of God
There by the lake of beer.
We'd be drinking good health forever
And every drop would be a prayer.
(from Brigid's Prayer in *Love of Ireland – Poems from the Irish*)

Although unannounced, this start to the show brought the mainly rock 'n' roll crowd to their feet as Clare Grady Walsh, the gracious young woman who runs Greenpeace in Ireland, read an ode to women and the Goddess. I was not the only person to have tears in my eyes as Noírín announced that the holy flame would be going with her and me to Beijing. No one seemed to want to go home that night – the audience or the artists. The *Evening Standard*'s heading SEX, NUNS AND ROCK 'N' ROLL AT LYNNE'S WOMEN'S FESTIVAL' seemed to sum it up and when I was asked to go on the stage at the end of this incredible night I acknowledged to the audience the power of the Goddess that had brought this event together.

With hardly time to get any sleep I left the next day for Beijing. I've learnt that the more expectations I have of a person or an event the more disappointed I am and I had a lot of expectations with regard to the Beijing conference. Officially I went there as correspondent for VIVA! and sent back daily news reports for the breakfast show. Unofficially I was networking, listening, learning, informing and generally hanging out. At many large conferences, it's the unofficial agenda, the private meetings, the networking and connecting that really creates change in the long term.

The most inspirational women I found there by far were the flamboyant Africans who wore their vibrant printed cottons and braided hair like symbols of their positive survival in the face of extreme adversity. On the whole they were the ones with least money who had overcome the greatest obstacle to get there. Even though in some cases it meant selling clothes to pay for their food, their larger-than-life energy gave sustenance to us all. We less resilient Westerners traipsed off to the local department store to buy bright-coloured plastic cycling macs and little rubber wellies to protect us from the unseasonal rains that drenched us to the skin through our summer clothes.

The area turned into a muddy swamp as the days progressed. Roofless buildings leaked everywhere and tents collapsed. We tried to keep our spirits up but it was almost impossible. Hillary Clinton swept in with her entourage to make a big speech. A select few hundred went inside to hear her while the rest of us hovered outside in the wet.

Eventually we gave up and went to the press room. I felt a bit better when I sat down next to a bedraggled Jane Fonda, who also hadn't made it to Hillary's speech. Her streaked blonde hair was as wet as mine and her beige suede jacket and snakeskin boots were the talk of the afternoon amongst bored and frustrated journalists.

I visited as many small meetings as I could. I listened to women with HIV from Nepal who'd been sold into prostitution by their families as children. I heard the early feminists of Sweden explain how things had gone wrong as well as right in their socially advanced society, with their men drinking too much and becoming violent in the need to assert themselves. I saw women from the Pacific islands dancing around in grass skirts with conch shells, honouring the power of God and nature, and I heard a group of Jewish and Arab women from Israel explain how they are trying to work together against all odds. I was impressed when I met Jordan's first woman mayor, a humble, quietly spoken lawyer, at a British Council reception and moved when Noírín and I took Brigid's flame to the peace tent at Huairou.

One of the more amusing stories that came out of Beijing was how a Chinese delegation had seen a group of militant Canadian lesbian activists take their clothes off at one of the preparatory conferences in Vienna. The government then warned the local hotels and taxi drivers to keep sheets and towels handy to throw over mad Westerners as we were all likely to do the same.

I had the feeling that the Chinese regretted offering to host the conference. I was told they'd been offered the women's conference as a consolation when they failed to win the Olympics and they must have felt they'd won the booby prize. Their culture was so different from those of the women delegates from overseas that there was very little mutual communication or understanding. They tried to be as hospitable as they knew how but there was suspicion and mistrust on all sides. At the same time one in five women in the world is Chinese, one in five people in the world is Chinese, and we all have to learn to work and live together harmoniously on this planet of ours. Certainly the younger Chinese students I met were hungry to learn about our lives and I felt that if we could get past this communication blockage and look for some mutual understanding, particularly in the area of human development, we could go forward together positively.

I felt sad that there was not more spirituality evident at the non-governmental organisations (NGO) forum. There was only one tent for peace with a somewhat bedraggled altar although I'd assumed that love, nurturing and a spiritual consciousness would be present. I am sure that many there felt like I did: that a women's conference needs to look beyond politics.

Apart from the unexpected hurricane weather, the hardest thing to face was that the NGO forum had been put out at Huairou, forty miles outside Beijing. The 30,000-odd NGO delegates either had to stay in apartments nearby or travel in every day by expensive taxi or irregular buses. Back at the UN conference at the smart facilities within Beijing there was a far more organised air. Having easy access with my press pass I did manage to get to see Hillary Clinton, who made another speech, this time on human rights being women's rights and women's rights being human rights. She also talked movingly about the importance of micro enterprise where small unsecured loans and credit can be granted to women. There have been some very successful projects like this in Asia, especially the Grameen Bank in Bangladesh and the SEWA Bank in northern India. SEWA – Self Employed Women's Association – was uniquely run by women for its women members. Each had operated a micro credit system for some twenty years and both had a payback rate of more than 90 per cent. 'After all,' argued Hillary, 'whether it's a cow in Calcutta or a computer in Chicago women need to be given a chance.'

I was told by her advisers that her speech had not been approved by the American administration, which had not even wanted her to attend, and I felt she was a woman of courage as well as vision. I also heard an inspiring speech from Benazir Bhutto. She spoke passionately about the need for women to receive education and reminded the Muslim countries that nowhere in the Koran does it say that women should not work. She is a beautiful woman and looked dignified and elegant in her traditional blue salwar kameez. I had to remind myself that however sincere she was she represented a corrupt regime where women had very little power.

Gossip and rumours abounded around the snack bars and rest areas. There was bad feeling about a few Nigerian male delegates who'd made sexual advances to some of the women delegates. There was also a fair amount of derision for Jack Lang, the former French Minister of Culture. A sexy French man who was there as adviser to the UN, he made a patronising speech showing he'd done no research and overrunning his allotted time by thirty minutes. His constant repetition and posing resulted in the cancellation of the press conference that was scheduled to follow. His posturing did not go down well at a women's conference. There was no time for bullshit here.

I don't know in retrospect if the Beijing conference really achieved anything. It was certainly a world talking point and I'd like to think that at least a match was struck for the fire that could light up world consciousness of the injustice women receive all over the world. But even after the language of the conference's Platform for Action was agreed; even after the unlikely alliance of the Catholic Church and the fundamental Muslim states including Iran backing down on the abortion and contraception issues; even then, would it really make a difference? We were all constantly being told by the official delegates that even if all the nation states signed the conference document very little would change unless pressure was put on governments by the NGOs, the grassroots organisations, and indeed by women and men in the street.

I left Beijing exhausted and deflated but with the hope that this was just the start of a long journey towards a balanced society based on partnership.

What had become very clear to me through my experiences with VIVA!, What Women Want and finally the Beijing conference was that if women try to take on the patriarchal system head-on there will be no change. Women and men have to undertake an internal transformation before they can look forward to a harmonious future of unity. Women are no more suited to sorting out the problems of the world than men unless they start thinking in terms of values of a different nature.

As Germaine Greer said on stage at What Women Want, 'The opposite to patriarchy is not matriarchy but fraternity.' Sinead used this speech at the beginning of her album, *Universal Mother*, and the phrase stayed with me.

I had spent the whole summer on the battlefield and had started to lose touch with my inner self. It was time to go inward, to look for silence and reconnect with the divine source.

I'd found out that we – women and men – have to tap into the innate power of our true selves, let go of our egos and change the core of our social system not through gender status and competition but through love, trust, wisdom, compassion, honesty and respect.

10

Journeying with the Wise Women

Candles flickered, casting shadows on the walls of the small chapel as one by one the women present affirmed their prayers of intent to honour the Mother. I was on the remote Scottish island of Iona at the invitation of Eleanor Dettinger, the American-born founder of the Wise Women Council of Great Britain and a benefactor to many spiritual and progressive initiatives. Eleanor had invited me with my daughter Jessica to join a small group of wise women including Irish singer Noírín Ní Riain to come to this sacred place at the time of the ancient Christian festival of Michaelmas and meditate together.

It was a few weeks after coming back from Beijing and I badly needed some spiritual sustenance. I'd met Eleanor at a Wise Women meeting some months earlier at the north London home of her co-chair Baroness Edmée Di Pauli, a passionate Austrian-born aristocrat in her early eighties, who for many years had been one of the mainstays of the esoteric movement in the UK alongside her friend Sir George Trevelyan. They embraced ideas from ancient and modern schools of thought which reflected a spiritual and philosophical awakening. I thought of them as the matriarch and patriarch of the British 'New Age'.

Synergetically Eleanor was a patron of Noírín's, the singer of sacred and ancient Celtic music who'd become a major part of the What Women Want concert at the suggestion of Sinead O'Connor. Through this unlikely connection and unbeknown to me, Eleanor. Edmée and other wise women had tracked the progress of the What Women event and had brought their friends and family to the Festival Hall to enjoy the evening.

Eleanor had rung me just after I'd got back from Beijing and had asked in her breathless little girl's voice if I'd like to join her and some friends for a weekend on Iona with no fixed agenda. Since I'd always wanted to visit this holy island, which is said to have been the first British home of Christianity, I jumped at the chance. Eleanor, a statuesque middle-aged woman dressed in long flowing clothes, met Jessica and me at Glasgow airport with her fellow wise woman friend, Irish nun Mary Hall, who ran a multi-faith centre in Birmingham. Apart from my ex-husband's aunt in Australia I'd never really spoken to a nun and found the strength and clarity of this attractive redheaded woman in her early sixties stimulating and inspiring. She explained to me how she was able to have far deeper relationships with men precisely because there was no possibility of a sexual dimension.

Eleanor drove us through beautiful highlands around the Scottish lochs until we arrived at Oban and took the ferry to the Isle of Mull. We then drove for another hour across countryside, beautiful in its bleakness, then took another short ferry trip across choppy seas to the Hebridean island of Iona. We felt as if we were at the edge of the world, and in a way we were.

This tiny island on the Atlantic Ocean, said to be the oldest rock above sea level, has just a few fishermen's cottages, some sheep farmers, a general store, a postbox, a couple of B&Bs, a small hotel, some ruins and one of the oldest abbeys in the world. Once adopted as a centre of religion by sun-worshipping Druids it was here the early Christian monk St Columba came from Ireland in 563. Sending all the women of Iona away he created a sacred space for men to worship Christ. However, at some point the women must have come back as there still exist the ruins of an early nunnery.

Apart from having a family home in Holland with her Dutch-born husband, Jacques, Eleanor has a small house in Iona where she spends several months of the year. Having brought up her large family of five children, and now with several grandchildren, she has set herself a different agenda, travelling the world and playing an important, behind-the-scenes role in the global movement for change. 'I love my husband and children dearly, Lynne,' she told me, 'but I do feel they are now more than capable of looking after themselves. I have chosen instead to dedicate my life to serving the planet.'

There is definitely a feeling of the High Priestess about Eleanor as she strides powerfully round the world with her classically beautiful face, hair pinned back, cloak fastened by a traditional Celtic brooch thrown over her shoulders and bold medallions hanging from chains around her neck.

Her cottage, though small, was warm and friendly and although she seemed comfortable enough it was obvious the island was a harsh home for the residents during the winter months. She had booked a cosy room in the nearby hotel for Jessica and myself, spreading her other guests throughout various B&Bs and hostels around the village. There were about twelve of us altogether, mostly from Ireland and Wales, plus three rather strange-looking women in white saris. I was told they were Brahma Kumaris. I didn't connect with them much, never thinking that within a few months I would be enjoying a visit to their centre on top of a holy mountain in India.

The first night Eleanor took us across the dark fields to the Benedictine abbey where we celebrated the eve of St Michael's, a major event in the Scottish Church. The service was taken by a young woman cleric and even though other women featured prominently in the service and Noírín sang beautifully, the language was entirely male. We sipped the wine representing Christ's blood and ate the bread representing his body – a ritual I'd never experienced before and found quite unnatural. As soon as we could, our group, with some other local women friends, left the larger abbey and went to the smaller St Michael chapel next door. Here we voiced our discomfort

with the male language of the service and as Noírín sang we spontaneously made our affirmations and meditated together in a more
female way.

The rest of the weekend we went on long bracing walks
around Iona's harsh hillsides, warming up with healthy home-cooked
meals, meditating and enjoying ourselves. My witty Irish companions
kept me laughing through every meal and Ann, my new Welsh friend,
told me stories of sacred sites near to her home which she said I had to
visit. My Irish friends also wanted me to visit them and see for myself
the power of their holy places. I realised how little I knew of the sacred
sites of Ireland, Scotland and Wales and decided to follow up these
invitations to find out more about their ancient Celtic energy.

It wasn't until I got back to London that I became aware of
how much I'd been affected by Iona. Its remoteness and austerity had
awakened something in me which resonated at a deep level. I'd been
so London oriented that I'd never appreciated the spiritual energy and
the connection with Mother Earth that I could find in my own
country.

Noírín lived in County Tipperary, close to the mouth of the
Shannon, in the middle of a nature sanctuary, rich with exotic wildlife.
Her home, a splendid Georgian country house, was situated where the
earliest inhabitants of the island are said to have lived. It is a very magical area not least because legend has it that the River Shannon was
formed by the goddess Sionna who on seeing the hazelnut of wisdom
by the Shannon Pot reached out and accidentally knocked it into the
water. As a salmon swam to get the hazelnut the water turned a purple colour and so mesmerised was the goddess that she too fell in. At
this point, according to the legend, the Shannon Pot overflowed and
the source of the river was formed.

Noírín met me at the airport and next day, together with
Eleanor, we set off for a remote guest house standing in the shadow of
Newgrange, one of the world's oldest spiritual sites.

Eleanor advised me not to go into Newgrange for the first
twenty-four hours but to settle slowly into the energy. We drove up

and had a look at this stone chamber fronted by a guardian rock covered with ancient spirals. I felt as if I'd come into an intense energy force and a band of pain settled round my head. As I backed away apprehensively I understood exactly what Eleanor had meant.

I seemed to be growing increasingly sensitive to the energy emanating from places as well as people. It was almost as if my vibrational level had been heightened to open me up to a new awareness and whenever I was near places with ancient spiritual history I'd get intense physical reactions. By the next day my body seemed to have settled into the local energy field and at ten o'clock that morning the seven of us went up to Newgrange. We were just north of Dublin at Drogheda in the Boyne Valley, known as the Valley of the Kings of Ireland.

Newgrange is said to be a transformational death and rebirth chamber about seven thousand years old – older even than the Egyptian Sphinx. It is built on one of the powerful energy lines running through Ireland and had originally been used as a place of initiation and as a sun observatory. The site was discovered by one of Cromwell's generals and some time after named Newgrange but the Irish name, Uainh na Greinne, actually means womb or tomb of the sun. The ancient spirals are thought to indicate male and female energy and this awesome site, in such a remote and beautiful area, seemed to have a powerful hold over me. Eleanor said she would hold the energy outside while the rest of us, together with our young female guide, went in. My friends had all been here before and I really felt that this trip was in my honour.

Our guide explained that for five mornings of the year between 19 and 23 December the rising midwinter sun casts a narrow beam down the 60-foot length of passage to illuminate the inner chamber. The symbolic meaning of a shaft of light piercing the darkness of an underground chamber was clear to us all and had been experienced by Dolores Whelan, the writer and sacred site expert, who was one of our group. She told us how, on the winter solstice of 1986, she had been given a place to watch the sun appear in the inner chamber – a privilege for which there is apparently a fifteen-year waiting list. 'It was the high point of my life, the most stunning thing I've ever seen,' she said.

I examined the interior, tracing my fingers on the patterns of the rocks. Three French tourists looked curiously at us but eventually left us alone. Without discussion we formed a circle inside the chamber with our guide, held hands and closed our eyes. All sorts of strange feelings went through me as I felt the power of my own death and rebirth. We stayed in silent meditation like seven priestesses of old until eventually Dolores and I simultaneously started a low chant that brought us all back to the present. We remained in silence as we rejoined Eleanor outside and I realised what a gift Newgrange and my friends had given me. Later I learnt that Noírín had come to Newgrange that day with a serious medical condition but the intense energy of this mystical site had worked its healing powers on her and from that moment on all her symptoms left her.

Later during the weekend, Dolores took me to Brigid's Well and the Hill of Tara, both important landmarks in Brigideen tradition, where I continued to experience a connection with Ireland's Celtic goddess energy in the shape of Brigid, the patron of poetry, learning, healing and craftsmanship. Such was Brigid's prestige that her name could be used as a synonym of goddess but perhaps paradoxically it is in the person of her Christian namesake, St Brigid, that the pagan goddess survives best.

Brigid's Well, in Faughart, north of Dundalk, is one of the many places said to be the goddess's birthplace. The Hill of Tara is Ireland's oldest sacred site. A mount with passages and crevices running through it, it is also known as the site of the High Kings of Ireland and has always been an important place of pilgrimage. Huge fires were once lit on this mound; according to legend they illuminated the entire countryside and could be seen across all of Ireland.

Dolores told me that increasingly the Irish people are awakening to the spirituality and esoteric meaning of Ireland's sacred sites, and that Tara's Hill was also referred to as a landscape temple corresponding with the chakras, or vortices of energy within the human aura. We started our walk at the place where the kitchens would have been: this represented the root chakra located at the base of the spine; we then walked through the long, narrow banqueting hall area up into the solar plexus chakra; and from there we moved into a different enclosure area which is the heart chakra and on to what is known as the Mound of Hostages which represents the throat chakra and is aligned with the rise of the harvest moon.

The green beauty of the Irish countryside, the mountains, rivers and lakes will stay with me for ever. I felt a very deep connection with Ireland whether in this life or, who knows, even a past lifetime and I knew I'd be returning for many years to come. Before leaving I arranged with Noírín to meet her in Wales where we would join another Iona companion, fellow wise woman Ann Lynon-Cowle.

Ann has restored a charming cottage overlooking the sea right next to St Davids Cathedral. She explained that St Davids was the smallest city in Britain with its cathedral built in the Valley of the Roses so as to be out of sight from sea raiders. On the first night we went to watch the bell ringers practise their ancient art in the old belltower of the cathedral. Ann's melodic Welsh voice flowed over us during dinner telling us tales from the *Mabinogion*, a rare collection of medieval tales written in Welsh in the fourteenth century which draws on old pre-Christian myths of Celtic Britain and contains some of the earliest surviving material relating to the Arthurian legend.

The next day she drove us, together with my friend Alex Fisher, the activist writer and road protester, through undulating countryside, to visit one of the oldest oak forests in Britain, hidden behind a hill a few miles from St Davids. As we walked through a sacred grove I could almost feel the spirits of the trees emerge from under the moss-clad branches covering the ground. The tall, upright trees with their gnarled branches are descendants of the neolithic trees which once covered the whole of the country, and the forest has one of the rarest collections of moss and fauna in the whole of the United Kingdom. There is said to be a cave underneath the ground which had acted as a hermitage for the Celtic saint St Brynach whose church is hidden in the valley down by the sea.

Eleanor once explained to me that when she thought up the name of the Wise Women Council she had intended WISE to include the initials of Wales, Ireland, Scotland and England and I felt that through her introduction I had connected on a far deeper level with the energy of my own country. The Council of Wise Women is a loose network of individuals working either in non-profit and spiritual organisations or on their own who come together to share information and support one another. I felt it was through my connection with them that I had connected with the wise woman inside myself. This archetype is inside all of us and contains our ancient memories of healing, ritual and magic.

Some five hundred years ago the wise women were so intensely feared by the church that up to nine million were killed throughout England, Europe and America. The arts of midwifery, herbalism and healing were lost to us as these millions of women, and some men, were either drowned or burnt at the stake as witches. Neighbours informed on neighbours as this genocide spread like wildfire.

It is only now that we are remembering the natural way of healing, understanding that the body, mind and emotions are really one and treating them with herbs and homoeopathy. Above all we're remembering to connect with the restorative energy of Mother Earth. Witches were never the pawns of the devil that the Church went to such pains to portray them as: they were ancient priestesses and priests, the keepers of true knowledge, and many of their secrets have been lost for ever throughout the British Isles. Of course, even priests and priestesses have their shadow side – as indeed do all human beings – but as every good witch knows if you use you powers to control or hurt anyone else there will always be a comeback.

These islands with their Celtic and Druid background, with the legends of Arthur and our sacred stones and sacred sites, hold important knowledge for the whole world and it's only by visiting these spaces, opening up to them and being in nature that we can try and restore some of the damage done to our magic land.

Stone circles, crop circles and other sacred sites have long been part of Britain's spiritual heritage. The giant sacred circles of Stonehenge and Avebury are said to go back to around 2000 BC. Since they seem too heavy to have been cut and positioned by the primitive people of that time, there are many theories of magical or even extra-terrestrial help.

Many sacred sites are said to fall on ley lines, old linear patterns in the landscape which integrate ancient monuments and sites with the natural features of the countryside dating back to a time when landscape, the heavens and the human mind were one interdependent whole. There are clear indications that the ancient shamen or tribal priests who first marked out these sites and sometimes linked them to others by paths made use of their mystical dimension as natural centres of magic.

British writer John Michell is considered the greatest living expert on British sacred geometry. A prolific man with an extraordinarily agile mind, he reminds me of Dr Who with his slightly vague out-of-world attitude and long scarves. I met him several times through mutual friends and he told me that the stone circles and other places of assembly formed an integral, country-wide network of ritual magic centres somehow in communication with each other. 'Since the prime use of every ancient temple was for invoking spirits,' he said, 'the form of communication between the megalithic ritual centres was presumably spiritual, involving the powers and vital energies of the earth under the influence of cosmic forces.'

Many people believe that the planet works on the same chakra, or energy point system, as the human body, and Glastonbury is said to hold the heart chakra energy for the world. Glastonbury also has many ancient Druid and Celtic connections. King Arthur's mysterious Isle of Avalon that exists in the world between worlds is said to have been located nearby. Certainly the energy of Glastonbury Tor, the ancient mound with its ruined tower on the edge of town, feels strangely otherworldly and I've heard of many uncanny experiences and sightings that people have had there.

This small town in Somerset has a special effect on me and I had an intense experience when I went there for the weekend at the start of my journey in the early 1990s.

I stayed in a local B&B said to be on the same ley line as the Tor: it had a crystal garden and various strange residents. I went there shortly after participating in Katrina Raphaell's crystal workshop on the recommendation of some other participants. The owner, a large, seemingly friendly woman in her early fifties, told me she used to be a PR herself but had given it up some years ago to work on less worldly matters.

'I'm trying to have a baby with my current lover,' she told me confidently as I looked at her in disbelief. Surely she was too old. And then as if to draw me in, she said in a softer voice, 'I'm a member of the Morganas, you know, and I might be able to let you into some of their secrets.' Knowing that Morgan le Fay was King Arthur's priestess sister, a wise woman whose story I had read in Marion Bradley's popular epic *The Mists of Avalon*, I assumed this was some local witches' coven.

In retrospect I wish I'd been more open to her but she alarmed me. She did however persuade me to come into her healing room for a reading. She looked closely into my eyes and started taking me through a visual meditation. 'You are at the bottom of the steps in a large building,' she said. 'It is a temple and as you come up the steps the High Priestess comes out of the golden doors. She is dressed in blue with lilac eyes and she is your spiritual teacher. Look deeply into my eyes and tell me if you recognise who this woman is.' It felt as if she was trying to hypnotise me or in some way take control of my mind.

I knew she wanted me to say the Priestess was her and that she was my spiritual teacher. Warning bells rang, but as I'm very short-sighted her penetrating stare seemed to have no effect.

Glastonbury wasn't the only place I visited where I had a strange experience. I'd been told by friends I'd met there about a drum and music festival which was taking place on a hill fort near Winchester, so I persuaded my musician friend Dominique to come out for the day and explore this area of Hampshire. I also arranged to meet my daughter Jessica and her boyfriend at the festival later on. But when Dom and I arrived there was no sign of any musical festival. A small street festival was taking place in the centre of town but it wasn't what we were looking for and no one we asked could help.

Unable to hear the sound of drums, we were both bemused. We went to the station to look for Jessica who had been leaving frantic messages for me back home with her brother in London. We continued to miss each other all day, Dom and I walking up one street, while Jessica and her boyfriend were walking down another.

I found out that Winchester was the centre of Wessex, another place claimed as the site for King Arthur's court at Camelot. There are several hill forts around Winchester dating back to the first millennium BC. We found some strange, pagan-looking symbols drawn in the ground inside an old forest on the crest of the first hill fort. Dom and I then heard about another hill fort a few miles outside Winchester on the way to Stonehenge. An increasing sense of mystery seemed to surround us as we continued our adventure and on reaching this old battleground we discovered people fleeing down the hill.

'Don't go up there – there's a swarm of giant bees attacking everyone in sight!' yelled one woman as she rushed past. We decided to walk up regardless. Again there was no sign of any festival but I could sense something was afoot. As we walked up the side of this hill in the late afternoon I looked to the right and saw strange circles and geometric shapes in the huge cornfield below me. I felt that a crop circle was what I'd been looking for all afternoon and stared at the shapes until they were imprinted on my brain. I didn't know on a conscious level if there was a message for me in them but somehow I felt they were another signpost to lead me further on my journey.

We got to the top of the hill to find the swarm of giant bees were indeed waiting for us. Dom started running with his shirt over his head as he made for a safe space beyond. I wasn't afraid and I walked slowly on with a sense of complete protection. I felt these bees were somehow the guardian of the site and knew I wished them no harm.

Finally I joined Dom unscathed at the top of the hill and as we looked around we became aware of a deep sense of silence. It was as if we'd crossed over to another dimension where we could just *be* and absorb the beauty of nature in this magical landscape. Eventually as the sun started to set on the horizon we made our way slowly back down the hill through the bees to our car and drove back to London.

Like all my adventures since I began to seek the truth, one event had seemed to lead on to another, and I realised that the more I trusted and allowed the natural flow of synchronicity to take over, the more I would encounter experiences of a transformational nature. It was as if I was undergoing a six-month initiation period in order to understand ancient wisdoms that I half recalled at a deep level within myself. I knew I was connecting with the Wise Woman inside me.

Rituals were starting to become a normal part of my life, especially when I was outside London. Celebrations of the full and new moon, acknowledgement of the solstices, awareness of the rhythms of Gaia or Mother Earth and cosmic patterns all put me in touch with my own body rhythms. I enjoyed the fun of rituals too – dancing, drumming, lighting candles and incense and meditating with other women, all of which brought me back to my centre.

London has its ancient history and sites too. Long before it was the Roman town of Londinium several Celtic towns were situated there. Even as recently as the last century, much of London was a pleasant place of meadows, fields, rivers and lakes. Now I feel that the only natural magic left is on Hampstead Heath. When I have to be in London for more than a few days I find it crucial to go up to the Heath for a couple of hours, to encircle Boadicea's Mound and ground myself by walking through the woods.

One of London's oldest sacred areas runs beneath King's Cross and St Pancras. I was fairly ignorant of the history of this area until I met poet Aidan Dun whose epic poem 'Vale Royal' explains the myths and legends of the area in depth. Aidan told me that the ancient Celtic city of Troynovant was sited under King's Cross as was the healing Fleet River. There were many secrets, he said, in the layers beneath the city and he'd spent more than twenty years living in squats in the area researching them. He told me that King's Cross was on the ley line from Glastonbury and was the Eastern Gate of King Arthur. It is even said that Merlin's tomb is hidden away in a deep cavern below King's Cross. Aidan's vision is that if you bring light, music and happiness back to this depressing, gloomy area full of railway sidings, gasworks and bedraggled prostitutes, you can change the energy of England.

His dream of King's Cross as an arts and healing centre may not be so far off. Already life is being breathed back into the area. The new Channel Tunnel link is based there and Richard Branson heads a consortium who have won the right to develop it. Trendy lofts in old warehouses are selling at high prices and the rich, crowded street life of Camden Town is spilling into the neighbourhood.

I met Aidan through Julie Lowe, another wise woman friend. A Boadicea-like figure herself, Julie founded and runs the Battlebridge Centre, a community development in the heart of King's Cross. Despite very little funding, she and her two teenage children, Charlotte and Danny, together with various volunteers and friends, have taken waste ground containing a huge old tram shed and transformed it into pretty gardens, individual eco-cabins for homeless young people, and a large centre for craftspeople, non-profit organisations, seminars and sustainable shops. They've also managed to create a vegetarian restaurant and a cosy home for themselves. Struggling against extreme hardship, Julie has continued her battle with budgets and the elements at Battlebridge, showing that determination and innate wisdom can truly create miracles.

During this initiation period of connecting with the wise woman inside me, I seemed to see magic wherever I was and connect with nature, even in the middle of an urban wasteland. I started to understand that if women and men connected with their archetypal or unconscious inner images of witches or wizards, we would be able to tap into the magic of transformation and reclaim our lost knowledge. We could create a new reality from the essence of our dreams.

11

Reconnecting with my Roots

We danced around faster and faster under the watchful full moon. The ancient shape of Jerusalem's Wailing Wall loomed over us as our circle gradually expanded to include all the religious Jewish women clutching babies and small children who had come with their husbands for the Shabat evening prayers.

It was the first Friday of January 1996 and I was in Israel with my children, my mother Angela, my sister Susan and her family from Canada as well as various of our cousins and friends. My son Joshua had brought me on this long journey back to my roots by deciding to become a practising Jew. He had had his bar mitzvah at the Wailing Wall the day before and my nephew Ben was due to take the same rites of passage to manhood the following morning.

We women had all meditated together in the hotel earlier that evening affirming our sacred power on the night of the full moon. In ancient times, the Hebrew tribe had regarded the moon as a goddess encompassing the archetypal unity and multiplicity of female nature, the giver of life and fertility. It was surely no coincidence that we were all in the Holy City of our ancestors at such a significant time. We had always been a family of powerful women and it was appropriate that we were gathered together here in Jerusalem to celebrate the ritual of our sons reaching manhood.

We arrived at the Wailing Wall as the traditional evening service was coming to a close. Then we silently put the prayers we'd written earlier, dedicated to the health and happiness of our loved ones and the planet, alongside the many others that had been placed in the cracks in the Wall. As we watched the Hasidic men bowing and chanting, we were aware that according to traditional Jewish law women have to keep their voices lower than those of men during prayer.

We found ourselves following their melodic voices as our bodies started to move with the rhythm. The high spirits of my sister took over as she grabbed my hand and together with my daughter, nieces and sister-in-law we started to dance. As we sang and spun round we were joined by the other women and children who danced with us until we finally collapsed on the floor in spontaneous laughter. The religious men who had been peering at us over the partition from their own far larger prayer area looked on surprised. We took no notice.

Joshua had first become interested in Judaism at the age of sixteen. I had felt it was up to the children to follow their own spiritual paths, as I was born a Jew but was a practising Buddhist during most of their childhood. My parents had become spiritual healers in later life and the children's father came from strict Catholic parents who later followed the teachings of Indian guru Sai Baba.

Hands-on healing had been part of my life for a long time. I'd grown up with my mother practising it for many years, so it had always seemed very natural to me. She had many grateful patients, but always refused payment. My father too was an effective healer before he came down with Alzheimer's. Sweet-smelling oil would appear from the palms of his great big butcher's hands during his healing sessions. To my surprise when I met my father-in-law in Australia I found he was also a healer and when my children were small they would run to their grandparents on both sides of the world for relief from pain caused by nasty falls and childhood illnesses.

My mother believes that we all have the power to heal. We have to learn how to focus our energy and send it into each other with loving intention. She calls on her spirit guides to help her and says they direct her to her patient's source of pain and discomfort where she can focus her healing energy.

My early upbringing was in a conventional post-war Jewish family. My parents, and particularly my matriarchal grandmother who lived with us in north London, expected me to attend our progressive liberal synagogue for weekly Hebrew classes and services until I was confirmed at fourteen. I don't remember relating much to the vengeful, angry Jehovah we were taught about. I felt more connected to the Bible's heroines like Esther, Ruth and Miriam. I couldn't understand why there were so few brave wise women portrayed in the Bible. Why were the wives so often perceived as manipulative and weak? Why was Lot's wife turned into a pillar of salt? And why was Eve blamed for Adam's downfall?

Indeed there are many dehumanising stories about women in the Old Testament. It is clear that women, whether wives, maid servants, concubines or their offspring, were considered male property. It was often justifiable to kill a woman found not to be a virgin when she married – as her virginity was part of her father's economic wealth. It was also acceptable for young girls to be offered in sacrifice to an angry mob, as Lot did with his two daughters.

The disempowering attitude to women is closely connected with the way that the worship of the Goddess disappeared from the history of the Hebrew people's religion. There is much evidence that the Hebrews, together with many other ancient peoples, moved from a religion that incorporated Goddess worship towards an exclusively male-led belief system. In Riane Eisler's book *The Chalice and the Blade* – an extensively researched look at the existence of Goddess culture – she quotes biblical and archaeological sources who have proved that the Goddess was 'an integral part of the religion of the Hebrews'.

My interest in studying Judaism as a teenager vanished when I discovered I had more fun using my time for dating. I first visited

Israel in my late teens to see an Israeli boyfriend I'd met in London. He subsequently married a more worldly American girl, had a baby, and then was tragically killed in the last few hours of the Six Day War. I've often wondered how different my life would have turned out if I'd been his widow.

I returned to Israel several years later, now married to Paul and running my still relatively small PR business. Through the connections of my Israeli cousins, I had been appointed the UK PR consultant for Israel's fashion and textile industry. At my initial meeting with my client, the director of the Israeli Export Institute, the first question he asked me was whether my husband was Jewish. 'We need all of you in the Diaspora to keep the Jewish traditions going and to bring your children up as Jews,' he told me.

I was amazed but soon learnt that this personal approach was very much part of the Israeli character. I worked for the Israeli government for some years after that, visiting often, making good friends and enjoying my time there.

Eventually our relationship came to a natural end but several years later I found myself working for another branch of the Israeli government, this time promoting tourism. By now I'd lost track of my Israeli friends and no longer identified with their cause. I wasn't in favour of their policies towards the Palestinians and believed that a non-confrontational approach from all sides was the only hope of peace in the Middle East.

And then it was Joshua's turn. Like me he'd watched the film *Exodus* on television when he was sixteen and got caught up in the pain of the Holocaust and pride in the concept of a new Jewish state. He was only interested in his school work if he could import a Jewish theme. His art project was full of Stars of David and photographic montages of our local Maida Vale Sephardic synagogue. His essay for his International Baccalaureate took him months to complete and was based on the justification of the founding of the State of Israel. He was a boy obsessed.

He was searching for his own identity and although it took me somewhat by surprise, I understood his passion. He was encouraged along this path by my mother who after years of being a liberated, intelligent woman began to show all the signs of being a proud Jewish grandmother.

Before going to university Joshua had his year off and immediately took off to Israel. He spent five months there, initially selling ice-creams at the beautiful kibbutz at En Gedi on the Dead Sea, and then travelling across Israel to end up at a yeshiva in Jerusalem for young Western boys like him who were searching for their heritage. He was taught a lot about the traditional history of the Jews, some of which was grounded in fact and some of which was outright propaganda. He used to phone me reverse charge for long philosophical discussions on such subjects as the appalling position of women in Jewish law – my point of view – and how God had written the Torah, the book of the Law – his point of view.

He came back from Israel to join me in Deia for the summer of '94 looking like a religious Jew from the ghetto. He had grown long sideburns and a beard, was wearing a *yamalka* and even the traditional religious undergarments underneath his T-shirt. I was a bit concerned, but as he was due that winter to travel to America via his father in Australia I was sure his enthusiasm would soon be tempered.

He told me before he left on his trip that he wanted to have his bar mitzvah in Jerusalem at the beginning of 1996 at the same time as his cousin Ben. Ben would be the traditional age of thirteen and although Joshua was nearly seven years older he was determined to experience the ritual too.

So here we were some eighteen months later in Jerusalem completing Joshua's dream. He'd had a traditional ceremony conducted by a rabbi friend of my brother-in-law's in front of the Wall. We'd managed to gather together the ten men necessary for Jewish ceremonies, and alongside many other boys of different nationalities Joshua celebrated his entering manhood. As mere women we were only permitted to watch from beyond the perimeters of the men's prayer area. After they'd finished the prayers we were allowed to throw sweets and make traditional Middle Eastern whoops of joy as Joshua was carried around on the men's shoulders. I was delighted for him and my mother was beside herself with pride.

We spent the afternoon celebrating in a Roman-style restaurant deep in the wall of the Old City and for the first time it really came home to me how Joshua's enthusiasm had brought me back to my roots. I recognised the magic of the city, the traditions and the mystery combined with the fear and the politics.

I talked to friends and discovered that the woman's role in traditional Jewry had not changed for thousands of years. I heard how the sister of one friend had run away from her bullying husband taking her small child out of Israel. He had applied to the rabbinical court to get the child back and under their laws my friends elderly parents were being threatened with arrest unless they appeared in court to disclose her whereabouts. Israel's secular and religious laws were the same as those in many of the Muslim countries: people's fate was being decided by archaic rules that had nothing to do with the twentieth century.

I met a liberal rabbi who had a vision of a multi-faith Jerusalem where Judaism, Islam and Christianity could co-exist happily and be a beacon of light to the rest of the world. I met women performance artists who were exploring the lives of the heroines of the Bible and the Torah through theatre ritual and I had conversations with lawyers who were working for a change in the law on women's rights. I heard of joint initiatives that gave hope for a peaceful future between Jews and Arabs, like the women-run children's nurseries and battered wives' homes. I met creative visionary women and men who saw that through finding inner peace they could work towards real peace for the Middle East.

But I also saw the anger, the fear, the young, inexperienced soldiers with guns and tanks, the burnt-out bombed buses, and realised that potentially this bustling city was a time bomb which could explode at any moment.

Joshua wanted to show Jessica and me the En Gedi kibbutz

where he had lived and we decided to take a few days off from the intensity of Jerusalem to visit the Dead Sea. It was unlike anywhere I'd been before. The crystalline air gave an unreal, almost mystical look to the stillness of the pale blue sea and the surrounding countryside. Everything seemed to be in hues of pink, blue and white and the unspoiled terrain must have looked much as it had done during the days of the Bible.

We visited the ruined mountain city of Masada. Joshua told us the story of how a tribe of Zealots had defended their freedom against the Romans in the one-time summer palace of King Herod. They had held out for four years before being surrounded by the Roman army. At that point the Zealot leader persuaded the 960-strong garrison to kill themselves and their families to avoid capture. When I closed my eyes it was as if I could hear the sounds of the men, women and children who had lived in that isolated community until the final sad end. We saw their water reservoir, ritual baths, watchtowers and living quarters, as well as the remains of Herod's elaborate mosaics, and imagined what it would be like to be trapped there without hope. We saw the caves where the Dead Sea Scrolls had been found, thus casting new light on the history, literature and religion of the time of Jesus, as well as on the nature and beliefs of the Essenes, a Jewish pacifist, pre-Christian mystical movement.

The mysticism of the Jews fascinates me. According to traditional Jewish law, the kabbalah, the source of its secrets, is forbidden to women and may be read only by men over forty. Yet the kabbalah itself, I was told by a learned rabbi, states that the Messiah will return only when female energy is back to its full universal strength. In the kabbalah, God is separated into ten elements, balanced between male and female energies, the most famous of the latter being Shekhinah. The female element is the receptive, co-operative, contemplative, nurturing energy and the male is aggressive, reactive, imminent energy.

In order to empower women in Judaism, radical feminists have been calling for the reconstruction and recreation of a tradition which would include Shekhinah as the female divine energy. My worry is that the traditional concept of Shekhinah as a merciful mother, obedient wife and dutiful daughter is limiting. Besides, many Orthodox women happily accept their conservative role in Judaism and have no wish for a female God.

Interestingly, pictures of Shekhinah holding Moses in her arms have been found in ancient synagogues and there is evidence that many female rituals, including the new moon ritual of Rosh Hodesh, were widely recognised. Even as late as the sixth century there is evidence that women worshipped the cult of the Mother Goddess in Jerusalem.

However, as Christianity grew, Judaism was forced to redefine itself and it did so by reverting to Orthodox scriptural teachings and presenting Judaism as a strict monotheistic religion where there was no concept of a female God. This greatly strengthened the position of rabbis in Jewish life – men of power and knowledge, charismatic leaders and experts in the Torah who founded their tradition on the ancient books. Judaism therefore became entirely scripture-based and anything other than the male, all-powerful God interpretation of the deity was viewed as heretical. It appears that in order to create a social organisation scholars and rabbis banished all references to Goddess worship, so that in effect the Bible was used by men as an ideological device to restrain women and safeguard the ideology of the monotheistic God as the great father.

In its own way the Christian Church also redefined the female role both as woman and Goddess. The role of Mary is of crucial importance in the story of Jesus and yet the Holy Trinity is of course the Father, the Son and the Holy Ghost. I believe that Mary was originally the third entity and that her story, together with that of Mary Magdalene, was completely rewritten several hundred years after they died. Many books have been written about the events two thousand years ago which differ from those in the Bible and Jesus himself taught the equality of men and women. The image of Mary often appears as a representative of the eternal mother in places where earlier Goddess-based religions worshipped. In *The Chalice and the Blade*, Eisler refers to Jesus's positive attitude to women.

I returned to Jerusalem determined to stay connected with the land of my genetic roots and be part of the feminine energy bubbling under the surface which I was sure could bring a positive future to this unsettled part of the world.

My rediscovery of Judaism was by no means over. When I got back to London almost immediately I was contacted by an extra-ordinary character called Shmuel Boteach. His assistant told me on the telephone that he was an American rabbi who was the director of the Oxford University and London L'Chaim Societies. She seemed surprised I hadn't heard of him and said they had organised a series of high-profile debates with speakers including former President Reagan, Gorbachev and several others. She told me they were planning to hold a London debate on whether women are discriminated against in Judaism. Yet again I marvelled at the timing of this call, having just seen for myself what was going on in Israel.

The extremely hyper Rabbi Shmuel Boteach arrived at my flat some days later armed with a variety of books I'd asked for on the Jewish law regarding women. He presented me with a copy of his own most recent book – *The Jewish Guide to Adultery* – the content of which he explained was the complete opposite of the title.

His personal story had been made into a major BBC TV special. He came from an excitable large American Jewish family and his parents had divorced when he was eleven. Determined that this would never happen to him, he turned to the ultra-conservative Jewish religious organisation, the Lubavitch, for succour and spiritual sustenance. By his early teens he had become a follower of their extreme views and started to study every aspect of Jewish law, first in the States and then in Israel. While working in Australia in his early twenties he met and married his sweet-tempered wife Debbie who, although only nineteen, was committed to the same life of Jewish service as him. She sees her life's work as supporting her husband in every way and has happily taken on the role of bearing endless children, running two large households and cooking delicious Friday night meals, sometimes for up to a hundred people.

Shmueli saw his mission as bringing the traditions of Jewish life into the heart of British academia by starting the L'Chaim Society, often confused by speakers with Oxford Union's famous debating society. Thrown out of the Lubavitch for being too controversial, Shmuel had definitely caused ripples in British Jewish society. His constant self-promotion and partiality for malt whisky had got him some negative write-ups in the Jewish press, but nevertheless he had strong supporters in the community who helped finance his dream.

Shmueli loves to name-drop and at our first meeting told me he was working on a film with Barbra Streisand and had a long session teaching Judaism to Erica Jong. I took his stories with a pinch of salt but liked the man enormously. His warm, infectious enthusiasm, his obvious sincerity and ability to laugh at himself won me over and I agreed to speak in his debate as the voice of Jewish feminism.

It was fascinating to read the material that Shmueli had left me. I found that a man was answerable by law to sexually satisfy his wife but he was not allowed to sleep with her for seven days after she bled, either as a virgin on the marriage night or after menstruation. The Jews are fastidious about health and cleanliness, hence the dietary laws regarding pork and shellfish, which tend to go off in hot climates; however, the attitude towards menstruation hasn't changed today and Jewish men still consider women to be unclean during and after bleeding. I remembered my own father living in a household of women and acting as if it was something dirty and not to be spoken of. I believe menstruation is a natural part of womanhood which should be celebrated.

I found out too that the first prayer a Jewish man makes every morning is to thank God that he was not born a woman. I read that under traditional laws women are not allowed to inherit their family wealth and, most worrying of all, I discovered the get.

A get has to be granted by a husband to his wife when she wants a divorce. Outside Israel she can of course obtain a civil divorce but will not be able to remarry in an Orthodox synagogue. I met some of the women in England who suffered from this law and heard story after story of how their husbands would not grant them a get for years until they were paid off by their former fathers-in-law or by the women themselves.

There had been enormous controversy about this law and promises from the rabbis that husbands who took this route would be shunned by the community. However, nothing had really changed and these women were adamant that they would not be forced to give up their Orthodox Jewish practice by their blackmailing former husbands.

Shmueli's debate took place in Regent's College and was a sellout. Chaim Bermant, a highly knowledgeable and witty columnist from the *Jewish Chronicle*, and I were to speak on the side of women who had been discriminated against. The other members of the panel taking the opposite position were Lady Jakobovits, the wife of the former Chief Rabbi, and Rabbi Shlomo Riskin, one of the stars of the American right-wing rabbinical scene. As always with Jews, there was a lot more talking and arguing on both sides of the panel as well as among the audience than we really had time for.

There was no question that my side had a clear victory. It was obvious that women had always been discriminated against in Judaism. I've heard Jewish men laughingly explain that their wives are already so strong that if they'd been allowed to study the law and pray alongside them they would have taken over completely.

We women are equally to blame since we have always given priority to the boy child. The old joke of 'my son the doctor' or 'my son the lawyer' never applied to the daughters and despite the many extraordinarily intelligent Jewish women academics and intellectuals over the centuries, education was always directed towards the men.

The Jews certainly have no monopoly of this attitude. Religions and races all over the world put the emphasis on the superiority of the boy child. But even if Orthodox Jewry is stuck in the dark ages, things are changing rapidly in the Reform and Liberal synagogues. The progressive Jewish renewal movement which started in the United States has brought many wider philosophies and practices together with Jewish traditions. Packed synagogues offer meditation and healing combined with joyful dancing and singing, all of which have encouraged young people back to Judaism in droves.

Here too women are playing a far greater role, with many female rabbis leading the way. I met Rabbi Shohama Wienen on a plane travelling back from an SVN conference from Colorado to New York. She told me she was the head of an academy which trained men and women rabbis and she herself practised healing and meditation. She had expected some hostile reaction when she first started teaching at seminars but had always got positive feedback.

While we were on the plane she started using a crystal pendulum to send absent healing to sick friends. I realised that women like her could really start changing the face of traditional Jewry. In the UK too we now have a handful of women rabbis.

After the Regent's College debate I started being asked to speak by other Jewish organisations, interviewed for Jewish publications and generally felt as if I was being reclaimed. But I knew that supportive as I felt of this movement for change and despite still being interested in discovering more about the mysticism of Judaism, I had to continue on a broader path to find the answers I was looking for. I am a Jewish woman who celebrates my heritage but I see that until we can break through our fears based on the beliefs of the last two thousand years and feel the power of Shekhinah's energy rising we will be stuck in the old ways.

Rules and traditions endorsed by patriarchal religious organisations are holding people back from moving into a balanced, progressive society. Women should be able to embrace their birthright alongside men but in a position of full partnership and respect.

Women and men together should ensure that never again will wars of violence occur in the name of religion and that we can use our spiritual beliefs to inspire us to a life of peaceful co-existence with our neighbours.

Following the Path of the Shakti

Yet again I found myself under the full moon at a sacred place in a far-away country, honouring the Goddess. I was meditating on the top of a holy mountain in Rajasthan together with two hundred other women of all ages and nationalities watching the sun disappear into a glorious sunset over the India-Pakistan border.

It was the night of the March full moon, the Hindu holiday of Holi when the legend of good conquering over evil is celebrated by adults and children alike throwing coloured paints over each other's clothes and hair in a wild frenzy.

Later that evening I experienced tremendous feelings of freedom and liberation and celebrated with the young Indian sisters. I spun around faster and faster in my dance, with my vivid green and orange traditional pleated skirt swirling around me as I learnt the local Rajasthani steps from my laughing companions.

I was visiting the Brahma Kumaris Spiritual University in Mount Abu for their conference on the Four Faces of Women and together with the other delegates from all over the world spent the early part of the evening of Holi in silent praise and acknowledgement of the beauty of Mother Earth and the divine energy that surrounds her.

Eagles soared below us as I stood up to leave and the full moon was shining high in the dark blue sky as the last of the sun's rays set in the west.

'Let's go before the locals start throwing the coloured paint,' urged Shelley, the wholesome English girl dressed in a traditional white sari who'd been told to look after me. As we made our way down from the mountain peak and walked round the vast still lake that made this small town of Mount Abu unique, I looked back on the last few days and realised how much I'd changed.

I'd met the Brahma Kumaris some months before through Eleanor Dettinger on the island of Iona and although I found them rather strange at first, I grew to trust and love their gentle manner and dedication to service. Some months later I'd sat next to Sister Jayanti, the European director of the Brahma Kumaris, at the Council of Wise Women's annual lunch. The radiant smile of this friendly Indian woman in her white sari seemed to strike me right in my heart. She explained that her London centre was in north-west London, not far from where I lived, and she invited me to visit her there and meet Dadi Janki, their senior administrative head.

A couple of weeks later, I took her up on her offer. I went over to Willesden and met the tiny eighty-two-year-old Dadi Janki. Although totally uneducated, the vast intellect of this woman held me spellbound. She spoke in Hindi, communicating through a translator, yet I felt the intensity of her words. She told me of the importance of connecting with God, and then added, 'A life based on service can bring great benefits and happiness.' I left feeling that this was the start of a new friendship with both her and Sister Jayanti and I felt keen to know them both better. Shortly after this I received an invitation from the Brahma Kumaris to attend a women's conference at their Indian headquarters at the top of Mount Abu in Rajasthan the following March. I knew I had to go.

Despite being a women-led spiritual organisation, they'd never held an event exclusively for women before. They usually hosted inter-national conferences where they'd regularly invite world leaders, academics and businesspeople of both sexes.

I travelled with some of the British and Canadian delegates accompanied by some helpful Brahma Kumaris (BKs) on a nightmare journey which involved us almost missing our plane in Delhi when the taxi took us to the wrong terminal, getting screamed at by harassed airline officials, having to make several airline stops and changes, luggage getting lost, long delays and what seemed like an endless and exhausting coach ride to our final destination. We were frazzled and wrung out but Shelley and the other BKs managed to keep calm and affable throughout.

We were greeted with cool drinks and flowers when we finally arrived at the Brahma Kumaris' World Spiritual University – a series of buildings set in a well-designed compound sympathetic with the beautiful nature surround it. There were fairy lights and neons everywhere, plus an artificial rockery with a fountain on top. We were allocated our rooms and I was relieved to see I had my own Western-style bathroom and no room-mate. What bliss!

As I slowly got my bearings and looked around the complex I discovered some beautiful small meditation domes and little eco-buildings as well as several large imposing halls, all with translation facilities for almost any language. The centre was looked after by Brahma Kumaris brothers and sisters who came from all over India to clean and cook for us, performing their duties with love and gentleness. I found so much to learn from these quietly impressive people, particularly their commitment to service.

After a few days I started meditating with them in the morning and was able once again to connect with that place of silence and peace deep inside myself. Wearing my locally bought thin white cotton clothes, I felt cleaner and clearer than I ever had before.

We were invited to join one of the Indian morning ceremonies. I saw the community receive guidance from their leaders and all of us were given sweetmeats and presents. Then two young Rajasthani girls, dressed in ornate traditional white, silver and gold outfits and looking like two beautiful Indian dolls, danced for us – and all before breakfast. I noticed an enormous difference between this conference and the UN women's conference in Beijing. Here in India it was about connecting with the feminine and finding the Shakti, or Goddess within.

The Brahma Kumaris had been founded some sixty years before by Dada Lekhraj, a successful diamond merchant from the Sindi community in what is now Pakistan. After spending his life building up his business, he lost interest in commercial activities and started to spend an increasing amount of time in deep contemplation. Then after a number of profound visionary experiences, he saw the world going through a traumatic change but one which would ultimately lead to a much more peaceful way of life. He also saw a time when it would be necessary for a women-led organisation to help bring spiritual values into the world.

At that time women in India and Pakistan were treated with even less respect than they are today. They were considered possessions of their fathers and husbands with no free will of their own. By teaching the young women in his community about the power of the feminine and of a different way of life he encouraged many to leave their families to set up a new self-sufficient community based on the principles of love and service. Some men and children came too, and for fourteen years the founding group of three hundred lived in celibate isolation spending their time in intense spiritual study, meditation and self-transformation.

Dada Lekhraj was not very popular with his former community for encouraging the young women's independence and in 1951 the group moved to an ashram at the peak of one of India's most holy mountains, Mount Abu. Bap Dada, as he was now known by his followers, continued to develop the group's philosophy and belief structure, giving daily guidance until he finally left his body at the age of ninety.

The two administrative heads of the organisation – Dadi Prakashmani in India and Dadi Janki based in London – are now in their eighties but were just young girls when they became founder members of the group. They are from peasant backgrounds and never received any education but have two of the smartest and most active intellects I've come across. There are 3,500 Brahma Kumaris centres throughout the world in sixty-five countries. They do not expect their dedicated lifestyle of abstinence and sacrifice to appeal to everybody but are willing to support and work with many people who are like-minded in their dedication to creating a better world.

What I found particularly inspiring was that although the Brahma Kumaris women are quietly spoken and feminine, they effectively and efficiently run the equivalent of a major multinational company. The men too are unique. They are certainly no wimps but are gentle and strong at the same time. They are comfortable and balanced in both their male and female energy and don't feel threatened by the women.

Their celibacy doesn't make them any less loving and affectionate but does give them the energy to handle the tremendous workload they all seem to take on. They are up by 3.30 a.m. every morning in time to meditate by four and come together again by 6.30 for their morning classes and meditation. They often work for several more hours on Brahma Kumaris activities before going off to do a full day's work in a normal job.

They live as brothers and sisters in the way that historians claim Jesus commanded within the early apostolic communities. He taught them to practice *agape*, or brotherly and sisterly love, just as Baba taught the BKs. They believe that physical relationships detract from their focus of service, which is crucial for this lifetime at least.

Brahma Kumaris are especially active in the areas of education, prison reform, health and peace initiatives. They are associate members of the UN and received a UN peace award for their role as principle co-ordinators of the Million Minutes of Peace during the 1986 International Year of Peace. In 1988 they launched their 'Global Co-Operation for a Better World' initiative from the British Houses of Parliament seeking to increase co-operation and understanding between nations, communities and people. They have a presence at many of the international UN conferences but also work with individuals who are going through pain and unhappiness, helping them attain a more balanced life.

The conference I attended in spring 1996 with two hundred other women delegates was organised as a dialogue on the four different faces of women – modern woman, traditional woman, eternal woman and Shakti woman (or woman in her divine power). Each section was started off by a masked dancer representing the imagery of each type of woman. The modern woman, in a shirt and tie, combined holding a baby with working on a telephone and computer, looking harassed. Traditional woman, in the beautiful colours of the local Rajasthani peasant clothes, made her own bread and looked after her family, eternal woman acknowledged her strength, and finally the Shakti woman took off her mask to expose the Goddess within.

After the dance we would stay in the auditorium while a small group would have a dialogue on the stage discussing what the theme meant to them. I was one of the platform speakers for eternal woman and discussed how we were remembering our feminine strengths and wisdom from a time when women were in true partnership with men.

I spoke together with an Aboriginal spiritual leader, a nun and a Russian professor from Moscow University, who specialised in gender issues. We were then randomly allocated to smaller groups, all with Goddess names, where we could discuss the various aspects of ourselves and how we could integrate them into today's society. I spoke with women of all ages from all over the world and we learnt much from each other despite our cultural differences.

I connected deeply with a women's activist from Brazil, a tribal leader from South Africa, educationalists from Canada and San Francisco, a politician from Mauritius and businesswomen from Singapore and Sweden. We started a dialogue on how we could keep our connections, creating some form of network to exchange information and support each other's projects.

Sister Jayanti told us that they had been inspired to hold this conference by their disappointment at the women's conference in

Beijing. It had been run on typical conference lines with all of us bustling around in our masculine energy.

I was already working on the development of What Women Want as a global infrastructure. I left India with a far clearer idea of my direction and a new group of friends and associates to work with.

When I came back to London I started meeting every morning with Sister Maureen at the Brahma Kumaris centre in Willesden just ten minutes from where I lived. Maureen Goodman is a lively young woman of Jewish descent with whom I formed a close friendship. She coached me on the history of the Brahma Kumaris and their belief system, and gave me some good objective personal advice. Later I gained great spiritual sustenance by going to their centre at 6 a.m. every day to meditate and listen to their morning teachings. The stress of London life seemed to just fall away and I didn't need anything else to sustain me. I started eating healthy food and went to bed earlier every night. I didn't get strung out or tired as much and life seemed calmer and more pleasant in every way.

However, I did find some of their teachings difficult to reconcile with my own belief system. They teach that the planet and human race is on a constant five-thousand-year cycle that goes from a time of peace, love and harmony through to chaos, anarchy and back again. Although I do agree that we are in a time of chaos and anarchy and would love to think we're going into a golden age, sadly my logical, rational self just can't accept the eternal repetitive cycle. Of course a lot of Eastern spirituality is metaphorical and I believe we Westerners can still learn much wisdom from it. The Brahma Kumaris are sincere, pure souls who have shown me and many other people nothing but love and friendship.

Following their example I decided to stop drinking alcohol and smoking marijuana – although I would never criticise anyone for doing either. I felt it was blocking me from both physical health and spiritual clarity. I was also guided by Dadi Janki to refrain from relationships for a while and decided to try a period of celibacy. It was such a relief and made me feel focused and relaxed. All these things combined to create a deep fundamental shift that was noticeable, according to my family and friends. Perhaps with the support of these wonderful people I'd put Edina Monsoon behind me once and for all.

I believe that I met them at the right time in my journey. I knew that living the life of a Hindu nun was not appropriate for me in the long term but their friendship and guidance gave me an opportunity to clean up a lot of the bad patterns that still stayed with me.

Another female spiritual leader I wanted to visit was Mother Meera, a young Indian woman considered by many as an avatar, or enlightened being, who lived in the middle of Germany.

Like many people worldwide I'd found out about her through reading Andrew Harvey's book *The Hidden Journey*. I knew he had now renounced her because she'd refused to bless his 'marriage' to a male photographer called Eryk Hanut, accusing her of being homophobic, but I wanted to see her for myself. Many of my friends had visited her and had interesting experiences. Photographs of Mother Meera always showed her intense eyes almost piercing through you off the page and I couldn't wait to find out what she was like in real life.

I'd been invited to visit her several years before by Marianne Williamson, the American teacher and writer I'd met when helping to promote her book, *A Woman's Worth*. Marianne too was a woman who embraced the Goddess within and her book had inspired me so much that I'd given it to many of my women friends. Visiting one Shakti woman accompanied by another was obviously something I wasn't ready for then and I found myself unable to go.

Perhaps it had not been the right time before but I decided to take my daughter Jessie with me just before my forty-eighth birthday. On some intuitive level I'd known since my forty-fourth birthday that the following four years would bring about a tremendous shift in my life. Looking back I could see an almost 180 degree change and felt that visiting Mother Meera at this time would signify some form of completion.

We left Deia where we were spending Easter and flew direct to Frankfurt airport from Palma. Germany had never been a favourite place of mine to visit as I always felt a very uncomfortable energy there. This was apparently the reason why Mother Meera had settled there too, intent on shifting what she considered had been the spiritual damage done to the country during the horrors of the last war. We took a train and cab journey to the local pub where we were staying, in a tiny hamlet in the middle of a forest. We dropped off our bags and took the cab on to a car park in the nearby town of Dornburg-Thalheim where all Mother Meera's visitors were asked to meet.

Mother Meera was born in southern India in 1960 and from as young as three found she was able to go into the state of *samadhi* – a form of meditative trance. At six she fell senseless for a whole day, an experience which she later said taught her complete detachment from human relations. While still a child she came under the protection of a distant relative, Mr Reddy, who recognised her divine powers as the Mother energy. Her reputation quickly spread and soon people from all over India were coming to her for help. When she was nineteen she started visiting devotees in other parts of the world and in the early eighties when Mr Reddy suffered kidney failure in Germany she decided to settle there with him, looking after him until he passed away. She bought a modest house in the quiet village of Thalheim where she lives and works in order to show people 'that the transformation is normal, can be done anywhere and in daily life'.

We were greeted by a serious, tall, thin German man who explained that we were all to walk in a column quietly through the streets and queue up when we got to the door of Mother Meera's simple suburban house. You had to let them know before you came and when our names had been checked off a list we were allowed inside. We saw lots of chairs packed into a very small space and quickly went and sat on two of them at the back of the room. In about half an hour the room, corridor and staircase were jam-packed with a couple of hundred people. We then had to sit quietly until Mother Meera appeared.

We found a piece of paper on our chair telling us not to move or make any sound and we sat in the increasingly oppressive space waiting for *darshan*. *Darshan* is Sanskrit for seeing and is used in Hindi in the context of seeing a master. This was a one-to-one experience where we would individually kneel and bow before Mother Meera. She would place her hands on our head for a few seconds. Once she'd lifted them we were to raise our head and hold eye contact with her until she nodded to indicate that our time was up.

Eventually a tiny young Indian woman in a pretty multi-coloured floral sari stepped gracefully into the room with her eyes downcast. You could feel an energy shift sweep through the audience.

There was no order as to when we went up: we made our way to the front when it felt right inside. I'd been told that when she placed her hands on our heads she unblocked stuck spiritual energy and connected us through her eye contact with the energy of the divine.

It certainly was an extraordinary experience. I didn't hear any voices inside my head or have any physical reactions as so many had reported but I felt lighter and very peaceful. Looking into her eyes was like looking into the eternity of life itself. I saw no guile or agenda, just an out-of-world clarity that seemed to sweep through my body.

Jessie too had an intense experience and we left the physical discomfort of the close little room on the first night spaced out and strange. I felt Mother Meera could be an enlightened human being but that our own expectations and projections can create much of what we experience.

Jessie and I were allowed back for three more sessions as first-time pilgrims and had many magical experiences over the next few days. We'd walked in the forest every day watching the leaves dance around us, following the butterflies to the beds of wild flowers where we lay in the afternoon sun. We became closer than ever and exchanged details of our vivid dreams. We climbed a hill to a local sacred chapel and meditated at the font made from a dramatic black meteorite. I noticed that my fingers tingled and swelled after seeing Mother Meera and a definite feeling of energy seemed to move up my spine. We continued to experience the physical discomfort of the three hours we sat still in order to receive *darshan* and, like everybody there, fell in love with the purity that Mother Meera emanated.

The area that most concerned me was the rather sinister group of young German men who surrounded her: though polite, they seemed cold. I was also uncomfortable with the obvious adoration felt by so many of her visitors. I watched as devotees genuflected by her chair after she left the room or just sat there breathing in her energy long after her physical presence had gone.

I liked Mother Meera and am delighted to hear that she's building a far bigger ashram in the area for the visitors. However, the time for putting gurus – whether women or men – on pedestals, for relying on them totally, is past. I accept she could be a manifestation of the Mother energy in human form and am happy to receive whatever gifts she can give me. But I agree with writer Andrew Harvey: it is up to each of us to empower ourselves and each other.

Visiting Mother Meera was a profound experience. As Jessica and I left our hotel on the last morning at 6 a.m., a rainbow appeared behind us. It was full of more prisms of colour than I'd ever seen and stayed for the full hour behind our cab as we drove to Frankfurt airport.

Some weeks later back in London I was driving back from my morning's meditations with the Brahma Kumaris listening to Radio 4 when I heard on the *Today* programme of a new coalition for peace in Northern Ireland organised by women from all religious, social and professional backgrounds. The initiative seemed to fit in with an idea I had for organising a What Women Want peace concert in Ireland and I determined to get in touch with them.

By another extraordinary example of synergy I found a message from them when I got back home asking me to contact them to see if we could work together.

Several weeks later I was due to go to Dublin to do a talk on ethical marketing from a futurist perspective as well as a public lecture on my journey and What Women Want. I arranged to meet the Northern Ireland Women's Peace Coalition while I was there.

I started the weekend off with my talk to the Irish Marketing Society. I met many of the guests before dinner and they all seemed a friendly, open lot. But the evening was a long, protracted affair, a large amount of alcohol was consumed and by the time I got up to speak they just wanted to be entertained by Edina from *Ab Fab* and seemed confused by my sober, earnest approach.

Absolutely Fabulous seemed to follow me round as the weekend progressed. Some Irish newspaper articles had come out announcing my visit and of course drawing on the *Ab Fab* connection – not, I suspected, that most people needed reminding.

I went to stay in the country at the beautiful home of the hospitable U2 manager, Paul McGuinness, and his independently successful wife Kathy Gilfillan. I accompanied them to a hysterical dinner party at Desmond Guinness's crumbling but splendid mansion where again I was quizzed about the TV programme. The whole situation started feeling like an episode out of *Ab Fab* when I bumped into my close buddy Ruby Wax, who was also up for the weekend. She was accompanied by her friend Carrie Fisher, who was due to play one of the lead parts in Roseanne Barr's American version of *Ab Fab* until it was judged to be too outrageous for the American networks.

'Small world,' I said as Ruby dragged me through to her bedroom to fill me in on all the goings-on between the large crowd of Guinnesses present and the other famous guests. I sat next to Mick Jagger and opposite Paul McGuinness as they discussed the economics of large stadium rock shows and watched Van Morrison sink smaller and smaller under his big Stetson as his girlfriend Michelle Rocca made some loud personal remarks. Marianne Faithfull, who I'd long been a fan of, told me that it was the first time she and Mick Jagger had been in this house together since they were in their late teens, and I renewed my acquaintance with Rolling Stone Ronnie Wood, whose PR I'd once done, and his bubbly wife Jo. J. P. Donleavy talked to me endlessly about indoor tennis, and a gaggle of gorgeous teenage Guinnesses and their friends danced around the tables after dinner.

The Guinnesses, very much like the royal family of Ireland, are extremely hospitable, lovely people and I'm not surprised that friends fly in from all over the world for one of Desmond and his wife Penny's famous dinner parties. I really did feel I was on the set of a TV show with me as the only sober member of the cast – ironic, given my reputation in Ireland as the continually stoned Edina.

The next day Paul McGuinness and I went to another wonderful lunch party with the same crowd and on the way back stopped by a bizarre sign stating in bold letters YOUR LIFE WILL CHANGE HERE. It turned out to be the opening day of a cosmic theme park founded by an eccentric Irishman who'd been a monk in India for the last twenty years.

'I want to bring Hindu mythology here and mix it with Celtic legend,' he told me enthusiastically as he showed us round in the pouring rain. Enormous statues of Shiva and Ganesh, the elephant god, made out of black alabaster had already arrived and had been set up in a damp Irish field. He showed us his plans for importing many more giant-sized Hindu statues, and some of the little jokes he had made, like the computer disc subtly carved on the back of Shiva. Paul and I were highly curious as to where the finance came from but he kept changing the subject or quietly chanting 'EU, EU'. Of course he might have been telling us the truth – everything in Ireland seems to be financed by the European Union.

The whole episode seemed to bring together my love for India and its Hindu traditions with the closeness I felt for Ireland and its Celtic history. It was all a message from the universe but I couldn't yet work out what it was supposed to mean.

The next day I went back to Dublin – an exciting, bubbly Eurocity – to give a public talk to a crowd of some eighty professional women, many from the world of marketing. I told them the importance of having quality time for themselves as well as their family and work. I also said I felt it was time for women to take their power and create a new style of business – the feminine way. 'It is time to bring values into the workplace, working in a non-hierarchical structure. It is time for dialogue – listening as well as speaking – throughout corporations as well as families and it is time for a more nurturing holistic approach to the art of making money. It is time for partnership between businesses, their staff and their market and a way of working together which will create satisfaction and well-being for all as well as a healthy profit.'

A group from the Northern Ireland Women's Peace Coalition had come to hear me talk. They were to stay on for a meeting with members of the Irish Republic women's movement. The women from Belfast were a mixture of academics, housewives, social workers and businesswomen between the ages of the late twenties to mid-sixties.

They explained that they believed the only way forward was through conciliation and communication and that most of the women in Northern Ireland were committed to peace, regardless of their religion. They told me how they had initially financed the launch of the movement through their own credit cards and about the tremendous support they'd had from other women. They told me that of the thirty-one people sitting round the table at the Northern Ireland peace talks, only three were women. They were hoping to increase this to five at the forthcoming elections.

I was astonished that this ridiculous disparity between men and women which disqualified women from debating their and their families' future had not been more widely publicised. I pledged my support and we talked about creating an event in Ireland to show that women of all backgrounds and religions could work together in a positive way without conflict.

I went back to London inspired that there were women in the world working together, committed to making changes and creating peace. I just hoped they would be given enough support and resources to make a real difference. I thought how the Northern Ireland Women's Peace Coalition, like the Brahma Kumaris, were working together without egos and hierarchy and with the same aim of creating a peaceful future from dialogue and not conflict.

The old patriarchal ways of confrontation and aggression had to change and women and men had to work together for world peace regardless of race, religion and geographical boundaries.

Women will only be ready to take their place alongside men and show them the new ways when we connect with the Shakti woman inside. We have to be in our power knowing that we can make changes through conciliation and love.

13

Searching for a Sustainable Future

Another city – another adventure – another full moon, this time shining down on the Bosporus. I was sitting at a large table in a delicious fish restaurant on the European side of the exotic city of Istanbul, having dinner with a noisy group of old and new friends. We were full of constructive ideas on how we could work together in the future and busy exchanging information we'd learnt over the last few days.

I was here for HABITAT – one of the UN's major themed conferences of the nineties – to discuss the crisis of the world's rapidly growing cities and how to create sustainable 'shelter' for the ever increasing global population.

Unlike the organisers of the Beijing women's conference, the secretary-general of HABITAT, Doctor Wally N'Dow, considers spiritual values an essential part of visionary thinking and he had brought together a unique group of principal players from the worlds of business, ecology, politics, finance, city planning and community, as well as visionaries and spiritual leaders to discuss how to work together for a positive future.

Marcello Palazzi, a friend and associate from Social Venture Network, had invited me to speak at the World Business Forum, a conference within a conference looking at 'Enterprise, the City and Sustainable Development'. My area of expertise was information and media and I was chairing a panel of experts from media and technology, among them John Bird, managing director of the *Big Issue*.

John told the audience the story behind the success of his magazine. He'd set up the *Big Issue* with his old friend, Gordon Roddick of The Body Shop, some five years earlier as a way for the homeless to have an income: by selling it directly on the streets and keeping the profits to survive on. The magazine. which has a high editorial standard, had done increasingly well and by the summer of 1996 editions were being produced in Australia, South Africa, Scotland and Ireland, with New York to come.

John told us: 'We sell 300,000 copies fortnightly in the UK and are the only genuine British-based media organisation other than the BBC. We've got two hundred people in offices across the country and have five thousand homeless or vulnerably housed people selling the magazine on the streets.'

He added: 'All our profits go into a foundation that finances housing and health care for the homeless as well as training and education. We've got our own film and video unit and from our offices administer the International Network of Street Papers funded by EU money to look after thirty-two street newspapers and magazines across Europe.'

John and I had become friends during What Women Want, which he'd supported by turning an edition of the *Big Issue* into the official programme, and I'd come to respect his views. He is a Napoleon look-alike with an abrasive 'man of the streets' manner. But I soon found out he was a real softie underneath, with a keen intellect and compassionate heart.

Also on the panel with us was Nicholas You, a member of the UN Secretariat for HABITAT. He told us about the Best Practices initiative he had been working on which gathers information and monitors success stories of sustainable urbanisation from across the world.

'We need to hear more good news about what's happening,'

he said and told us how the Best Practices campaign was going out over the Internet and on a CD-ROM. We talked with the other delegates about how to change public awareness in more innovative ways, and Nicholas You told us how he had put simple, green messages on all the commercially rented videos in Sri Lanka when he was posted there.

He told us about a neighbourhood partnership programme in Poland – a community-based development where residents work together with city planners to improve the urban environment of their neighbourhood; about a new sanitation scheme in Senegal where the traditional horse-and-cart system has been adopted to clean up a serious refuse problem which was affecting the health of the city; and how women in Brazil are being trained to build their own homes, supported by local government to buy land and building materials, and create an infrastructure.

We heard from other technology experts about the innovative ways they were using computers to visualise the future, so they could not only plan sustainable cities and towns but could actually, through virtual reality, 'experience' what it's like to live in them. We were also told about systems accommodating data input on all areas of urban planning, including sewage and waste disposal, recycling, population densities, fuel consumption, transportation and electricity which could be available on-line anywhere in the world.

Technology could also map out potential draining and pollution of a city's natural environment and, most extraordinarily of all, it could use declassified images from satellites belonging to the US and Russian intelligence agencies, as well as more peaceful observation sources, to help get a real picture of what's happening in the world. About time all that expensive information was being used for positive ends!

In between learning about the different potential aspects of our future – some positive but some very worrying – I visited as much of the city as I could fit into my busy schedule. HABITAT had chosen the perfect venue. Istanbul has been the capital of three world empires and has thirty centuries of urban tradition. It is a melting pot of people from many ethnic backgrounds – Turks, Kurds, Greeks, Armenians, Jews, Levantines, Poles, Albanians and Bosnians – all living in this crowded city where East meets West.

Half in Asia and half in Europe, today Istanbul is a cultural and commercial centre and a focal point for the new nations of Eurasia. The combination of the ornate palaces with their elaborate, now empty, harems, the huge domed mosques and the famous covered bazaars packed full of enticing Turkish jewellery and ceramics make it one of the most fascinating cities I've ever visited.

But Istanbul, like many of the cities of the world, has its problems too. Refugees in shanty towns have swelled the population to a point where the infrastructure, such as sanitation and transport, just cannot cope and precarious high-rise buildings are being constructed illegally to cater for the influx of new communities.

Back at HABITAT we were told that over the next few years refugees from war zones and poverty-stricken rural areas will be flooding into many of the world's major cities. By the year 2000 the world will for the first time become predominantly urban and by the year 2030 the numbers living in urban areas will be double those in rural areas.

The irony is that in the more affluent countries, the middle classes will be able to choose where they live and work because of the new technology and many will move to safer, healthier areas in the countryside.

But it will be in urban areas where most of the world's population will live and work, where most economic activity will take place, where the greatest pollution will be generated and where most natural resources will be consumed. In fact the conference felt that the urban agenda will be the most pressing challenge facing humanity in the next century. We also discussed the large divide of wealth and poverty between the northern and southern hemispheres. We were told of the evidence that at least 600 million people, mostly in developing countries, live in squalid and life-threatening conditions; at least

250 million urban residents have no easy access to safe piped water and 400 million lack sanitation.

I felt overwhelmed by what I was hearing. Like others, I saw that the only way forward was for governments to create partnerships with businesses, NGOs, community groups and local authorities. Only through dialogue could we stop this downward spiral of so-called social progress.

As always at these conferences, the networking outside the meeting rooms over coffee, lunches and dinners proved as important as the official agenda. Marcello had managed to attract a good cross-section of business people from Europe, the States and Japan, together with community leaders and people from the worlds of technology and communication. I spoke to many of them about the role of women in business and community. I was concerned that there were no women's groups at the World Business Forum and decided to arrange a women's circle when we visited the Garden City, a new urban development outside Istanbul.

The Garden City, a bland, characterless modern development which our Turkish hosts believed was the answer to all big city problems, is situated an hour from the city. Residents could live, eat, work and be educated in this self-contained, ready-made community. It had obviously cost millions and they showed it to us with pride. The idea was you never had to leave the complex and for this reason alone it didn't surprise me at all to learn from a fellow delegate who was a Greek urban planner that in her experience this type of sterile environment was a breeding ground for suicide and depression.

I'd given out flyers earlier in the day at the Garden Centre asking women and men from the Forum to meet me during the afternoon to discuss the subject 'Women, Communication and Community'. I felt that a less rigid discussion, looking particularly at the problems facing women in the developing countries, would be a valuable addition to the schedule, and I was determined not to leave out men.

About twenty or so like-minded women and men as well as some of the dynamic young business students who were attending the conference gathered together. I started off with a few minutes' silence and an informal introduction session before we all expressed our views and visions of how women in the West could help their sisters from the Third World, many of whom were being exploited.

The men who turned up were very supportive and again I had the opportunity of being with people from other cultures and learning about their countries' problems and solutions. We determined to keep in touch and I added their names to my increasing global network of associates and friends.

The Brahma Kumaris had a strong presence at HABITAT and Dadi Janki was personally invited as one of the Vision Keepers, the senior spiritual statesmen and women who were asked to address the main assembly. I started off each morning by going to meditate with them at their small apartment, accompanied by Brian Bacon, an extraordinary visionary business consultant who was staying at my hotel.

I had met Brian recently in England and had been invited to introduce him at a Self-Managing Leadership conference held at the stately country retreat run by the Brahma Kumaris in Oxford later that summer. Together with his business partner, Frenchman Mark Fourcade, he had developed the SML training programme to provide a framework for personal strategic planning. 'It empowers the individual to realign with the changing environment and subsequently develop greater self-esteem and self-control in terms of new attitudes, style and behaviour,' he explained to me. 'It helps you clarify your personal purpose, values and vision and become a better leader.'

SML concentrates on personal responsibility and development, bringing spiritual values into the workplace. Brian's clarity, charisma and communication skills have taken SML into large organisations around the world and have helped many individuals. He spends his life constantly travelling from country to country, working as management consultant to many top multinationals, as well as fulfilling his other role as president of the progressive World Business Academy.

He was in Istanbul with Mark working with his associates from the International Labour Office in Geneva and the Danish Ministry of Social Affairs on planning a conference to create 'A New Partnership for Social Cohesion'. Like many of the delegates, they were developing the concept of business working in a socially responsible manner, using partnerships and networks to create a sustainable global society. The uniqueness of the Danes' initiative was to encourage governments everywhere to take on a completely new role, supporting business processes in a way that would effectively meet social challenges.

Over breakfasts, joint taxi rides and a dinner by the Bosporus on his birthday, I discussed with Brian the importance of sustainable women's enterprise in the developing countries and how, using our mutual contacts, we could take the training and educational aspects of What Women Want to a global level.

Brian also told me about his background in advertising and marketing. Like me, he'd had a very successful business while still in his early twenties. Then in his native Australia living a jet-set lifestyle, he'd realised he wasn't happy with this way of life. He decided to make a major change and give up all his material possessions to dedicate his life to service. His new goal was not based on financial success or personal power but on a genuine desire to contribute positively to a better world.

Another inspirational person I spent time with in Istanbul was Jane Nelson, there in her capacity as a director of the Prince of Wales Business Leaders Forum. Prince Charles had set up the Forum as an international extension of his effective Business in the Community organisation. The Forum is a network of international business leaders who work together recognising the long-term value of good corporate citizenship and sustainable development, particularly in developing and transitional economies. The Prince of Wales's business initiatives, both in the UK and internationally, have created many positive changes and his efforts have been vastly undervalued.

Jane is a dynamic young woman in her mid-thirties who left

the world of banking to enter the non-profit sector on half her former salary. Like Brian, she travels constantly, committed to bringing together the business world with the public sector and community. Her passion for her work and her clear and far-sighted vision have taken her into the forefront of a new global network that was being consolidated all over HABITAT. Working with multinationals, the World Bank, non-profit organisations and local governments, Jane played a central role in many of the meetings and we too committed ourselves to working together in the future.

HABITAT was a unique opportunity to meet women and men from all over the world who would inspire me and take me to the next stage of my journey. I gave and received business cards at a fast and furious pace and we all agreed our e-mail would ensure we kept in touch. Privately I determined that I'd better learn how to use mine when I got back.

Istanbul wasn't my only new discovery in the spring of '96. I was about to venture into Scandinavia for the first time to visit Sweden's phenomenally successful women's fair, Kvinnor Kan – Women Can – and look at post-Communist Central Europe at a Social Venture Network meeting in Prague.

When I got to Prague I could see how many habits had infiltrated from American capitalism just on my way from the rapidly expanding high-tech airport. Amongst the beautiful architecture of Wenceslas Square I saw four McDonald's, and nearby were huge advertising boards and tall factory chimneys, bellowing out environmentally unfriendly clouds of industrial smoke. The Czech Republic is the most polluted country in Europe and acid rain has devastated many of its forests, ancient statues and monuments.

Despite this, the beauty of Prague's squares, palaces, parks and statues, together with the fifties-style American jazz clubs and noisy 'dumpling' restaurants, has attracted an enormous influx of tourists since the fall of Communism. Music and art festivals seem to be on for much of the year and at any given time the natural population of 1.3 million residents is swollen to 5–11 million. The shops selling wooden puppets and traditional coloured glassware are constantly packed and it's difficult to get a room at either the bland international hotels or the local picturesque ones near the centre of the city.

Prague's two most famous sons, printed on all their tourist T-shirts, are melancholy writer, Franz Kafka, and Golem, the clay or wooden servant of local Jewish legend who ends up getting out of control. Their dark energy doesn't seem to curb the natural exuberance of the city.

Prague has the oldest active Jewish synagogue in Europe and the remains of a ghetto that goes back hundreds of years. In the synagogue I was in tears as the elderly woman tour guide told us that just a handful of the original Jews from the many thousands who'd passed through the Prague ghetto had survived and they were all now in their eighties.

I saw an exhibition of ghetto children's art which looked as if it had been done yesterday. There were the usual childish pictures of a house with a chimney, four windows and a front door, a mummy and daddy and the children standing outside. The only difference was that underneath each picture was the name and age of the child and the death camp they'd perished in.

Coming to Prague and seeing the tragic legacy of the Holocaust for myself brought it vividly to mind. We are so overwhelmed by today's problems that it's easy to forget the past. But we must remember, if only to ensure we don't make the same mistakes. I thought of more recent genocide in the name of religion and race – such as the horrors of Bosnia and Rwanda – and prayed that we humans could change from aggressive, warlike people to the nurturing, loving men and women we could learn to be.

The SVN spring conference was launched with a presentation by the American director of the Institute of East West Studies, Stephen Heintz. Although obviously sincere, he presented a paper in a disturbingly positive fashion talking up the so-called development of countries in Central and Eastern Europe. I was concerned that since free enterprise had arrived here, progress has been viewed in terms of a capitalist society where bigger is always best and profits are the priority, at any cost to people and the environment.

We heard more encouraging comments at a talk given to us by visionary statesman, Vaclav Havel, President of the Czech Republic. He told us that it was important for conscious business people to promote enterprises that set examples of the new way of doing business – the responsible way.

'When changing an economic system it's easy to forget man's natural relationship with the planet resources,' he told us. 'In my opinion, business cannot be reduced to mere egoism or monetary gain but must have close links with humanity and the existing natural order. Legislation must be smart enough in a changing monetary system to be immune to fraud. However, respect for the law cannot be ensured by the law itself but by climate and the extent to which moral values are taken seriously. It is a cultural and civil matter and is down to the behaviour of politicians, media and the educators.'

We were all enthralled by this charismatic former poet and playwright as he talked about the importance of spiritual consciousness and a redistribution and sharing of wealth. 'Solidarity works best at a local level,' he added. 'Businessmen should be putting up hospitals in their own cities instead of paying government taxes. It's by helping one person, one village, one community that we begin to change the world.'

This is what we'd come to the Czech Republic to hear, and as we stood up to give him a standing ovation I wondered if his visions were shared by his far more right-wing government. There are few statesmen with the wisdom and foresight of Vaclav Havel. Silently I sent him support and love for his courage and strength.

Certainly the demise of the USSR has resulted in an economic crisis as well as horrendous environmental damage which will take years to fully comprehend. However, if we in the West just implant the worst of our materialistic habits in this vulnerable area of the world we are going to cause more long-term destruction.

According to Hazel Henderson, the futurist economist, who

was also in Prague, the Russians and other former Communists had studied outdated Western textbooks about how free markets supposedly work but few had actually visited the West to see them in action. They didn't realise that twentieth-century capitalism had already 'evolved within a myriad of rules at local, state and national levels of government'.

With the amount of corruption, bribery and violence that is soaring in Eastern and Central Europe it seems obvious that the so-called freedom from Communism and advent of democracy has only brought chaos. I saw how far away spiritual values and a trusting society were from daily life here and felt again that positive change could be initiated by the women.

Sadly there seemed a lot of disillusionment amongst the women academics and activists from the different countries in Central Europe that I met at the conference. They told me that it was a real struggle to find support for the women's movement and that many women just wanted an easier life. Under the Communist regime they'd been required to work as hard as men while still often taking on responsibility for the home and family. Now they just wanted a rest. I was told that it was the younger women who wanted positive change and were dialoguing with many of their sisters in the West, particularly with women from Scandinavia.

The Prague conference was my first opportunity to meet two other men who had long been heroes of mine. David MacTaggart, the low-profile Canadian founder of Greenpeace, and Jonathan Porritt, the British environmental campaigner.

David, now in his early sixties, had come out of his so-called retirement in Italy to visit the conference *en route* to his eleventh visit to Chernobyl, the scene of the disastrous nuclear explosion in 1986. He'd stopped off at SVN in the hope of raising some money for serious study of the changes necessary to ensure that no further explosions occurred there.

He told me that the Ukraine government did not have the billions of dollars necessary to make Chernobyl safe and the reactor plant could blow at any time. He believed that this crisis could be avoided only if American contractors, with experience and know-how, were allowed to make the necessary repairs. This would cost a vast amount of money but he was prepared to spend time and to use the many major connections he'd made over the years to help raise sufficient funds.

A former contractor himself, David believes that Chernobyl is potentially one of the most dangerous situations we have in the world right now. 'It's far worse than all the nuclear weapons and plutonium that are being smuggled and sold out of Russia. We know they are getting into the wrong hands. I've proved it by getting together all the components for a nuclear bomb myself but these are nothing compared to the devastation that could happen all over Europe if Chernobyl blows again.'

Not the usual veggie, leather-sandalled environmental activist, David is an attractive flirt, who has children aged from forty to four. He chain-smokes and drinks a lot of wine and whisky despite health problems. But his commitment to saving this planet from man-made destruction is second to none and I wouldn't hesitate to follow him on one of his pirate adventures on the Greenpeace boats in the Pacific.

Jonathan Porritt is also different from the usual 'greenie'. An old Etonian, he is smooth and articulate and makes the most controversial statements seem common sense. And in most cases they are. To me he is 'Mr Sustainable', constantly urging the world of business and the consumer society to stop wanting more possessions and bigger profits at the cost of the long-term damage we are doing.

Turning from the world of politics, he'd recently set up Forum for the Future, with fellow directors Paul Ekins and Sara Parkin, where he felt he could create more positive change. He told me over dinner that the Forum was the central link for a variety of projects including a consultancy with the business world on green issues, a *Green Futures* magazine, a best practice database, a network for others involved in sustainable development and Forum scholarships for young people covering environmental issues. It seemed ambitious to me although urgently needed.

My network of extraordinary and inspirational individuals dedicated to a positive future was growing rapidly and I knew this invisible web was part of an infrastructure that would need to be in place as the world shifted into a new way of being.

It was through Jonathan Porritt and other members of SVN that I first heard about The Natural Step, a non-profit foundation based in Stockholm and founded by visionary doctor, Karl-Henrik Robert.

I was hearing more and more stories of interesting Swedish organisations committed to social change and decided it was time to go there myself and meet some of the players. Of course it was no coincidence that one of my new friends from the Brahma Kumaris Mount Abu conference, a bright, progressive Swedish businesswoman called Monica Linstedt, had just told me about the forthcoming Kvinnor Kan – Women Can – event. And so almost as soon as I got back from Prague I set off again, this time to Scandinavia.

My first meeting when I got to Stockholm in May 1996 was with The Natural Step who told me how they started. Dr Robert was then head of the leading cancer institute in Sweden and it was through his work with human cancer cells that he became frustrated with what he considered to be the out-of-date complexity of most scientific debates on environmental issues. He passionately felt the need to simplify the message for a sustainable human society.

He managed to get the Swedish scientists behind him, together with many top Swedish entertainers, the Department of Employment and Swedish television. He even got the King of Sweden to agree to be patron and eventually after tremendous effort and total commitment he raised the funds to distribute copies of a pamphlet and audiotape containing his statement on the environment to every school and household in Sweden – 4.3 million copies, reaching 8.7 million people. In the process the corporate leaders who sponsored the programme became the founding board of The Natural Step.

'The message seemed natural to me,' Dr Robert told me. 'Start off with the smallest unit of life, the cell. Cells don't care about ideologies or politics. Cells only care about the fundamental prerequisites of life. No matter what our values, we should therefore still be able to join forces to defend the interests of the living cell. In a biological sense we are neither the masters of nature nor its stewards but a piece of nature ourselves just like the animal species. If these species have become threatened with extinction in the space of a few decades because of our environmental pollution, we too are threatened. We have enough knowledge to say that the only way of reversing this process is to avoid introducing substances into nature that it cannot process and to learn to live cyclically – just like cells in nature.'

The Natural Step's consensus programme supports a shift away from linear, resource-wasting, toxic-spreading methods of material handling and manufacturing towards cyclical, resource-preserving methods. Achieving this goal, they say, is necessary in order to preserve the prerequisites for the existence of all life. Rich industrial countries, including Sweden, have a special obligation to find worthy and sustainable solutions, the organisation declares. The strategy of The Natural Step is to lend active support to good examples of eco-cyclical development in households, companies and local governments. Its vision is to transform Sweden into a model of an attractive eco-cyclical society.

Today the organisation is working with industry all over the world advising on environmental matters, as well as instigating and advising more than a dozen Swedish networks committed to sustainable change, ranging from farmers to lawyers and nurses. It also runs an intense educational programme, including the European Youth Parliament for the Environment.

My next stopover in Sweden was Kvinnor Kan, which was established in 1982 by a group of angry women after the broadcast of a major TV debate on important social matters with only male participants. The women decided to arrange debates for themselves, without inviting men.

214

Their concept was to demonstrate women's abilities and values and to present women as role models. They established a secretariat and raised financial backing from both the private and public sectors. At the first fair, in Gothenburg in 1984, over 30,000 visitors attended. Since then they have held fairs every two years, growing constantly larger. The one I attended took place in Karlskrona, a small military town on the Swedish coast.

Like The Natural Step, Kvinnor Kan work very closely with sponsors both promoting their involvement with the fair and training them in how to work and communicate with women.

I'd arranged to meet Bonnie Bernstrom, the chairperson of the fair, the afternoon I got there and found her on her mobile phone, looking bedraggled and rather stressed. The intensive rains and winds had almost flattened the tented city of Kvinnor Kan and the visitor attendance was not as good as they had hoped. The Swedish press, which had always given Kvinnor Kan a high profile, were buzzing round like vultures waiting for their prey, hoping to run big disaster stories. I felt sorry for Bonnie, a pretty, dark-haired woman about my own age. It reminded me of the attitude of the British press towards What Women Want and I told her that the women's conference in Beijing had been far more flooded and that Sinead O'Connor had explained that water was a sign of the Goddess.

She showed me around the enormous fair area and told me that there were six hundred exhibitors, some commercial companies selling their wares and others there for PR and research. I saw a wide variety of messages mixed up in a fairly chaotic way. There were small craft enterprises, food companies, Volvo cars, plus the police force and event sponsors, the army and navy. All the stands were run by women with a women's message, but with men and women visitors.

I felt it would have benefited from a more organised layout but one of the early founders, now there in an almost tribal elder way, told me that they deliberately mixed different types of exhibitors to encourage the visitors to shop around, whether for products or messages. The town, itself one of the sponsors, was also the host for many debates and seminars on women's interest areas. Young women had their own exhibition seminar area and there was a local award scheme for women entrepreneurs.

I felt there was a lot to learn from Kvinnor Kan but that they too could learn from others. They seemed to be stuck in a bit of a time warp in having such a competitive attitude with men. It was the eternal problem – creating a space where it was safe for women to become empowered and creative but at the same time not excluding men. I told them I was convinced that women and men had to work together, not separately, to bring about positive change, even if women have to take the lead at times. Certainly their debates could examine that problem. Swedish and Scandinavian women in general are very strong and progressive, but these first true feminists still face a lot of opposition from their men. I feel this comes from fear and that the way to combat it is by strong feminine, nurturing communication rather than head-on conflict.

I had good meetings with many of the organisers, one of whom showed me their web site on the Internet, and I told them about the history and success of my What Women Want event. We decided to work together on international projects and when I left after two days I received a warm goodbye from my new Swedish friends.

Back in Stockholm I spent my time admiring the beautiful city as well as having further meetings with like-minded souls. The weather there was warm and the sun was shining. I was seeing Stockholm at its best. My small, comfortable hotel was in the middle of a park by the port and after early morning meditation at the nearby Brahma Kumaris centre I would wander back by the water's edge, floating along in a peaceful haze. I watched the sun sparkling on the water and the shining rocks at my feet as I stopped to admire the view.

Like other futurists, including Brian Bacon, I was sure that many of our most progressive humanist ideas were coming out of Sweden. However, my Swedish friends told me they felt the missing link in their country was a spiritual one. The austere, closed Lutheran Church did not encourage spiritual openness yet there was a hunger for new ideas. Many of the American New Age celebrities and world spiritual leaders attracted sellout crowds when they came there and *The Celestine Prophecy* had swept the country like wildfire.

'The thing is,' said Monica Linstedt, 'we're such a small country that if a new idea is recognised by a small group of people everyone gets to hear about it.'

I thought of the UK, also a small country, where ideas seem to take much longer to get off the ground and in any event are controlled far more by the politics of our national newspaper proprietors.

Sweden has other problems, though. There has been a political backlash to their tax system which pays for all of their excellent social services. Their transport system, health service and child care are of the highest standard but unlike their Norwegian neighbours they do not have access to oil. When the recession of the early nineties hit them there was an inevitable reaction to their expensive cost of living.

One of the most charming stories I heard was from Anders Olsen, a Lynne Franks PR Swedish advertising associate, who told me about a campaign he'd organised for an ecological washing powder, under the theme 'Water is the Source of Life – Don't Destroy It'.

'My six-year-old son came home from school and asked me if I realised that we drank the same water that the dinosaurs peed in and space doesn't send us any more,' he told me. He had decided to use it for the next part of the campaign.

Marilyn Mehlmann is an Englishwoman married to a Swede who has lived in Stockholm for almost thirty years. I met this warm, friendly woman in Istanbul and she told me about Gap – Global Action Plan – which had been started in 1989. It is an innovative international, Swedish-based non-profit organisation dedicated to making ecological change at household level. They work in an underground resistance way, through local cells, with householder training householder in the simple ecological rules – such as rubbish disposal and product packaging – that collectively can bring about far-reaching change. They were now based in fourteen countries including the UK,

USA, Ireland, Turkey and Iceland. Marilyn told me in her focused, soft-spoken way of the many initiatives that they'd either started or were participating in. They almost seemed the feminine version of The Natural Step.

I left Sweden with my head buzzing. In just a few weeks I'd visited so many countries and heard many new ideas but the message coming through was basically the same. To create a sustainable, positive future we have to change attitudes in business and the home by clear communication and information. Whether politicians, businesspeople, community leaders or women and men in the street, we all have to work together, combining resources and energy in a spirit of love and co-operation.

If we can balance the problems and the damage to the planet with an equal amount of sustainable environmental solutions we will secure the future for the human race.

14

The Summer of Love

I stood on the stage looking out at the colourful mix of parents with small children, orange-robed Buddhist lamas, dreadlocked teenagers and glamorous rock 'n' rollers enjoying themselves in the sunshine. I was co-presenting a concert, spiritual and cultural event at Alexandra Palace in north London.

'This is London at its best,' I thought. 'Happy faces, good music and a beautiful day. What more could we have asked for?' I looked around the large field and saw many familiar faces from the journey of the past four years of my life, all gathered there in celebration.

I saw wise woman, Eleanor Dettinger, who'd come up from her home in Iona; Kari-Ann Jagger, my companion at Glastonbury and many other gatherings, and her husband Chris who'd organised the music for the afternoon; their friend Hal, the owner of the big yurt and Turkish bath where I'd stayed at the Glastonbury Festival; Patrick Nash who was in charge of the day and who'd been running Findhorn when I first visited there; Lama Yeshi, the jovial, good-natured abbot of the Samye Ling Buddhist monastery in Scotland; Sarah, another Gabrielle Roth tantric warrior; Jasminder Love and TV producer Jo

Sawicki, both of whom had also done Chuck Spezzano's relationship workshops in Hawaii, and Spencer Style, a young TV producer with whom I'd had a short relationship after I'd got back from Hawaii and with whom I'd remained great friends. He was now living with film director Beeban Kidron and had brought their young son Noah along to the concert.

I ran into Alex Fisher, my tree-living friend; Jahnet, the sacred hooker, who alongside Caroline Aldred had taught the tantric sex session at the What Women Want festival; Helena Norbürg-Hodge, the radical ecologist I'd met at a transpersonal conference in Ireland; Claire Farman and her young musician boyfriend, Jamie Cato, who had been close friends of mine through all the dramas of the past four years, together with their baby, my goddaughter India Rose; and Sister Jayanti accompanied by Sister Maureen and several other Brahma Kumaris who had come along to give a blessing for peace on the stage together with the Dalai Lama and an assortment of male spiritual leaders.

Sinead O'Connor, my great supporter from the What Women Want concert, accompanied by her friends and young son, Jake, performed some songs and later I introduced her to Annie Lennox and filmmaker husband Uri Fruchtman who with their two young daughters have become good friends and holiday companions of mine when we're at our respective second homes in Mallorca. Pink Floyd's Dave Gilmore was also performing and I chatted to him and his ex-journalist wife Polly about the days when we lived on opposite sides of the canal in Maida Vale.

I thought of all the strange coincidences and awakenings that had occurred during my adventures and celebrated the synergy of having so many of my friends all together at one time. The day seemed to mark the end of one phase of my journey and the beginning of the next. I was about to go back to Deia for the summer and I knew I was on the brink of something new. What I didn't know then was that that afternoon I was to meet the man who would become my companion during the many adventures I still had to come.

From the beginning of my journey I had known there would come a time when I'd be ready for a partner who I'd be able to grow with, someone who would be equally committed to making a positive contribution to society, who would be a friend to travel and have fun with and a lover to hold and cherish me.

I knew that I wouldn't be ready to meet him until I was centred, clear and happy to live on my own. Past feelings of neediness had been as offputting to the men in my life as my need to control. I still hadn't been ready to 'trust and receive' and my lack of self-esteem had attracted me to the unsuitable and emotionally unavailable.

And so when I finally met a man who was attractive, available and eminently suitable, I backed away nervously. I was happy on my own, felt good about myself, and was enjoying life tremendously. Meeting a man was the last thing on my mind at the end of the concert, so I wasn't very attentive when Jo Sawicki came to find me backstage bringing with her a tall, good-looking American, whom she introduced as Tom Blakeslee.

'I write books on popular psychology,' he told me. 'I'm on my way to Germany to do some research and then I'm looking for a place to spend the winter where I can write and live in a beautiful environment.'

'You should try Deia, where I live,' I offered, immediately regretting my words. He'll think I'm coming on to him and he might even turn up, I thought as I handed him my phone number. I wandered off feeling slightly uneasy but with other things on my mind.

My summer of love continued when I got back to Deia. I was surrounded by loving friends and my children, who had grown into two bright and amusing companions. The usual interesting international crowd of old and new friends kept me busy having fun in my home or at other parties around the island. Life was good. I had been on a ten-day fast and had never felt healthier or more energetic.

I'd had a few phone calls from Tom Blakeslee but didn't pay much attention. I'd even given him the phone number of an attractive woman in Heidelberg where he was staying. I was more interested in spending time with penniless artists or musicians than with an interesting, intelligent man who might turn out to be a serious threat to my independence.

Finally it was time for the children to leave and I had invited a variety of friends and business associates to spend working holidays with me in Deia during the last few weeks of my stay.

Mysteriously and coincidentally they all started phoning me from around the world cancelling our arrangements, as they had got caught up in complicated business commitments. I was happy to spend a few weeks on my own but thought during a sunset meditation that it would be even better, although not very likely, if I was in a relationship by the time of our traditional village August full moon party the following week. I had chosen to be on my own for the past six months and felt it was time to let down my defences.

When I got home after the meditation there was just one message on my answerphone. 'Hi, Lynne, this is Tom Blakeslee. I've bought a ticket to Mallorca and I'm arriving next Saturday.' I was amazed. My children were leaving on Friday and it was the full moon party on the following Wednesday. What had I got myself into?

I phoned up our mutual friend, Jo. 'What's he like?' I asked her. 'I don't even know this man and now suddenly he's coming to stay.'

'He's wonderful,' she reassured me. 'He's a considerate and helpful house guest, pays his own way, is a good cook and very pleasant to be with. You'll have a great time.'

I wasn't so sure and decided not to get too excited. There are lots of beautiful women of all ages in Deia and I hardly knew him. He could go running off with any of them as soon as he arrived for all I knew and anyway, I was happy on my own.

Saturday came round and I persuaded the crowd of friends I was with to leave one party and come with me to the bar to meet Tom before going on to the next one. I hoped I'd recognise him and I was pleasantly surprised when this attractive grey-haired man with a suitcase and several bags arrived in the bar and walked towards me.

He explained that he was travelling light. He'd rented out his apartment in Santa Monica, put most of his belongings in storage and had managed to fit his two computers, lots of paperwork and some clothes into a few bags. We stuffed them into my car and made our way to a party that my Australian friends Sandra and Bob Jones were throwing with their two teenage sons.

Another great Deia party with good music, friendly people and lots of dancing. Tom seemed to fit in immediately as I introduced him to some of my friends and he joined me on the dance floor moving to the exciting salsa music.

At last we got back to my house, put his bags in the guest room and went down to the swimming pool for an early morning dip. The inevitable happened, and although I suggested we get to know each other slowly, in the event the guest room was never used.

We knew almost immediately that we'd fallen in love and were phoning all our friends and relatives within days to tell them. They thought we were crazy and told us to slow down. Tom told me his marriage had split up about the same time as mine and he too had been in business partnership with his wife. He'd been travelling the world, having different relationships, but just before he met me he'd decided he was ready for a serious commitment.

I realised how important timing is in our lives. We had both healed from the break-up of long-term marriages, had got the need to play the field out of our system and were free to travel and work alongside each other. We had both run big businesses and had large houses with all the accompanying material possessions but both now wanted a far simpler lifestyle. We were financially independent of each other and our children were old enough to look after themselves. If we'd met each other any earlier I certainly wouldn't have been ready and I doubt he would either.

I believe that Tom and I were meant to find each other that afternoon backstage at the concert and that all my friends dropping out of visiting me just as he had decided to come was also meant to be.

Again, as I'd felt so often during the past few years, circumstances had been created which were more than just chance. As James Redfield writes, in his hugely successful book, *The Celestine Prophecy*, there is no such thing as coincidence.

I've had too many synergetic signs and events that led to the next part of my journey. I'd found that the more open I was to accepting the process and the more I let go of control and went with my natural flow, the more my life progressed and the nearer I came to my truth. I was happier too.

Tom has a far more scientific approach to life than I do, which is why I think we balance each other out so well. He believes coincidences are simply coincidences, but even he had to admit his amazement at one incident in Deia shortly after we met. A wind suddenly blew through the bedroom window as we were making love and knocked over a picture next to my bed representing the two Hindu female and male deities, Lakshmi and Narayana, who represent the perfect male and female. I had kept it there to represent the ideal relationship between a man and a woman and the perfect harmony of our male and female energies within. The picture fell straight on the floor face down and the wind immediately disappeared.

'If you make something like that happen regularly,' said Tom, 'even I'll start believing in magic.'

Now I had what I was looking for – an adult relationship with a loving, affectionate man who fitted all my requirements. I was nervous but knew that if I could remember all I'd learnt, take life one step at a time and stay in the present as much as possible, I would have an opportunity for great happiness. I knew that commitment was required to sustain intimacy and trust and that when there was a misunderstanding or some hurt it was important to communicate and express how I felt instead of running away.

I believe that the healing and growth that can take place through a loving relationship is the biggest challenge I've had to face. I now know that the sacred love that two people can feel for each other can connect us with a divine energy and that it had been necessary for me to learn through my own experiences the importance of true communication in partnership.

Conclusion:

The Pieces of the Jigsaw Come Together

Back in London I thought over the past four years and reflected on what I'd learnt about myself and the world I lived in. I remembered how it all started after my two closest PR friends died and how I realised it was a matter of life and death for me to get off the crazy *Ab Fab* merry-go-round I had created. I'd come to understand that material success and recognition means nothing if there isn't inner peace and quality time for loved ones. If pressure and stress push us constantly into the future, our health and relationships will suffer and we will never be happy in the present.

I remembered the painful experience of facing my fears and letting go of everything I'd spent twenty years building – my business, my marriage and my home. I acknowledged how my beautiful village of Deia had been so important in giving me the strength to heal myself. It was there, surrounded by nature, that I'd found the courage to begin the journey to find my truth by connecting with my inner self.

I thought of all the places I'd visited over the past four years and how significant each experience had been in bringing me closer to understanding myself and others. My journey to Hawaii was the start of healing my relationship blockage after the painful end to my marriage: the work I began there, together with subsequent short-term relationships, made me appreciate that we can all create unity through duality. I had found out that I would only be ready to receive a partner with unconditional love when I could feel that love for myself.

After years of neglecting physical exercise I learnt to get out of my head and into my body. Working with Gabrielle Roth in California, together with my daughter Jessica, I learnt to enjoy the ecstatic movement and rhythm of her Wave. The dancing, and the experience of the naked hot tubs at Esalen, had given us the freedom to appreciate our bodies. Our egos had allowed us to lose our self-consciousness and realise we didn't need to look for outside approval to feel good about ourselves.

My own physical experiences led me to the understanding that the toxins we put in our bodies through stress as well as food are killing us and we have to be far more responsible and conscious about the food we eat, the water we drink and the air we breathe. I saw that exercise and lifestyle are vital in creating the sense of well-being that will ensure a healthy mind and healthy body.

Spending so much time in the small, friendly village of Deia and visiting other communities such as Findhorn had made me understand just how much we were all missing in today's urban society. I'd seen how community can become a supportive extended family and believe that if we can recreate this sense of tribal belonging in city environments, we can overcome frightening social problems now being caused by the isolation of urban living and the breakdown of the family unit.

PR is often about creating illusion, and my quest is about searching for the truth. I compared hype to faith and saw they were both a matter of believing in something that you want to believe in. I saw that integrity and honest information make good business sense and should be an intrinsic part of any communication strategy.

I wanted to be part of an industry that was dedicated to

contributing in a positive way to people's consciousness and attitudes, whether using the latest technology or one-to-one dialogue.

My recent travels across North America and Europe had put me in touch with many other like-minded entrepreneurs who believe it is possible to create ethical business practices and partnerships. I had discussed visions of a new kind of business philosophy where a double or even triple bottom line is evolving that is as much about consideration of human values and protection of the environment as it is about making profits.

I'd started working on what I was calling conscious marketing ideas, where enterprise could create projects that would benefit the communities they work with or sell to and at the same time take their message out to the consumers. I was now passing on to the marketing industry, through talks and seminars, the importance of letting go of eighties hype and outdated aspirational marketing which I'd been so involved in myself. I now saw how it affected the consumer's self-esteem and that the future of communicating the integrity and message of a brand was far more effective when in creative partnership with the public. Business and the marketeer have to learn to work together with the consumer, not exploit and manipulate.

My journey of discovery had cost me a considerable amount of the money from the sale of my business. It was time to go back to work – but using the knowledge I'd gained during my search. Now I am determined to use my creativity, my communication skills and wealth of contacts to bring about positive change.

During my summer of feminism, when I launched VIVA! Radio, created the What Women Want festival and attended the Beijing UN women's conference, I realised that women cannot afford to make the same mistakes as men if they want to change society in a positive way. The future of the feminine way, for men and for women, is to learn to work and live together in full partnership, not competing for position and power. Men and women have to be in harmony with each other, as do the inner male and female energy inside all of us.

My initiation into the Celtic sacred sites with the wise women had woken up the magician inside me. I'd connected with the land and understood the importance of ritual and ceremonies that reawaken ancient memories of a time when we all knew how to heal ourselves and others.

My son's urgent need to connect himself with his Jewish ancestors had taken me on a journey to Israel where together with my family I was able to celebrate my roots, while questioning the whole position of women in the Judaeo-Christian and Islamic societies. Social progress and peace have been held back for too long in the name of religion and it is time to let go of a distorted history and bring a balanced spiritual view to everyday life.

My association with the women-led spiritual Brahma Kumaris organisation and the Northern Ireland women's peace movement again reminded me that it is only when women can be in touch with the Goddess inside and know our strength that we can convince men that we can all work for peace in love and conciliation.

My global network of similarly minded business people, communicators, politicians, academics, futurists, spiritual leaders, visionaries and representatives of non-profit organisations was growing all the time. We shared information through conferences, e-mail and faxes, committing ourselves to work together sharing resources and energy to build a sustainable future for this planet. I saw the importance of people like ourselves becoming bridges between business and society, helping to create a vision of common interest for both.

All these experiences and more have brought me to the awareness of an invisible thread that is weaving its way through the world, helping to create a huge shift in consciousness. Embodied in this wave is hope for the future. The old structures don't work any more, new truths are emerging – and new ways of viewing reality. Whether a single parent or a top executive, all of us can make this shift.

My vision is of a world where big is not always beautiful and where business and community can work together for a sustainable future; where women and men play an equal role and where true partnership exists in all areas of life – the home, politics, business and the inner and outer self. It is a vision of a new way of living and working where the best of feminine and masculine energy combine to create a world where we all learn to trust our intuition and connect with our soul. It is a time to stay attentive and be true to yourself. This period is not about giving away our power to gurus, businesses, institutions or politicians, but about understanding that we are our own and each other's teachers.

Addresses

All Hallows House
Centre for Natural Health and Counselling,
Idol Lane, London EC3R 5DD
Tel/Fax: 0171–283 8908

Brahma Kumaris, World Spiritual University,
Global Co-operation House, 65 Pound Lane, London NW10 2HH
Tel: 0181–459 1400 Fax: 0181–451 6480

Centre for Media Literacy,
4727 Wilshire Blvd, Suite 403, LA, CA 90010, USA
Tel: 213–931 4177 Fax: 213–931 4474

Children Now,
1212 Broadway, Oakland, CA 94612, USA
Tel: 510–763 2444 Fax: 510–763 1874

Council on Economic Priorities (CEP),
30 Irving Place, New York, NY 10003, USA
Tel: 212–420 1133 Fax: 212–420 0988

Esalen Institute,
Highway 1, Big Sur, CA 93920, USA
Tel: 408–667 3000 Fax: 408–667 2724

Fenton Communications, Inc.,
1606 20th Street, NW, Washington, DC 20009, USA
Tel: 202–745 0707 Fax: 202–332 1915

Findhorn Foundation,
The Park, Findhorn Forrest, Moray IV36 0TZ, Scotland
Tel: 01309–690956 Fax: 01309–691387

Forum for the Future,
227a City Road, London EC1V 1JT
Tel: 0171–251 6070 Fax: 0171–251 6268

Global Action Plan (GAP International),
Stjärnvägen 2, S–182 46 Enebyberg, Sweden
Tel: +46–8785 3145 Fax: +46–8768 8397

Institute for Alternative Journalism,
77 Federak Street, San Francisco, CA 94107
Tel: 415–284 1419 Fax: 415–284 1414

The International Council of Wise Women,
21 Fleetwood Court, Madeira Road, West Byfleet, Surrey KT14 6BE
Tel/Fax: 01932–343614

Kvinnor Kan Foundation,
Östermalmsgatan 33, S–114 26 Stockholm, Sweden
Tel: +46 (0)8–723 0707 Fax: +46 (0)8–791 8834

Liberty Hill Foundation,
1316 Third Street Promenade B4, Santa Monica, CA
   90401–1325, USA
Tel: 310–458 1450 Fax: 310–451 4283

Linn, Denise (seminars)
PO Box 75657, Seattle, Washington 98125–0657, USA

The Media Foundation (*Adbusters* magazine),
1243 West 7th Avenue, Vancouver BC V6H 1B7, Canada
Tel: 604–736 9401 Fax: 212–677 8732

Mother Meera,
Oberdorf 4a, 65599 Dornburg-Thalheim, Germany
Tel: +49–(0)6436–2305 Fax: +49–(0)6436 2361

The Natural Step,
Amiralitetshuset, Skeppsholmen, S–111 49 Stockholm, Sweden
Tel: +46–8–678 0099 Fax: +46–8–611 7311

Nichiren Shoshu Buddhism (now the Buddhism of Nichiren Daishonin),
SGI–UK, Taplow Court, Taplow, Maidenhead, Berkshire SL6 0ER
Tel: 01628–773163 Fax: 01628–773055

Raphaell, Katrina (crystal healer),
PO Box 3208, Taos, New Mexico 87571, USA

Roth, Gabrielle (information on books, tapes, videos and workshops),
c/o The Moving Center, PO Box 2034, Red Bank, NJ 07701
Tel: 201–642 1979 Fax: 201–621–2186
ravenrec@panix.com
htlp://www.ravenrecording.com

Samye Ling Tibetan Centre,
Eskdalemuir, Langholm, Dumfriesshire DG13 0QL, Scotland
Tel: 013873–73232 Fax: 013873–73223

Second Wave
Ya'Acov and Susannah Darling Khan
Nappers Crossing, Staverton, Totnes, Devon
Tel/Fax: 01803 762255

Self-Employed Women's Association (SEWA),
SEWA Reception Centre, opp. Victoria Gardens, Ahmedabad-38001, India
Tel: (91) 079–5506477 Fax: (91) 079–5506446

Skid Row Access Inc.,
PO Box 21353, Los Angeles, CA 90021, USA
Tel: 213–624 1773 Fax: 213–624 1849

Social Venture Network (US),
PO Box 29221, San Francisco, CA 94129–0221, USA
Tel: 415–561 6501 Fax: 415–561 6435

Social Venture Network (Europe)
Valkenburgerstraat 188, PO Box 937, 1000 AX Amsterdam, The Netherlands
Tel: +31–20 5353250 Fax: +31–20 6221608

Spezzano, Chuck,
c/o Psychology Vision, Townsend, Poulshot, Devizes, Wiltshire, SN10 1SD
Tel: 01380–828394 Fax: 01380–828590

Vispassana Meditation,
Christopher Titmus, c/o Gaia House, Totnes, Devon

WEDO (Women's Environment & Development Organisation),
355 Lexington Avenue, 3rd Floor, New York 10017–6603, USA
Tel: 212–973 0325 Fax: 212–973 0335

World Business Academy,
PO Box 191210, San Francisco, California 94119-1210, USA
Tel: 415–393 8251 Fax: 415–393 8369
wba@well.com

Youth Empowerment Project,
1373 West 29th Street, Los Angeles, CA 90007, USA
Tel: 213–735–2295 Fax: 213–735–9629

235

Bibliography

Adilakshmi, *The Mother* (Mother Meera, Germany, 1987).

The Body Shop Values Report (The Body Shop, Littlehampton, 1995).

Boteach, Rabbi Shmuel, *The Jewish Guide to Adultery* (Pan, London, 1995).

Bradley, Marion, *The Mists of Avalon* (Penguin, London, 1993).

Buckmann, Christina and Spiegel, Celina, *Out of the Garden: Women Writers on the Bible* (Pandora, London, 1995).

Caddy, Eileen, *Flight into Freedom* (Element, Brisbane, 1995).

Chopra, Deepak, *The Return of Merlin* (Century, London, 1995).

Council on Economic Priorities, *Shopping for a Better World* (Sierra, San Francisco, 1994).

Cunningham, Nancy Brady, *I am Woman by Rite: a Book of Women's Rituals* (Samuel Weiser, Maine, 1995).

Curtis, Susan and Fraser, Romy, *Natural Healing for Women* (Pandora, London, 1991).

Dass, Ram, *Be Here Now* (Hanuman, Alburquerque, 1978).

Devereux, Paul, *The Ley Hunter's Guide* (Gothic Image, Glastonbury, 1994).

Dunn, Aidan Andrew, *Vale Royal* (Goldmark, Uppingham, 1995).

Eco-Villages & Sustainable Communities (Findhorn Press, Scotland, 1996).

Eisler, Riane, *The Chalice and the Blade* (Pandora, London, 1993).

Goldstein, Joseph, *Insight Meditation* (Gill & Macmillan, Dublin, 1993).

Gottlieb, Lynn, *She Who Dwells Within: A Feminist Vision of a Renewed Judaism* (Harper, San Francisco, 1995).

Graves, Robert, *The White Goddess* (Faber & Faber, London, 1961).

Harvey, Andrew, *Hidden Journey – A Spiritual Awakening* (Rider, London, 1991).

Harvey, Andrew, *Return of the Mother* (Frog, Berkeley, CA, 1995).

Houston, Jean, *A Mythic Life: Learning to Live our Greater Story* (Harper, San Francisco, 1996).

Ingerman, Sandra, *Soul Retrieval* (Harper, San Francisco, 1991).

Ingerman, Sandra, *Welcome Home: Following Your Soul's Journey Home* (Harper, San Francisco, 1993).

Kennelly, Brendan, *Love of Ireland – Poems from the Irish* (Mercier, Cork, 1996).

Kenton, Leslie, *Passage to Power: Natural Menopause Revolution* (Ebury, London, 1995).

Linn, Denise, *Sacred Space* (Rider, London, 1995).

Linn, Denise, *Signposts* (Rider, London, 1996).

McWhirter, Jane, *The Practical Guide to Candida* (All Hallows House Foundation, London, 1995).

Michell, John, *New Light on the Ancient Mystery of Glastonbury* (Gothic Image, Glastonbury, 1992).

Mother Meera, *Answers* (Mother Meera, Dornburg-Thalheim, Germany, 1991).

Raphaell, Katrina, *Crystal Enlightenment*, Vols 1–3 (Aurora, Santa Fe, New Mexico 1985, 1987, 1990).

Reder, Alan, *75 Best Business Practices for Socially Responsible Companies* (Tarcher/Putnam, New York, 1995).

Redfield, James, *The Celestine Prophecy* (Bantam, London, 1994).

Roddick, Anita, *Body and Soul* (Ebury, London, 1991).

Rossbach, Sarah, *Interior Design with Feng Shui* (Rider, London, 1987).

Roth, Gabrielle, *Maps to Ecstasy* (Mandala, London, 1990).

Schultes, Richard Evans and Hofman, Albert, *Plants of the Gods: their Sacred, Healing and Hallucinogenic Powers* (Healing Arts, Rochester, Vermont, 1992).

Shiva, Vandana, *Staying Alive: Women, Ecology and Development* (Zed, London, 1989).

Spezzano, Chuck, *If it Hurts it isn't Love* (Arthur James, Evesham, Worcestershire, 1996).

Starhawk, *The Spiral Dance: A Rebirth of the Ancient Religion of the Great Goddess* (Harper, San Francisco, 1989).

Starhawk, *Truth or Dare: Encounters with Power, Authority and Mystery* (Harper, San Francisco, 1990).

Starhawk, *The Fifth Sacred Thing* (Bantam, New York, 1994).

Tannen, Deborah, *You Just Don't Understand: Women and Men in Conversation* (Ballantine, New York, 1991).

Vallely, Bernadette, *What Women Want* (Virago, London, 1996).

Williamson, Marianne, *A Woman's Worth* (Random House, New York, 1993).